KERENSA JENNINGS is a storyteller, strategist, writer, producer and professor.

Kerensa's TV work took her all over the world, covering everything from geo-politics to palaeontology, and her time as Programme Editor of *Breakfast with Frost* coincided with the life-changing events of 9/11.

The knowledge and experience she gained in psychology by qualifying and practising as an Executive Coach has only deepened her fascination with exploring the interplay between nature and nurture and with investigating whether evil is born or made – the question at the heart of *Seas of Snow*.

As a scholar at Oxford, her lifelong passion for poetry took flight. Kerensa lives in West London and has developed a career in digital enterprise to help inspire young people across the UK and unlock their potential.

Seas of Snow is her first novel.

SEAS OF SNOW

Kerensa Jennings

This edition first published in 2017

Unbound
6th Floor Mutual House, 70 Conduit Street, London W1S 2GF
www.unbound.com

Typeset and text design by Ellipsis Digital Limited, Glasgow

A CIP record for this book is available from the British Library

ISBN 978-1-78352-311-5 (trade hbk)
ISBN 978-1-78352-312-2 (ebook)
ISBN 978-1-78352-313-9 (limited edition)

Printed in Great Britain by Clays

1 3 5 7 9 8 6 4 2

Dear Reader,

The book you are holding came about in a rather different way to most others. It was funded directly by readers through a new website: Unbound. Unbound is the creation of three writers. We started the company because we believed there had to be a better deal for both writers and readers. On the Unbound website, authors share the ideas for the books they want to write directly with readers. If enough of you support the book by pledging for it in advance, we produce a beautifully bound special subscribers' edition and distribute a regular edition and e-book wherever books are sold, in shops and online.

This new way of publishing is actually a very old idea (Samuel Johnson funded his dictionary this way). We're just using the internet to build each writer a network of patrons. Here, at the back of this book, you'll find the names of all the people who made it happen.

Publishing in this way means readers are no longer just passive consumers of the books they buy, and authors are free to write the books they really want. They get a much fairer return too – half the profits their books generate, rather than a tiny percentage of the cover price.

If you're not yet a subscriber, we hope that you'll want to join our publishing revolution and have your name listed in one of our books in the future. To get you started, here is a £5 discount on your first pledge. Just visit unbound.com, make your pledge and type thesea in the promo code box when you check out.

Thank you for your support,

Dan, Justin and John
Founders, Unbound

For Ella, Anya, Rahul and Scarlett

'Be patient toward all that is unsolved in your heart and try to love the questions themselves, like locked rooms and like books that are now written in a very foreign tongue. Do not now seek the answers, which cannot be given you because you would not be able to live them. And the point is, to live everything. Live the questions now. Perhaps you will then gradually, without noticing it, live along some distant day into the answer.'

Rainer Maria Rilke

With special thanks to Ajaz Ahmed, Gi Fernando,
Pat Jarvis, Matthew Jukes and Seven Hills

Contents

Prologue

Its low, guttural kraaa pierced the air and echoed into nothingness.

Powdered whiteness bleached the horizon.

A silver sun hung low in the sky.

Something glinted on the ground, discarded in the snow.

The chill of a wing's breath swooped past.

A trace of something lingered on the breeze.

Claws

She could still feel the lingering stench of his presence. Soap suds were melting away around her, softly. The cold water shivered into her. His darkness had breathed into the room and the ash-bitter foulness of him enveloped her small, white form. He had reached down and seared her skin with his touch.

She looked down and tucked her chin onto her knees.

Of course, the picture she presented to the world was a mask. What choice did she have?

The rain trickled into dropleted patterns down the glass. Rivulets darting about – fat luscious large ones and tiny, sparkly, little ones. Almost swimming. A kind of kinetic energy which belied the mistiness of the rainfall.

Outside, the view was hazy through the spray. Splashes of green and grey. The odd moment of purple or yellow.

Spring then.

Her heart was beginning to beat with that familiar anxiety. Inside, she knew she just had to get through it. Again. Deep breaths.

There was a straggly set of daffodils squatting in a white

china vase downstairs. The Formica gleamed. A scent of polish lingering in the air. Harpic and Jeyes fluid. Bitter. Piercing. It was a house that looked like one of those dream homes you saw in pictures. But this wasn't a place anyone could call a home. Wasn't *home* meant to mean something warm and inviting? Safe and cosy. Hearth and heart. Home, sweet home.

This house was a dream that never was. A game of make-believe. Of nightmares.

The daffodils caught the sunlight with a cheery yellowness. She bowed down and smelled them. Strangely chemical rather than floral.

I wandered lonely as a cloud . . .

A whisper of a thought crossed her mind but disappeared in a vapour.

'You ready, then?' he asked.

She looked up, nodded.

The sense of not quite being able to breathe constricted her. She wasn't sure if she could speak.

The man wore a long, black coat and a long, stern face. He had slightly raised eyebrows, as if questioning.

Her mother's brother.

She couldn't bring herself to call him uncle – that would have been as much a lie as calling this house a home.

She collected her things and walked through the door he held open for her. The cold rain lingered on her cheeks and clung to her eyelashes. Her soft hair began to feel damp.

Joe had been in her life for the last eight years. He turned up when she was five. She remembered how it happened.

*

It was bath time. School was still a novelty in those days and it had been a day of painting and sunshine. Mam was sloshing the water around and it felt warm and delicious.

The doorbell rang. Mam hurriedly gathered her up out of the bath and wrapped a rough, peach towel around her. She gave her a little kiss and said she would be back in a minute. 'Won't be long, pet.'

Then, a gasp which became a kind of squeal. Like an animal, but Mam.

She peeked her head around the banisters and looked down. A man was standing in the doorway. Mam was clasping her hands to her mouth, though it was hard to tell if it was shock or joy or something else.

The man came inside and grasped Mam tightly, his hands clasping around her. There was murmuring – she couldn't hear what was being said . . . then another exclamation.

'Gracie, come and meet your uncle!' her mother called.

Still wrapped in the rough, peach towel, Gracie toddled down the stairs. She eyed the man.

He looked at her. She was about as sweet and precious and lovely as an angel. Her blond curls were damp about the neck.

'Give your Uncle Joe a kiss, pet.'

He swooped her up, a tiny towelled-up bundle, and his raspy, scratchy stubble itched her skin.

She smelt like lemons.

Gracie had never heard of an uncle before. But then again, you don't know everything when you're five.

She looked at her mother and saw something different in her

eyes. They were shining like glass. They looked a bit like the eyes of her baby doll, Victoria – you couldn't tell if she was happy or scared, but you could make believe any story you wanted and it would fit.

Joe said something about not having set eyes on the little one before. One ... two ... three ... four ... five ... Gracie counted up how old she was.

She didn't remember much about her first few years. There was the agonising morning when she knelt down onto the ground and the grass bit her. The pain was more horrible than anything you could imagine. The grown-ups said something about a wasp, but Gracie didn't know the word, and frankly didn't really care. She just wanted her knee to stop being red and angry and sore.

The other memory she had from those days were those precious times she and her Ma spent reading, squished together on the doorstep if it was a nice day and snuggled up on the sofa if it was chilly or wet outside. Well, it was Gracie's Ma who did the reading, but the pair of them would sit for hours with storybooks and nursery rhymes. Fairy tales with magic, beautiful princesses, evil monsters – and happy-ever-afters.

She felt safe and warm and happy. The sound of her mother's laughter was a tinkling comfort, and cuddling up with each other felt just perfect.

The years went by and there were more memories. Mostly everything seemed a bit beige or grey, but there were flashes of colour. She thought of roses. White roses.

Blood-orange-purple-black inside her eyelids as she ran away blindly from a boy who had tried to thrust a dead blackbird down the back of her blouse. His cackling like something from a storybook.

Her heart had never been tested like this. It felt as if it had gone on fire. She ran and ran and ran. She thinks she screamed, but she can't be sure. A private, empty scream that nobody heard.

The scratchy feathers had got tangled up in her hair and pointy sharp things were digging into her neck. The bird's lifeless body still felt warm. She couldn't see it, but she could feel it, a lump of oily deadness with coarse blades penetrating her skin. Its sticky, almost-living roughness felt tepid beneath the cotton collar of her blouse and forced her into violent shudders.

She tried to dislodge it, panic setting in as the nightmare cleaved ever tighter. Why couldn't she get rid of it? Why was nobody helping?

Even as she ran, the limp body slipped slightly further down her back, revolting her with its warmth and making her retch uncontrollably. Sheer terror seized her. Acid gagged into her mouth. Her whole body froze.

And then, the monster freed itself and fell with a thud to the ground.

Gracie uncoiled, her throat burning from the vomit. She saw the shiny black heap of feathers, a yellow beak daring to point itself at her. A twisted neck distorted its shape into a comma of coal. Staring eyes looked out pointlessly, and its claws seemed to be hooked onto an imaginary prey.

Tears prickled into Gracie's eyes and her cheeks burned. She realised she was out of breath, and gulped down some air to try to make herself feel better. But the waves of sick didn't go away.

For the rest of her life, the flutter of a bird's wings would cause a swelling of nausea in her stomach. She didn't mind birds at a distance. Could almost sense their beauty. At a distance. But even a dead bird lying in the lane would grip her with its cold claws and threaten to stifle her. And that day, after bath time, she strangely felt the same. Uncle Joe had come into their life and it was as if something was clawing at her heart.

Tears

Everything took on a routine. Uncle Joe more or less moved in. But there were times when he would disappear for ages and ages. Whenever he left for one of his long trips, her mother would look out of the window after him and sigh, deeply. Gracie always sighed, too, with relief. When he came back it was as if a little bit of life drained away from them both.

At first, her mother would smile at him when he came through the door. A tentative approach, a stroke, what looked like a clumsy attempt at a kiss. He would barely look at her, pushing past and muttering about supper.

She began to act as if she didn't know what to do or say.

He would smell of ash and dirt and a dark, treacly bitterness Gracie couldn't identify. Come up to her and bury his head into her neck. Kiss her with his prickly face and stare at her with his hooded eyes.

It was like being watched by that dead bird. Made her shudder.

Her mother would gaze on and the sparkle of her eyes gradually disappeared. The tortoiseshell green that glowed and shone when Uncle Joe first arrived became a watery shadow. The light faded into nothingness.

Sometimes Gracie heard her mother sob with wretched, fuggy-throated gulps. She would emerge later with a face riven with lines. Blotched, red, mottled and old.

She seemed to be getting thinner, too.

Sometimes she'd spend ages layering clothing to cover up the latest blue-purple bruises. Blouses and cardigans and high-necked dresses. Scarves came in useful. On days when her face wore black shiny memories of the previous night, she would stay at home and cry some more.

All the while, she would look at Gracie with the wisp of an apology around her lips and in her lifeless eyes. But she said nothing. May Close. North Shields. Tyneside. With Uncle Joe. This was now their life.

Gracie pondered on what was happening. Friends at school with brothers and sisters sometimes fought with them, sometimes hated them, but always seemed to love them, really.

Gracie had often wished she could have a little brother or sister of her own, but it never happened. She had never had a Da. Not like some of the children at school who had once had a Da but lost him when he died in the War or anything. She had just never had one.

So the chance of having a little brother or sister was about as likely as getting good at spelling. Or ever trying one of those bananas her teachers talked about. Or a real egg.

She didn't know much about it, but when she visited her friends, it seemed as if brothers and sisters teamed up together. Played together, laughed together. Had jolly good fun together. Mucked about together and teased each other about silly things like having to wear too-big hand-me-downs. It was noisy and boisterous and involved lots of play-fighting. But it always looked fun.

Her mother didn't seem to have much fun with Uncle Joe. They never played or laughed. He just hurt her and he made her cry. Then he'd pretend he hadn't and he'd come up to Gracie and grasp her and breathe her in with a fierce intensity she hated.

He usually disappeared again then for a while.

The memories flooded back. One day, her mother took her out onto the back doorstep, as they'd gone a hundred times before. She had brought a bowl of soap and water. And began blowing bubbles.

Gracie was almost seven on this occasion. Bubbles felt a bit like a little girl's game, but she humoured her mother. It was the first time they had sat down together for as long as Gracie could remember.

It was a sunny day, so the colours were as bright and beaut-iful as they could be, and the reflections of their pebble-dash house rose high into the sky and merged with the blues of the sky. The oily spheres had a life of their own, spiralling upwards, gleaming with a thousand rainbows. Nothing in the world could be more magical. Even now, as a big girl, she loved watching them float into the air, then disappear in a puff of invisibleness.

'Gracie, pet, what do you think about us having a little baby?'

Gracie looked at her mother. There was a wise curiosity in her eyes.

'So we could have our very own baby Victoria, only real?' she asked.

'Mam's got a baby growing inside her tummy, pet. In a while, we'll get to meet it. How about that, pet? Would you like a little brother or sister?'

Gracie wasn't sure what to make of this. It reminded her of a terrible time a few years ago – before Uncle Joe appeared. She had been woken up in the night by the sounds of her mother crying with desperate, animal yelps.

She had tiptoed downstairs. Her mother was weeping un-controllable, jagged tears.

She pulled Gracie to her tighter than you can imagine, stroking her hair and clasping her as if she couldn't bear to let her go.

Gracie looked up at her, and with a tiny finger, traced a tear running down her mother's cheek.

'Oh my darling, my darling, my pet,' she said, rocking the little girl backwards and forwards.

'Violet's lost her little one,' she said, crying and crying.

It was some time before Gracie properly worked out what was wrong. Violet – Mrs Sherwood from number 16, was expecting a little brother or sister for Catherine and Michael and Mark. But something bad happened and now the baby was in heaven. Gracie didn't even think it had been born or any-thing.

She looked at her mother now. She was blowing bubbles, and there was the faintest trace of a smile in her eyes.

'Are you going to be happy now, Mam?' Gracie asked.

'I don't know about that, pet, but let's wait and see.'

Shadows

Billy next door was Gracie's special friend. A couple of years older than her, he'd never minded the fact she was just a girl. Ever since they were little, he'd wanted to look after her. He thought about the time when she was three and he was five. He'd invented an adventure game for them. He knocked on her door, and waited.

Gracie had scuttled across the floor to say hello. In May Close, everyone used to leave their front doors open when the weather was all right. A small cul-de-sac, but everyone knew everyone and that was no bad thing. The wives who had been left behind in the War did their best to help out with elderly neighbours, when they needed odd jobs doing. It wasn't easy, but they did their best. Billy was lucky – he was proud of how his Da was big and strong and had one of those smiley faces you couldn't help but like.

His Da had always been round the other houses, helping out and laughing and being strong and big for everyone. But not right now – he was away with all the others. Billy always felt sad when he talked about his Da being away. But today wasn't a day for being sad.

'You coming out?' asked Billy.

'Mam says it's okay,' said Gracie.

'Come on then.'

He'd often delight her with new and exciting games. Life was like one long happy playtime, with different adventures tumbling into one another. Billy Harper was the best thing in the whole wide world, and she adored him.

Yellow sunshine flowed everywhere. Twinkled through the trees and bounced off the grey stone walls of the houses. Sprigs of daffodils clumped together in the front yards and along the road. Pockets of dazzling brightness nestled in the grass and the dirt.

He took her hand and they pottered off down the lane, oblivious to the click of a camera behind them. Her in a smock dress, him striding manfully by her side.

Gracie looked at Billy and thought nothing in the world could make her feel like bursting with smiles more than her big friend.

They walked into the woodland behind the Close and he led her into a dappled area with dark green trees all around. In the distance was her favourite bit – a small pond which caught the light on a good day and danced with glitter. It was like that today – dashes and darts of sparkles jostling for attention.

'Right, we're playing dragons and princesses today. I'm the scary dragon and you're the princess and I'm really your friend but you don't know it yet because I'm being all scary and frightening and stuff.'

'What's my name?'

'What do you want your name to be? You can pick anything you want. I'm going to be The Dragon.'

'Alright then. I'll be The Princess. The bravest princess ever and ever!'

He began to chase her through the trees, roaring convincingly. Billy had obviously put some thought into his dramatic portrayal. He let her run off a little to give her some space, then rushed at her, fast.

'Stop, Princess, stop!'

She squealed and ran, skipping over the gnarled roots and uncurling ferns. Jumped over shadows and aimed for the bright bits. Princesses in storybooks always expected princes to come along and rescue them, but not this Princess. She was concentrating on toddling as fast as her chubby little legs would carry her.

Then, silence. She realised The Dragon had somehow disappeared. She looked around nervously.

'Dragon?' she asked quietly.

'Where are you?'

'Dragon?'

Silence. The wind rustled the leaves in the trees softly, purple and yellow crocuses nodded gently in the breeze. Little midges buzzed around, their tiny wings diffusing light into a mishmash of haziness.

The pond seemed to be very far away – all she could see was the silhouette of the great big tree that Billy and his brothers would climb up to launch themselves into the water in the summer.

'Billy, are you hiding? Are we playing hide and seek?'

She looked around her, peering around tree trunks and squinting into the distance.

Then she saw it. A black shadow. And out of the shadow, a beak, gleaming like polished, sooted metal. An eye, fixed on her. Claws gripping a branch, their pointed ends like pins and needles. A wing, raised slightly in anticipation.

Her heart began to beat so fast she could hear it.

The shadow shifted and the leaves parted slightly. A lone sunbeam filtered onto the shape, revealing the nightmare blackness within.

The beak parted slowly. The talons tightened their grip, glinting in the sun. Feathers made of blackened iron lined up like armour.

And the eye was looking at her. Intently. With a hunger that she couldn't understand.

She thought about the dead blackbird that had clung to her neck and wouldn't let go and that familiar sense of dread bit into her. This bird was also black, but bigger, with a fierce black beak that hovered half open. Sharp. Pointed. Lethal. It let out a deep, gravelly kraaa.

Paralysed, Gracie could do nothing. She tried to scream, but her throat was suffocating.

'Billy!' she tried to shout, 'Billy.'

Leaves

The silence grew thickly around her, layers of fog hovering in the distance. She became aware of a startling pain on her hands and her face. Hot and stinging, as if a hundred barbs were prickling into her. She had no idea where she was.

Rays of light were shimmering overhead, stirring softly through leaves. The brightness hurt her eyes. Puzzled, she realised she was lying down on her side. Fern fronds were tickling at her, and underneath the ground was warm but hard. A dizzy sensation overwhelmed her and she felt sparkles invading her eyes like tingles of light.

She drifted in and out of dreams – there was a calmness about her. Curled up like a small woodland animal, she slept for days.

When she stirred, the needles digging in penetrated her consciousness and ripped apart her calmness. She began to try to tear them out of her hands and her face, but realised, confusingly, that the needles weren't actually there.

'Gracie! Are you alright? What happened?'

Billy's voice felt familiar yet far away, even though he was standing practically on top of her.

'Is this some new kind of game, where The Princess goes hiding away from The Dragon?' he chuckled.

His voice felt as if it was echoing around her ears.

'I don't know what happened,' replied Gracie, truthfully. Tears gathered in the corners of her eyes and started streaming down her cheeks.

Billy looked at her, and thrust a manly arm around her. That's what Da did when he was trying to make his Mam feel better. Beyond that, he had no idea what to do or say.

'I think I've been asleep,' gulped Gracie, between tears, 'and my face and hands hurt, but there's nothing there. And there was a giant black bird and it wanted to eat me and it flew right on top of me and it killed a mouse and I'm scared.'

The last bit she gabbled so fast he could barely keep up.

'I only lost sight of you for about two minutes,' he said gravely, 'how did you cram all that in?'

She held out her hands to him, sobbing.

'Why am I hurting?' she asked. He looked carefully at her tiny, outstretched paws and the beginnings of some bumps were poking up, pinkly.

'Oh Gracie, look, I think you've fallen into some stinging nettles, no wonder you feel proper horrible.'

'What's stinging nettles?' she asked.

He showed her a clump, and pointed out the tiddly fronds that stick out of them.

'You're not supposed to touch them,' he said, by way of explanation. 'Come on, yer Ma's going to kill me.'

Dragons and Princesses would have to wait for another day.

'I've not been a very brave princess, have I?'

'You've been the bravest princess that ever lived. Ever,' he said, with extra emphasis on the 'ever'.

She smiled gratefully, then glanced skywards once more.

'The bird wanted to hurt me,' she said again.

Books

The fat, luscious raindrops were interlacing down the smoothness of the glass. Outside, the misty rain showed no sign of relenting.

The reassuring patches of yellow spring flowers offered a smile to her heart, but nothing would raise the gloom within.

She sighed, slowly.

It was a small room. Lavender paint on the walls. A glass vase of wilting daffodils sitting on the cabinet. Reminding her of something. A collection of old photographs jumbled together on the side. An empty tumbler. A couple of drab faux impressionist paintings on the walls. Like one of those grotty hotels that dressed itself up as better than it was.

There was a small bookcase. Her solace. She tried to sit up, and tentatively put some weight onto her feet. The pain shot through her like needles. She paused. The rain sputtered onto the ledge of the window, mockingly.

Another sigh. Another go. Come on you, you can do it, she muttered under her breath.

Her frail bones could barely carry her these days. Her body had become a sunken husk. Wispy white hair trailed down her back. Hands criss-crossed with dark green veins and distended knuckles. Her torso had become so light and shrunken, even the child-size knitted cardigan hung loose, dangling as helplessly as her life.

Mustering all the strength she could call on, she shuffled along the bed, slowly, towards the books. The rain beat down, harder. She couldn't even distinguish the green and the yellow anymore – obliterated now with a thousand droplets.

At last, her fingers reached for the small, brown book. Golden letters embossed on the spine. The familiar feel of leather and the scent of the pages – almost like cinnamon – transported her to another time, another place.

Her greatest comfort had always been books. Escaping to other worlds was the only way she could cope with living in this one.

Today, she wanted to reread an old poem that had been her companion for many years. It transported her back to the time she began to make sense of the three-year-old Gracie. The beginning of the rest of the story.

> *I wandered lonely as a cloud*
> *That floats on high o'er vales and hills,*
> *When all at once I saw a crowd,*
> *A host, of golden daffodils;*
> *Beside the lake, beneath the trees,*
> *Fluttering and dancing in the breeze.*

That heartfelt sense of loneliness, that ache. That wistful feeling of casting adrift, aimlessly. And then – suddenly – a sense of hope, of beauty. A shining array of yellow, bursting onto the scene like sunshine. Imbuing the landscape with colour and brightness and energy. The lightness of touch – fluttering and dancing. . .

There was a cheery optimism, a sense of freshness and delicacy. Of transience. How a rain cloud had blossomed out of its solitude into a new dawn of companionship – see the words 'crowd' and 'host' bundling together and giving an atmosphere of bustle and busyness. And even more explicitly, the word 'company' – right there on the page. . .

The emotion it prompted touched something profound within her. A longing, and a deep felt pain.

Her fingers flickered through the leaves of the book and the pages fell open at another familiar passage. Unlike Wordsworth, master craftsman and well known to school children up and down the land – this second one was from an obscure Bohemian-Austrian poet practically no one had heard of. It didn't stop the words lifting off the page and softly singing to her, their lyric loveliness hanging in the air like a spell.

How should we be able to forget those ancient myths
That are at the beginning of all peoples.
The myths about dragons
That at the last moment turn into princesses.
Perhaps all the dragons of our lives are princesses
Who are only wanting to see us
Once beautiful and brave.
Perhaps everything terrible is in its deepest being
Something helpless, that wants help from us.
So you must not be frightened

If a sadness rises up before you
Larger than any you have ever seen.
If a restiveness like light and cloud shadows
Passes over your hands and over all you do
You must think that something is happening with you,
That life has not forgotten you.
That it holds you in its hand.
It will not let you fall.

Soft, silent tears began to drop onto the page. This poem was like a prayer for the young Gracie. A Secret Key. She remembered all those times they had sat together, mother and daughter, reading this strange but lovely poem the little girl had been given by Mr Hall at school. What had started as a homework project took on a different guise. The words sang deep into their hearts, binding them together. Creating a thread to the past of an invisible optimism buried deep in the child she once was.

She remembered trying to be brave . . . more times than anyone could possibly imagine. Even before the poetry of Rainer Maria Rilke had come into her life, his philosophy connected to something in her.

Eight years old, pigtails. Scratchy grey school skirt and a white blouse with rolled up sleeves. A long time ago.

Gracie, Tish and Jo had been asked to pack up the hall after morning assembly. It was one of those jobs you just groaned at when you'd been picked. Okay, so it was something you could tell your Ma and Da and they'd be proud of you, being all grown-up and that. But it also meant you were a swot or a teacher's pet.

The girls had mixed feelings. They didn't want to be teased when they went back to class. Who would? Tish and Jo started whispering and giggling. They were really tight with each other. Did everything together.

Gracie wasn't part of the in-crowd really. She had Billy out of school but she hadn't made much headway with girls her own age. She didn't know why.

Humming to herself, she carried on putting away the books and stuff, oblivious to the others. The melody of 'All Things Bright and Beautiful' was barely audible, but it was in her head and now it was floating softly into the hall.

English started in a few minutes' time so she concentrated on collecting up the remaining books. But where had Tish and Jo gone?

Gracie made her tenth trek back into the store cupboard, loading up the shelves. Then something strange happened. The door closed. The light switched off. There was the sound of laughter bubbling up in front of her. Disembodied giggles penetrating the darkness.

She couldn't see anything. It was completely dark apart from a tiny window covered in moss and mildew up in the corner.

Gracie felt herself being bundled onto the floor.

'Shut up, don't squeal, Pastie Gracie,' said a voice. Tish, probably.

She felt her arms being held. Hot breath hovering over her.

24

She felt like she imagined The Little Girl Lost must have done in William Blake's famous poem. Giggles of innocence morphing into brutal experience.

> *Lost in desert wild*
> *Is your little child.*
> *How can Lyca sleep*
> *If her mother weep?*

Then a short, stabbing feeling down her left arm.

'What are you doing? Let me go!' she begged, as the little stabs bore down on her skin. 'Please stop, please!'

Remembering her pleases, even in the midst of attack, Gracie had no idea what else to do. Then in an instant, she felt herself being released. The door opened with a judder – blinding daylight flooded in. Two figures bustled out, laughing helplessly. There was the sound of a slam and the purple-black darkness once again ate the light.

Gracie was still sitting on the ground. She crossed her legs and thought. As her eyes grew accustomed to the blackness of the cupboard, she detected a lizard-green gleam filter through the moss above her.

She got up and tried the door. Even before she pushed, she knew. Locked.

She sighed, and felt tiny tears prickling in her eyes and a tightness grip the back of her throat. She rubbed her sore arm, wondering what on earth had happened, and why.

There was nothing to be done but pray, she supposed. Nobody at school would be able to hear her – the store cupboard was at the back of the hall and no one was having PE until the afternoon. She would have to sit. And wait. And pray.

Gracie wasn't terribly sure who or what God was, but she knew he was the thing Mam turned to when she needed something. Well, Gracie needed something now – she needed to leave this horrible, reeking place with its sickly, black-green muskiness.

'Dear God,' she began. 'I don't know why I am in here, I don't know what I've done wrong. But please let me out of here, please, please, please.'

She waited, but nothing happened. A fleet of angels failed to appear, and the door failed to open.

'Please God, I want to get out. Please don't leave me in here . . .'

She sat cross-legged and wondered what she should do now.

The darkness took her back to another time, when a shadow became a raven. Briefly, she wondered, fear flickering in her blood, whether there was any possibility that there were any birds in the cupboard.

She listened intently. Nothing. Nothing at all.

Trying to stop the sense memory of what happened in the glen was futile. It crowded into her head, taunting her with the possibility of being. She remembered the way the beak and claws had leapt into life, swooping down towards her. She remembered the throbbing of her pulse rushing through her, dizzying her. She remembered trying to move, trying to scream.

The bird had brushed over her head, the tips of its wing and tail scraping at her head. Her babyish curls were lifted, swept skywards, as the black shadow dived to the ground in front of

26

her, pounced on a small, furry mouse, then launched back past her again.

She would never forget the sound of its beating wings for as long as she lived. A harsh, almost noiseless, whirring and slashing. Sitting here quietly now, locked in the darkness, all she could think about was the petrified mouse, gripped in the talons of a shadow's vice, settling into stillness. Death hung in the air above her, and somewhere the raven cawed a low, guttural kraaa.

The greenish sheen began to imbue the whole space with a cloying mossiness. The blackness of before faded into what looked at first like a peculiarly comforting den of leaves. Like one of Billy's dens.

Lost in thought, Gracie began to breathe properly again.

She began to make out shapes. Sharp corners of shelves, the ribbed spines of the books lined up. What looked like a broom in the corner, maybe a bucket. Boxes and boxes stacked up together. A mop and some pencils sticking out of a tin. It was like a silhouetted other world, where she began to feel safe.

Pencils

The lavender walls were beginning to feel oppressive. When she first arrived at this place, they said lavender was calming. Would be restful for her soul. Would help her relax.

What did they know?

She glanced down at the poem in her hand.

> *Perhaps everything terrible is in its deepest being*
> *Something helpless, that wants help from us.*

She wondered if this could possibly be true. The myths of the world are scattered with demons. Real life had even worse monsters.

In life, it would always start with something small. The boy who would carefully peel the wings off a fly, to see what happened. Or maybe it would be to laugh and to mock at an inferior existence. Next he'd slice off the tail of a worm. Drown a cat. Kill a man. Where would it end? Does a boy like this want help from us? Is he *really* helpless? Is there hope for redemption, or is the soul of this boy tainted with an evil that can only grow?

What are we, in our deepest beings? What is the truth?

And how can we know? What certainty can I seek?

I've tried to live my life the right way. I've tried to do good. But the torment never fades or subsides. An invisible force, always there. The sadness rises and rises, and never falls. Larger than any I have ever seen. And it will always be so.

She was sitting cross-legged, hands joined together in prayer. Waiting. So far, it didn't look much like God was going to be able to help her out. She wondered whether this was because she didn't really know who he was – and she knew she had definitely never met him.

But then a miracle really did happen. Gracie started as the door began to rattle.

Someone opened it and the beautiful white light shone in like something from a fairy story. She got up and made her way out, stumbling clumsily because she had pins and needles in her legs.

'Gracie, what on earth are you playing at?' demanded the teacher.

'Miss, thank you, thank you!' was all Gracie could think to say.

'Explain!'

Gracie frowned slightly, weighing up the balance of telling the truth and getting the girls in trouble, or fibbing and hopefully preventing a kicking.

'Gracie Scott, will you please tell me what happened now!' bellowed Mrs Thomas.

Gracie felt rather frightened, and wasn't very good at fibbing anyway, so she came out with it.

'The others locked me in, Miss, it was horrible, I felt scared.'

Gracie knew there was no honour to be had for dobbing in Tish and Jo, but she felt she had no choice. Mrs Thomas looked as if her head was about to explode, it had gone all red like a tomato. If it wasn't so serious, it would have been funny.

Gracie stifled a tiny giggle – she couldn't help herself. Completely ridiculous, she knew, but for some reason it just burpled up inside her. She willed herself to concentrate, to remember how just a few moments ago she would have given anything to escape. But looking at that red tomato face was just too much.

'Sorry Miss, it's been a rotten morning and I'm feeling sick.'

It was the only thing she could think of.

'Well, straighten yourself up and we'll take you to the nurse. I thought you were cannier than that, Gracie, letting yourself get knocked around by those two. Be careful in future.'

Gracie breathed a sigh of relief. Her accidental giggle had mercifully gone unnoticed. She pulled down her sleeves and couldn't help but catch sight of dark grey pockmarks all over her left arm. She remembered the stabbing sensation and wondered what had happened. Puzzling over this sobered her up, and she went to see the nurse.

It was mid-morning break by the time she got back. She decided to keep herself to herself. Not that this was particularly different to normal, but today, it was deliberate.

Tish and Jo wasted no time in trying to find her.

Gracie had sat on the grass outside the classroom, making a daisy chain, reflecting on her morning. She was thinking about seeing Billy later, and filling him in. She knew he'd want to have a right go at the girls, but he was a good lad. If she asked him to leave off, he would.

'Oi, telltale Pastie-Gracie.'

The words broke her out of her reverie. She groaned inside.

She spotted the girls were each holding a pencil.

'Want some more, do you? Do you?' they challenged, waving the pencils around.

They grabbed hold of Gracie and pulled up her left sleeve. Jo whispered fiercely, 'Shut up, be quiet, or else.' She was holding on to her tightly.

Tish started prodding the pencil lead into Gracie's arm, adding to the other grey spots.

It hurt horribly. Eyes watering, Gracie looked away, as if somehow this would make everything better. It didn't. The pain bore into her and wouldn't go away.

Gracie glanced at Tish, who was laughing and sharing glances with Jo. Gracie had no idea in the world why they would want to hurt her like this. She got the feeling she wouldn't find out, either.

The rest of the day passed without incident, but Gracie was aware of the throbbing in her arm. As the bell rang for the end of the day and everyone poured out of school, she was aware of voices trailing after her, warning her to watch out.

She hurried home.

'Hello, pet, glad you're back, love, can you give me a hand with the mangling?'

Her mother's cheerful voice filled the air with comfort and safety. Gracie did a lot of helping out at home. Didn't mind at all – it's what everyone did really. It was one of the good days today. Joe hadn't been back for weeks, and Mam was beginning to be a bit like her old self again.

'Can I have a drink first, Ma?' asked Gracie.

'Wait for your tea, love, we're running out of powdered milk and I've got a nice crumble to look forward to later for afters. Let's pitch in and get this done.'

Gracie knew she'd probably have a spam buttie for tea – boring, boring, boring – but the promise of crumble for afters was just too enticing for words. She wandered over to the sink, rolling up her sleeves. 'Thanks, Ma, canna wait.'

'Gracie, pet – what's all over your arm, love?'

Gracie froze. For the second time that day, she asked God for help. 'What should I say?' she asked under her breath.

'Gracie?'

Gracie glanced down at her forearm. It was red raw in places and fleckered with lead. It looked as if some demented flea had been at her.

'I don't know, Ma,' was all she could think of saying.

'Are you getting into trouble, doing bad things?'

The wireless wittered on in the background, buzzing gently from the other side of the room.

''Course not, no, no.'

'Well, what the flaming hell is tha'?'

Oh God, please help me, what am I supposed to say – people think I'm so worthless they lock me in cupboards and stab me with pencils? I can't do that to Mam. She's so miserable herself, I can't make her sadder. Please God, please . . .

Gracie looked up at her mother and shrugged her shoulders. Her deep-green eyes gazed up with truth and innocence and sadness.

She heard the blow before she felt it. A devastating whack on the side of her cheek. For the third time that day, tears pricked and there was a suffocation at her throat.

Reason collided with hope in that instant. She stared in wonder at her mother. The world was going mad.

'Never muck about like that again, do you hear me?' the voice, muffled through the vortex of Gracie's terror, shrieked and screamed. It didn't sound like Mam.

Another slap across the face.

Gracie felt like a wounded animal, didn't know where to look, what to say. Had this God who she didn't even know decided today was 'hate Gracie' day?

'Oh God, pet, I'm sorry, I'm sorry, I'm sorry, I'm sorry.'

Suddenly, she was bound in her mother's arms, feeling the hot wetness of maternal tears in her hair and on her forehead.

She was being rocked backwards and forwards, backwards and forwards.

Some time later, Gracie wondered whether she being punished for the tomato giggle. Did God somehow find out about that, and want to punish her for not being grateful for his miracle?

Right now, all she could do was silently resolve to keep out of harm's way, as best she could. She was aching all over from the pressure of her mother's embrace. Her cheek was stinging, her arm was sore, her heart was pounding. But worse than all of that was the sense that life was never going to be the same again.

Lemons

The room felt close, stuffy. A tiny space for a bed and a chair.
All she had were her memories and her books.

> *For oft, when on my couch I lie*
> *In vacant or in pensive mood,*
> *They flash upon that inward eye*
> *Which is the bliss of solitude;*
> *And then my heart with pleasure fills,*
> *And dances with the daffodils.*

That precious moment when the sadness of loneliness is
transported away and replaced with the thoughtfulness – and
deliberateness – of solitude.

And her own inward eye paused and reflected on thoughts of
happier times. That sense of optimism, when everything seemed
possible. When life had meaning and light.

She wanted to capture that bubble of hope and wallow in its
dreamy pensiveness. Wanted that moment of reflection and sunshine to last and last . . .

Her thoughts turned to another line that resonated with optimism, and she clung to it, tightly, willing it into being . . .

Lemons

Perhaps all the dragons of our lives are princesses . . .

Imagine if deep at its heart there was something clean and true in everyone. Under the scales of hate and venomous teeth, a golden seam of goodness. Beneath the roar of anger or indignation, the gentle call of forgiveness and compassion.

Was evil born, or made?

Was innocence something we all hold in our souls, only to be blackened and turned rotten by experience?

Why were the dragons of real life so much more terrifying than the monsters of storybooks?

Rain shards sliced onto the grey stone paving slabs. She started . . .

It was humid, wet and muddled. Just like inside her head. Turbulent colours of early summer whirling outside and in, slashing marks into life and imagination. The whirring noise of thought blurred with the complexity of vision. Dizzying. She inhaled. Eyes closed. Just let me breathe . . .

Gracie could feel the wetness of her own eyes mingling with the moistness of the clouds' tears. All she could think about was the dreadful, horrible thing that just happened. The scent of bitter lemons hung in the air.

She had noticed Uncle Joe stare at her for some time now. There was a peculiar intensity to his gaze. His eyes were so dark you couldn't even tell what colour they were.

His eyebrows furrowed together with deep tracks across his forehead. There was a sternness about him, a steeliness that stirred a dark anxiety deep within her.

A memory of another shadow oppressing her sank deeply inside, slowly tightening her throat and beating hard at her heart.

Gracie was becoming accustomed to this fierce attention. And she hated it.

A few years after Joe started living with them, he was having one of his periods away. There was a lightness in the air as both Gracie and her mother felt the softness of the light, and the lightness of their togetherness. The absence of darkness.

Tea had been an old favourite – beef mince with gravy. Served with extra potatoes today. Mam had spent the day washing and cooking so was a bit tired, but tired in a happy red-cheeked kind of way.

Gracie asked if she could have a bath. She loved the lemony foamy scent of the liquid soap – it smelt like sunshine. Bathing in its sweet citric fragrance was like being in a dream world. The foam looked like great mounds of snow, curved in waves, gently undulating with the movement of the water.

She lay there blissfully, imagining a world where the snow was hot, and ice smothered you with warm fuzzy lusciousness. Her whole body was submerged in a sea of snow – a white, crystalline landscape of magic and crackles.

She listened as the bubbles began to pop in little fits and starts. Like fairies chuckling together – a poppling and crickling as the snow began to melt.

Lemon ice – in some strange alchemy, warm and comforting,

enveloped her very being. She felt herself drifting into her thoughts, finding peace and silence in the bubbling snow.

A creak disturbed her reverie. The door was pushing ajar. She looked up.

Uncle Joe.

She expected him to gruffly grunt and move away, close the door. She hadn't heard him arrive home, and she hadn't heard the familiar whimper Mam made when he would push past her, dismissing her as he would a runty dog.

He walked in.

Her bones felt grey and cold – frozen. She couldn't move, not the merest hint of a whisper.

He looked at her, unblinking.

Where is Mam? Why is he in here? What should I do?

He turned halfway behind him, and reached for the key. Locked the door, noiselessly. As he put the key into his pocket, the jangle as it tinkled with coins was deafening.

Oh God, what's he doing? Why has he locked the door?

A familiar dizziness was blurring in her head. The big, black shadow hovered over her, waiting.

He looked at her face. The soft wetness of her skin was peachy pink. Her dark eyelashes were dotted with water droplets. The deep, forest-green of her eyes looking up at him with such uncertainty, such fear.

Her cheeks were rounded and dimpled.

Damp hair gathered in ringlets around the base of her neck, bubbling over gently. Eight years old and quiveringly sweet.

He took in her small hands, her tiny shoulders. Her almond

milkiness. The perfect little nose and the rosebud mouth. Her scent . . . her freshly bathed lemon scent.

Condensation was dripping down the blue-painted walls. A ceramic bowl sat squatly by the sink, crammed with a hair brush, a small hand mirror and some bright red ribbons. An enamel pot – painted with golden splashes – held a fistful of withering stalks and week-old crocuses.

The fragrance of lemons overwhelmed him for a moment, as he caught himself and looked back down at the ashen loveliness lying in the clouds of whiteness.

Droplets of water gathered in blue streams down the blue paint. Puddles sploshed together at the rim of the bath as the dampness collected.

The snow was beginning to melt. Paralysed with not knowing, a stabbing in her chest incomprehendingly penetrating the core of her soul. Blue-black-purple stars prickling the backs of her eyelids.

The small mirror above the sink was hazy with mistiness. The floor was linoleum cold.

A chilly breeze seemed to hang in the air, at once motionless and stirringly real.

There was silence, save for the intermittent crackling of the slowly dissipating bubbles.

The snow was melting, revealing a pale form, a body.

Gracie's heart was beating hard from embarrassment and fright. Only once in her life had anyone other than Mam seen her private, secret self.

It was a night a couple of years ago. For some unknown

reason, she was rushed next door to number 28 – her mother gripping her tightly. A grimness set in her face, she looked in pain. Inaudibly, she seemed to be agreeing something with Mrs Harper, Billy Harper's Ma.

There were nods and an exchange of worried looks. Mam winced, her face contorting with some unknown wretchedness.

Then Mam left.

Mrs Harper bustled around, fussing noisily about the place.

'You'll have to sleep in the back room, but you won't mind that, will you, pet?'

Gracie wasn't entirely sure what was going on – why was she having to sleep anywhere other than in her own bed – and where had Mam gone?

Billy and his brothers tumbled through the front door shortly after that – a jumble of chatter and laughter and rough-and-tumble.

'Oi, leave off!' said Simon, tugging away from Billy.

'Gerrof!' said Billy, jabbing back.

The boys each took a stance – professional boxers would be proud – and launched in for another round.

'Grow up, you two,' John, the eldest chipped in. 'I'm tired, I want some tea.'

It was at this point that Gracie wombled into the front room. She'd been out at the back with Mrs Harper, helping her prepare some strawberry jam sandwiches.

'Gracie!' yelled Billy, and ran up to her. 'What are you doing here? Are you staying for tea?'

'Seems like it. Mam's had to go away so I'm staying here tonight. We can play princes and princesses!'

The evening passed with the energy and excitement you'd imagine when an unexpected playmate turns up. Jam sandwiches were the feasts of kings and underneath the dining room table was – of course – the secret witches' lair. The witches were trying to trap the prince and the princess – though the tricky thing was that they were completely and utterly invisible. The worst kinds of witches.

But the prince and princess were strong and true, and with pure hearts they found a way to defeat the evil witches. They made their escape, fortified with magic red jam made with magic red berries.

Then it wasn't long before the yawns began to take over and Billy and Gracie agreed that even princes and princesses needed their sleep.

Billy's house had three bedrooms. His brothers slept in one room, and he slept in the tiny, cupboard-like backroom next to his Ma and Da's. He thought of it as his very own fortress – and at the top of the turret, he loved the window looking out to the stars.

He showed Gracie the sparkling dots filling the sky with luminescent twinkles. The moon shone its golden cream milkiness onto the tops of trees in the distance. Far away, there was the sound of foxes crying.

The turret – just an ordinary window really – was a vista onto a world of secrets and magic. The sky, midnight velvet, was dense and thick.

Mary – Mrs Harper – had told Billy that he'd have to let Gracie stay with him tonight – and she joked with Gracie that she'd have to put up with Billy and his smelly feet.

They laughed in excitement at this very new adventure – Gracie couldn't ever remember staying anywhere other than home, and Billy was bursting with the privilege of looking after her.

The lights went down and the two of them chatted up close under the big furry blanket. Downstairs, Mrs Harper was pottering away, tidying up.

'Do you get scared sometimes Gracie, in the night I mean?'

Gracie paused, looking at him intently. The moonlight was flooding into the room and dappling onto the walls. Her eyes were bright with moonbeams.

'It's always the big, black shadow, Billy, the raven. He comes to me in my dreams and he looks at me. He won't stop looking at me!'

She caught her breath, transfixed with the memory.

Billy patted her gently on her arm.

'He won't hurt you, Gracie, it's just a stupid bird.'

Billy started to tickle Gracie to make her forget the bird. He'd wanted to tell her about his own fears, how he'd spend hours reliving those treacherous nights, wondering whether his Da was going to survive the War, wondering what *he'd* do if one day *he* got asked to fight.

Billy got scared in the night. Every night. It didn't help that his Da was away fighting for the first few years of his life. His absence was so real you could touch it. A Da-shaped hole where a Da should be.

The tickling seemed to be working. Gracie was giggling and the light in her eyes was dancing again.

'I know what would be fun, Gracie – have you ever wondered about boys and girls?'

Gracie had no idea what he was talking about. She knew boys and girls were different – of course they were! – but she didn't really know much other than boys grow into men and stink more and have shorter hair and when they're men have beards sometimes, where girls grow into ladies and smell lovely and have nice long hair. Ladies didn't grow beards, ever.

Billy attempted to explain, but crumbled into fits of laughter.

'What is it, what is it, Billy?' Gracie asked him, beginning to tickle him back.

'Oh Gracie,' he giggled, 'it's so funny, but it's a kind of secret. Boys and girls have got different bits – want to see? I can show you me if you show me you!'

Gracie thought this sounded brilliant. She had no idea she was going to learn mystifying things about life this evening.

Billy pulled down his pyjama bottoms and let her peek inside.

Gracie squealed as she looked at the wriggly pink worm half hidden in the dark.

'That's such a funny secret! Have Simon and John got the same thing?'

Billy nodded, 'And Da! But Ma doesn't. I've seen. Now show us yours then!'

Gracie pulled up her nightie and showed him.

They collapsed into giggles and talked some more and laughed some more and talked some more.

'You two, pack it in, go to sleep,' Mrs Harper's voice floated up.

It made them laugh even harder, with those funny silent

giggles you get when you're trying really hard not to make any noise. Punctuated with tiny snorts which made them laugh even harder, it wasn't long before the two of them dozed off, exhausted with playtime.

Ripples

Each little flower that opens,
Each little bird that sings,
He made their glowing colours,
He made their tiny wings.

Gracie hummed the words of the hymn inside her head. She thought concentrating would help her somehow. But she wasn't sure it was working. The fear gripped her, constricting her throat as it did before. Surely Uncle Joe wouldn't hurt her? But the blurriness of her vision was swirling.

Tiny wings.

Gracie started. *Wings.* The bird.

Joe was standing above her, the shadow of his huge form casting darkness over her. His eyes glinted with the reflections of the water. His mouth was set in a half-smile. The lines on his face seemed thrown into relief like an etching in an old book. The scratchy outline of his stubble was silhouetted against the faint twilight misting through the pane of glass. His nose, horned and stern. Hard. Avian.

And his stygian black eyes had a deadness to them – the

dancing light merely a glittery mask. A patina of life painted over the dullness of death.

A flicker stirred inside him. He was beginning to ache, looking at her, so pretty.

Her nipples were small and round and pink. Not developed at all yet – could have been a boy's. Her hips were slender, her arms softly tawny from last summer. Her limbs stretched downwards. But as she saw him casting his eyes down her legs, she drew them up to her chest and clutched herself, tightly.

Her tiny hands were whitening from the strain of holding her knees so hard to herself. Her eyes, fixed on him, posed a question he had no intention of answering.

His hands were clenched, the tension throbbing through his blue veins. Skin rough and scaly. Nails dirty and ragged. She thought about the little mouse, gripped in the talons of a dreadful darkness.

Blood surged through her head and her heart was beating so loudly it was causing little ripples in the water. The last of the snow was dissipating.

The wet dewiness of her skin beckoned him. He could sense her excitement. He could see her eyes darkened in want and in need – their greenness masked by the pools of shiny, tarry blackness of widening pupils. He could tell she wanted him . . .

She had never been so terrified. The way he was piercing her with his hard gaze, the clenching and unclenching of his huge hands.

Where's Mam? she wanted to know. Why hadn't she come

45

up? Why had she let Uncle Joe come into the bathroom? Panic rose up in her.

She glanced at the locked door and tried to work out what to do, still clinging desperately to herself, protecting her nakedness as best she could. She had no idea what Uncle Joe wanted, but she knew it couldn't be good.

It reminded her of that feeling, trapped inside the cupboard at school. She had no idea why the girls had been so cruel, but the moment she saw them huddling together and glancing her way, she knew there would be trouble.

Locked inside that small, damp room, she had felt helpless and bereft. Uncomprehending. Frightened. Alone. She had heard the blood pounding through her head on that day, too. And she had just as little clue then as now about why she had been singled out for bad stuff by bad people. Had she done something wrong? She was sure she was as good as can be, but for some reason things kept happening to her. A wave of nausea swept through her.

She decided she only had three options. She could either leap out of the bath and try to run away; ask Joe to pass her a towel; or lie there and find out what he was there for, what he wanted with her.

The trouble was, it looked as if he was waiting for something. His face was contorting into different expressions – seemingly in pain one moment and ecstasy the next. He continued to twist his hands, leaving white marks where he had pressed too hard.

If she tried to run away, he could catch her – most probably *would* catch her – and who knows what he may do. If she asked for a towel, he would laugh at her, mock her. She could feel the scorn boring into her. If she stayed, she didn't know what would happen . . .

The afternoon light was fading now and the raindrops had become intermittent spits and spots. Razor slashes melted into caressing kisses, rippling in puddles on the terrace. A stillness settled in the garden, and a calmness descended into the room, and in her.

The old, fragile woman reflected on the young girl's dilemma. An ensnared creature, imprisoned in every sense – and no way out. By that point, not a word had been spoken by either prisoner or jailer. A grim silence presided. The thick fug of anticipation – fear from one, excitement from the other.

The faded book was still in her gnarled hands. She traced the words again with a bent, twisted finger:

> *So you must not be frightened*
> *If a sadness rises up before you . . .*
> *You must think that something is happening with you,*
> *That life has not forgotten you,*
> *That it holds you in its hand,*
> *It will not let you fall.*

The old woman knew that it was this very sentiment that had sustained the little girl in the school store cupboard and later, locked in the bathroom with her uncle. In her heart, she believed she had not been forsaken, that somehow, some way, it would all be alright.

And then my heart with pleasure fills,
  And dances with the daffodils.

But right now, it was hard to see a way out. She certainly felt forgotten. And the dizziness that kept sweeping over her made her feel as if she was falling, falling, falling . . .

Flowers

The night at Billy's was a big adventure, but the next day Gracie's mother wearily came to collect her daughter. She looked tired. Purple shadows circled under her eyes, and her face looked worn and old.

'Mrs Scott, can Gracie come to stay again please? Please?' asked Billy, winking at Gracie. She trusted him and loved him more than life itself and, if truth be told, it was rather lonely just being at home alone with Mam all the time. She and Billy had promised each other that they would try to have more evenings like that – more evenings with princes and princesses and secrets and surprises.

Gracie's mother looked blankly at Billy and offered a weak smile. 'I'm sure we can arrange that, Billy, pet,' she said, softly.

'Now come on, you, let's get you home, Gracie.'

Years later, Billy would visit the lavender room, usually with a small posy of flowers. It was Billy who kept her going really, a link to a time when life had moments of real joy. That life was long gone now, of course. A faded memory to match the faded flowers, withering in the glass jar by the window.

'Thank you, Billy, dear, they're lovely,' her voice was rasping with the effort of speaking. 'The daffs are long gone, dear.'

Billy had brought her a small handful of freesias. Their scent wafted into the room, lifting the darkness of the walls with a momentary freshness. Billy busied himself, emptying the old flowers into the bin and rinsing the ceramic vase out. He ran the tap for a moment and filled the vase almost to the brim, stashing the flowers inside. Yellows and pinks, they were, a perfect spring captured – if not elegantly – then prettily in their new home.

'How are you?' he asked. Billy had always been so very lovely. She remembered him coming around all the time in those days, the eagerness and exuberance of youth – his voice excitable, his boisterousness exhausting.

'I've brought you a newspaper, thought you might fancy a read,' he said, handing her the paper. It was true, she liked to try to stay in touch, but there was such a wealth of dispiriting stories in the papers it hardly raised the soul.

These days, they didn't have all that much to say, but it was touching that he never forgot her, always visited when he could.

He'd made a very good living and was looking well on it, too. Billy Harper – who'd have thought it – ran his own business now, having worked his way up from sweeping the floor and learning the ropes from scratch. These days he owned a small components factory.

'Now the world needs computers, the world needs me,' he would say, touching his finger lightly on his nose. He'd cornered the market in a particular type of resistors for circuit boards – nobody could make them better, or cheaper. 'Secret's in the design, in the imagination of the design,' he would say.

Billy was always one for a vivid imagination. He just had to close his eyes and he could invent new worlds, new games, new adventures. In the blink of an eye you would be a unicorn or a goblin or a ballerina – your kingdom, forest or stage unveiling before your very eyes. Dragons and princesses, magic and mystery.

Where he retained a youthfulness and sunniness, she had become a bird-like shadow of herself. An old woman. Terminally ill and waiting for the inevitable. Bitterness and sorrow creasing in every line across her face.

His ruddy cheeks burst with smiles, usually, but today, glowed with embarrassment, because he had no idea what to say to her.

'What've you been up to?' he asked.

'Oh, you know, there's so much going on here, so much going on, I can't keep up.'

These days, her memory was more and more unreliable. Partly a consequence of the life she had been dealt – she had wanted to obliterate so many memories . . . And partly the treatment. Such invasive medical procedures were bound to have their consequence. But it was also partly age . . . she had withered physically and mentally in the last few years. The books were both a solace and a source of torment . . .

Her mind drifted away.

The shadow hovered above her, and she saw Uncle Joe slowly reach for his belt. Eyes fixed on her, he carefully stroked the

metal buckle. Backwards and forwards, backwards and forwards, it seemed as if he wanted to polish it.

He began to undo the buckle, let the harsh leatheriness of the
strap pass roughly through the spokes. The thud of leather
against metal was a sound she would never forget.

He seemed to hesitate. Was it that he wanted to beat her? She
knew that at school naughty children were beaten with a belt.
She racked her brains – had she been naughty? Had she done
anything that someone thought was naughty?

Suddenly, she realised with an explosion of recognition that
this must all be her fault. Like being locked in the cupboard,
like being stabbed with pencils, like being slapped by her
mother. It must all be her fault. God must think – somehow –
she wasn't sure how – that she was a bad person.

She tried desperately to think what she had done that was so
wrong. She loved her Mam, she tried hard at school (although
spelling was always a chore) and she did her best to be helpful
and kind. She said her prayers, even though she didn't particularly know who God was, really, and she always did what
she was told. So what was it?

Her eyes widened as she wondered at her fate. She watched
the big man, familiar and yet unfamiliar, his belt hanging
loosely down his sides. She sensed his breath coming fast and
heavy. She smelt that old stench of bitter treacliness. Everything
about him disgusted her.

He put one hand inside his trousers and let out a deep, dark
groan. His dancing eyes closed for a moment.

She watched him move his hand up and down inside his
trousers, faster and faster. With a sickening dread, she knew

what he must have inside there – the same as Billy's, but different.

He paused and looked at her, approaching the side of the bath with the stealth of a beast approaching its prey, silently. But this was in full view – she could see him. He could see her. She could hear his breathing . . . he could hear hers.

He touched the top of her head, stroking her hair softly. He circled his fingers along her temples, tracing downwards towards her ear. Back to the top of her head, stroking, stroking. Teasing her wispy curls. Stroking, stroking.

She made herself focus on the petals of the yellows and pinks, shoved carelessly into the small white pot by the sink. Small, perfect, pretty. Spring captured.

The strains of a musical phrase echoed inside her . . .

Each little flower that opens . . .

She wasn't quite sure what happened next, but whatever it was proved to be her lifeline. The bird flew away.

Myths

Billy's visits were something she looked forward to. Sometimes she momentarily lost herself, forgetting who he was or how he knew her. Sometimes she would ask him questions of such apparent obviousness, she would dissolve into embarrassment when she realised what she had said.

Her face would crease with recognition when the answer came back, the lines etched deep around her eyes and across her forehead searing with age and memory; her eyes flickering with recognition.

A flash of pain would indicate she'd suddenly remembered something.

Billy would look at her, barely recognising her. An old woman, a frail, bird-like creature with wizened limbs and a hollow chest.

Seeing her like that would make him feel so deeply sorry for her. There was nothing much he could do – other than come along from time to time and try to brighten her day.

The trouble was, there were so many awful memories; seeing her would stir his own thoughts. Usually, for days after his visits, he couldn't sleep properly. There was too much sadness, too much damage. His own heart never properly healed, probably never would.

'Remind me what those flowers are called, Billy?' she asked.

'Freesias, they're called freesias. I remember you used to have them in your bathroom at home.'

'Oh yes, yellows and pinks. I remember. They used to make everything smell pretty, like spring. I think I can still smell them . . .'

She inhaled and slowly closed her watery eyes. She would wince from time to time, agony coursing through her body.

She looked like any other little old lady. Gentle, soft, rather sweet. Her voice trembled as she spoke – it had got progressively raspier with age. It almost sounded as if she was speaking with two notes at once, like the strings of a cello played at the same time.

Billy reflected that she had been through so much, it was a wonder she had survived this long. Her illness was excruciating, debilitating. Her treatment had been long and extreme. There wasn't much time left.

He wondered what she could still remember. Did she sometimes think about Joe? He shuddered at the thought of him. About the old house? About old times?

'Do you want me to read to you? Or would you rather chat today?'

'I've been reading some poetry again. Perhaps you could read a little out loud for me? I'm not sure what I am in the mood for today . . .'

Billy had never been one for poetry, but he remembered once in English, in between the Wordsworths and the Shakespeares and the Byrons, there was a little Rilke poem tucked away that he'd been given as homework. It didn't make much impact on him – he much preferred a nice old traditional sonnet by one of the greats. Especially because the homework piece was part of a series of letters from one unknown poet to another random young poet who he'd never heard of. But he did remember that somewhat obscurely, Rilke had been a favourite of Gracie's. Why she had latched onto him, he wasn't sure. But something about it gave her comfort and solace. And that can only be a good thing.

When they were at school, she'd told him she and her Mam used to read one of the pieces out loud, like it was a prayer or a wish or something.

Much later in his adult life, he came across a reference to Rilke and felt inspired to find out a little more about him. It reminded him of Gracie, and anything that bonded him to her was special in his book.

His mind drifted off as he recalled what he'd learned. Born in Prague, at the time of the Austro-Hungarian Empire, Rilke lived through a terrible childhood. Peculiar, it was. He'd been forced to wear little girls' clothes to compensate for his mother's earlier loss of a baby girl. Although he would become known as Rainer Maria, his mother instead called him Sophia. He went on to become – said the article – one of the world's greatest lyric writers. Wrote in German, apparently.

Rilke had eventually died, so people said, from an infection he'd contracted after pricking himself with the thorn of a rose.

A sad life, but an unusual one. An artistic adventure, threaded through with love and passion and withdrawal. Critics said his writing was imbued with such wisdom, mystery, depth and longing.

Much to his surprise, Billy recalled a quote of his:

Surely all works of art are consequences of having been in danger, of having gone to the very end in an experience, to where man can go no further.

Where was that place? Where man can go no further? He suspected Gracie had known – had been there.

He remembered the job in hand. 'How about those Rilke letters?' he asked.

'Oh yes, I love the letters.'

He remembered Gracie telling him as she got older, the joyous past time of blowing bubbles together with her Ma was gradually replaced by soothing, happy times together sitting and reading. Gracie had loved reading poetry out loud to her mother, and had developed a real passion for both Wordsworth and Rilke she wanted to explore and talk about. She told him how much she treasured those times, talking her Ma through her interpretations of poems. How her Ma had told her when she was a little girl, she used to like reading, too, but that she had never got the hang of poetry. Gracie thought that was funny, and in her knowing way would say that poetry held the Secret Key.

There was a particularly long period Gracie had told him about when Joe had disappeared for ages, and the two of them had pored over a book Gracie had discovered on a dusty shelf in the library. The Rilke. In a strange kind of way, Gracie had told him, they had taken such comfort and succour in the words, had almost lured themselves into thinking maybe this time, he wasn't coming back.

It wasn't to be.

He scanned the bookshelf and spotted the small, familiar volume. Its dark brown cloth cover well worn over the years, the colour of tobacco. He felt the gold lettering etched into the spine.

Billy turned to the page with the floral bookmark. An old, creased cardboard strip printed with a cascade of white roses. Why roses? he mused, a memory stirring somewhere . . .

> *How should we be able to forget those ancient myths*
> *That are at the beginning of all peoples,*
> *The myths about dragons*
> *That at the last moment turn into princesses . . .*

His mind drifted back to a sunny day when he'd invented a new game for his little friend. He knew Gracie adored him. It made him feel important, big, brave.

He would spend hours plotting clever new ideas they could play out together. He'd draw inspiration from fairy tales. But he wanted something better than mere stories, he'd wanted something real. He wanted to create a dream world where the two of them could escape for hours, perhaps losing themselves forever.

It would be one way to keep the nightmares at bay. Every evening, as darkness fell, he would feel the familiar beat of his heart. He'd fret about war. He'd anxiously worry about his Da.

He'd think what would happen to his family, if there was another war. He'd feel sick, wondering whether one day he'd be called to fight.

Inventing games was one way he used to run away from his night fears. He would try to banish the thoughts by thinking up new things he'd be able to play with Gracie. He'd remember the story of Hansel and Gretel, and wonder if he could come up with something where a boy and a girl would find themselves in a wood. He'd remember the stories he'd heard – ancient legends and myths where dragons would turn into princes and princesses, and plot how to make them real.

The first time they played dragons and princesses had ended with terror and tears. It started off well enough. Beautiful sun-shiny day, Gracie chuckling with pleasure.

They started the game, and the two of them were having the time of their lives.

He let Gracie advance further into the woodland, to prepare the secret surprise of the game.

He sneaked away in silence, so that Gracie wouldn't see. He knew she would be pottering along, happily running onwards, away from the dragon. He wanted to surprise her with a collection of flowers. This was the big surprise – he wanted to impress her with his magic – how he'd transform the dastardly dragon into a perfect prince, and to prove it, present her with a suitably royal posy of white roses. It's not the kind of thing he would have dreamed of playing with his brothers, of course. The very idea of pretending to be a prince! They'd have never let him live that one down. But with Gracie he was free. He could be anything for her, and she would love him for it.

He meandered back out to the edge of the glen where the pathway was strewn with rose bushes. He reached out with chubby fingers and carefully twisted then snapped the flowers from the bases of their stems. He was very pleased with himself – she was never going to guess. He heard her chuckling away in the distance, calling his dragon name in delight.

He got lost in his thoughts for a moment, wondering whether to just collect white roses or to mix them up with other flowers. He was aware of the stillness of the air and the darkness of the shadows of the trees. He realised it was getting late, so decided he'd better hurry back to the cosiness of the wood and reveal to her the magical transformation from dragon to prince.

Suddenly, he heard her call out with a terrible scream. 'Billy!' The sound of it momentarily stopped the blood pumping to his heart. His ears filled with nothingness, as sheer, black fear gripped him. A primal fear as old as time itself.

'Gracie! Gracie!' he called, running in the direction of her voice. He couldn't see her, couldn't see anything. In front of him was a hazy rushed blur of green and brown. He was stumbling over roots and looking wildly around, unseeingly.

'Gracie!'

The trees were closing in on him and the sky became darker. The wind began to whistle above, as a shadow swept over the trees.

Nothing but branches and leaves. Nothing but mud. Nothing but silence.

At last, he saw her tiny body lying on the ground.

His worst fears rose up inside him. What had happened to her? Had she fallen? Had something frightened her?

Then, slowly . . . The most terrible question of all . . . was she dead?

He hurried to her side.

'Gracie! Are you alright?' She began to stir. He bent down to her, watching her as she opened her eyes. A sigh of relief overwhelmed his whole being.

'What happened?'

She was curled up as if she had been asleep. Her face had that sleepiness about it everybody has when they've just woken up.

He stood up, looking around. He pondered what on earth could have happened. And he wondered what he could do to make things better.

He looked at her frightened face, and had no idea what to do. He always panicked when he had one of his nightmares, the ones where your heart races fast and you wake up with your hair sticking to your forehead. She looked how he felt after one of those night terrors. He searched his mind for something to say.

'Is this some new kind of game, where The Princess goes hiding away from The Dragon?'

He tried to keep his voice nice and normal, and even managed a little laugh, as if he was teasing her. All he wanted was to make her feel better. To stop her being frightened.

He couldn't make any sense of what she was saying. Something to do with a bird and hurting hands.

He did his best to cheer her up, and they began to make their way home. As they walked back through the woods, he spotted the tangle of flowers he'd picked for her in a clump where he'd dropped them. They didn't look nearly as pretty anymore. Just a jumble of fading colour meshed with brown muddiness. Their freshness broken into crumples. What peculiar thing had happened here today? He decided to leave the flowers be.

Ladybirds

It was months later that Gracie found out the truth about some quite important things. It hadn't been very long since she had had to spend the night round at Billy's. That marvellous, fun-filled night when she learned a thing or two about anatomy.

Some time later, she overheard a conversation that perplexed her horribly.

'I lost the wee bairn,' she was hearing Mam saying. 'Probably for the best – it's all God's will. It would have been difficult for Gracie if it had survived – and Lord knows it's hard enough providing for both of us on the buses.'

Gracie had been dawdling on her way home from school, and had got distracted by some ladybirds which looked as if they were trailing after each other. Ladybirds were elegant, pretty little creatures, with perfectly formed dots on shiny red backs. Part of the beetle family, she knew that, and, she thought with a chuckle, she knew they did yellow poo from the times that she had held them in her hands. She loved the way they puttered about on their short stumpy legs, then at a moment's notice could fly into the sky in a haze of red fuzziness.

The ladybirds were dallying through the grass outside number 12, the Armstrongs'. Mam's friend Ivy, Mrs Armstrong, lived there with Mr Armstrong and three little Armstrongs. Gracie wasn't terribly keen on the three little Armstrongs – they were the sorts of kids that stared a lot and didn't say very much. They were either very very clever, or very very daft, and Gracie hadn't made her mind up which was right.

The door to number 12 led straight into the kitchen area, and Mrs Armstrong was leaning on the Formica counter with a cup of tea in her hand. Gracie's mother couldn't be seen from outside, but the strains of her voice fluted onto the air and drifted outside.

Gracie looked up from the ladybirds, and listened.

'You poor, poor thing. Here, give us a cuddle,' she heard Mrs Armstrong saying. She heard her mother muffling into Mrs Armstrong's arms and stifling a tear.

'It's alright, you can cry, you can cry pet.'

And with that, she saw the door push slowly shut, and the story hung in the air.

The ladybirds were continuing on their way, apparently unabashed by what had just been said. Their shiny coats blazed in the sunshine and their grassy path was a jungle of adventures. They ploughed on unawares.

Gracie, on the other hand, was forced to sit herself down. She squished into the green tufts, taking care to avoid any ants and dandelions. She knew her mother hadn't been looking after any other children at home, so she couldn't have lost one there. She contemplated the possibility that she'd been tasked to look after someone on the buses and had managed to lose him or her there. But why would that have had anything to do with Gracie

– and why was Mam saying it would have been hard on her 'if it had survived'? It was all a complete mystery.

Later that evening, as Gracie began helping clearing away the tea things, she thought she would broach the subject.

'Ma, when did you lose a wee bairn?'

Her mother looked at her, barely disguising the surprise she felt. 'What do you mean, pet?' she asked, gathering her thoughts.

'I was looking at the ladybirds and heard you saying you'd lost one. And that it was for the best. So I wondered what had happened?'

Gracie's mother sat down at the dining room table. The old lace cloth looked rather tired and worn these days, its crochet holes looping rather too large in places. The dark wood grain underneath felt solid and warm, as old as time.

Gracie watched her Ma glance around the room. She followed her gaze. The orange walls were suddenly too bright, too bold, and as for the curtains . . . She suddenly hated their floral pattern. Why were things feeling so strange today?

'Oh Gracie, pet. As you know, I've been growing a baby inside my tummy. We were going to have a little brother or sister for you, pet. But God decided it wasn't the right thing to happen, so it didn't happen. That's all. Now come and give me a hug.'

Gracie stared at her mother. Her tummy was still much more round and big than normal, it had been gradually swelling as the baby grew. The little girl felt torn between feeling horribly sad for her Ma, who was clearly devastated about this revelation

. . . and feeling incredibly sad and confused on her own behalf. Where had this new baby brother or baby sister gone? What happened? And why? Then – a panicked thought – did her Ma lose the baby because God thought Gracie wouldn't want it? She walked slowly towards her mother, twisting with guilt and upset and empathy.

They hugged for the longest time. Silence embraced them, bringing them close and snug. Mam buried her face into Gracie's soft skin and they sat there, Gracie curled into her lap, each drawing comfort from the other.

After a while, her mother began weeping hard, jagged sobs, breaking down with dreadful, noisy inhalations, gulping for air between tears. She stayed buried in her daughter's warm, milky neck, her mind filled with untold memories and sadnesses.

'Is that what happened to Violet, I mean Mrs Sherwood, Ma, you know, when her baby went to Heaven?' Gracie asked, quietly.

At that, her mother collapsed into deep, uncontrollable retches, and she was rendered helpless and speechless.

Gracie couldn't think what to do, so she just sat there, holding on tight, stroking her mother's hair as gently and softly as she could.

Something in the back of her mind was joining the dots between all the adults in her life; and the notions of Heaven and joy, life and death. She wasn't sure what to make of any of it, but she realised it was a terribly sad thing when God decided not to let you have a baby after all.

It made her think about the day they had sat outside, blowing bubbles. The day she had learned Mam had a baby growing inside her tummy.

She knew now that she would never meet the baby after all.

Moonbeams

The bath water was beginning to feel cold. Gracie began to focus on the room again. The flowers sat reassuringly in their vase; the stumpy ceramic pots were in their place. The door was slightly ajar. But other than her, the room was empty. She breathed out.

Gracie touched the top of her head gently, water droplets trickling down her arms. He'd only stroked her softly, but it felt as if he'd left gouges of scent – almost something physical of himself, tangled up with her hair.

She plunged deep into the water, scrubbing herself fiercely with the Lux soap. Only when her skin had become pinkly raw did she stop. She realised she was crying.

She stepped out of the bath and wrapped herself tightly into a towel. The mirror – only a small, tarnished old thing – showed a little girl with fear in her eyes. And those eyes were red with tears.

Gracie bent to let the water out of the bath and waited, listening until the very last dribbles swirled out. The snowy foam had long melted, but the lingering aroma of lemon soap bubbles hung in the air. Mixed – tainted – with the dirtier smell of a man's sweat and breath. Something profound had happened here today – even the air knew it.

She went into her bedroom and began to dress into her nightie. It was white cotton with small, pink bows sewn into the neckline, had short puffy sleeves, and went all the way down to the floor. A modesty she appreciated somewhere deep in her being on this day, even if she couldn't quite articulate why.

She plonked herself on top of the bed and reached for her beloved knitted rabbit. Baby Victoria was looking up at her from the cradle on the floor, but Samson was more cuddly. More than anything right now, Gracie wanted a cuddle.

She wanted to go and snuggle into her mother's arms, but she didn't want to see Uncle Joe again, and she wasn't sure what she should say to Mam about why she was so upset.

She peeked around the doorway and listened. The house felt silent. Making her way to the top of the stairs, she risked a glance over the banisters. She couldn't hear Joe snoring, which is what he seemed to spend most of his time doing, but she also couldn't hear anything else.

The silence hummed and buzzed in her ears as she waited and wondered. Everywhere had got dark. The blood pounded noisily around inside her, as she willed her own body to be quiet. Even her own breathing seemed loud.

She began to work her way down the stairwell, wincing at each and every creak. She passed the plates mounted on the walls, their gilded rims gleaming in the moonlight. She was aware of the intensity of the darkness, and the brightness of the moonbeams casting fierce light in streaks around the lounge.

To her relief, there was Mam, sprawled across the settee and sleeping. No wonder she hadn't stopped Uncle Joe – she was asleep.

Gracie made her way across the floor, her feet tap-tap-tapping against the lino. She went up to her mother's head and knelt down beside her, the tears beginning to prickle again in her throat.

'Wake up, Mam!'

Her thoughts were willing the sleeping figure awake but she remained silent. That beautiful face looked so serene in this light, she almost didn't want to tell her, to disturb this calmness. But then, a trickle of black blood glinted up at her. She realised with a sudden shock that her mother wasn't just sleeping, but had been hit and was bleeding.

All thoughts of her own misery floated into nothingness as she tried to rouse the grown woman lying in front of her.

'Mam, wake up! Wake up! Mam!' she said out loud this time.

The first stirrings of recognition flickered across her mother's forehead. Slowly, she began to squint and open her eyes. One of them was crusted with blood.

'Are you badly hurt?' asked Gracie, her small hands trying to wipe away the blood.

'I'm alright, pet, I'm alright. You're a canny bairn. I'll be alright.'

She tried to sit up and shuddered from the pain.

'Should I go and get someone? Do you need help?' the little girl wondered.

Her mother looked at her – the pain a heavy veil hanging over her eyes.

'No, pet, I'll be alright. Run along, dear. It's late. Why don't you go to bed and I'll clear up here . . .'

It was sometime later that Gracie learned Joe had struck her mother on his way out of the house, just after he'd abruptly left the bathroom.

Gracie supposed she had been in too much of a dazed state to hear or see. She remembered feeling as if time was in suspension. All she was conscious of were the petals of the flowers, and the ripples in the water as her heart beat with a continuous, butterfly rhythm. All sounds were banished in this slow-motion world. And it wasn't long before her vision was likewise relegated into oblivion.

She had no idea how long she had been in this neverland. A minute? A day?

She remembered realising that Joe had definitely gone as her eyes refocused, bringing noise and sight back into the real time world.

At that moment, she could not comprehend what had taken place, couldn't explain the hunger in his eyes, his grunts of – what were they? Pain? Or pleasure?

And she had no idea at all why he had put his hand inside his trousers.

She had no idea why he had looked at her as if he almost wanted to devour her – a famished man hungrily surveying his first sight of food. The wildness darting in his eyes made him look like a mad animal.

She felt a pang of despairing regret as she thought perhaps Joe had lashed at her mother because he was angry with *her*.

She still didn't understand why her mother had somehow allowed him to come upstairs and enter the bathroom when she was in there. That just wasn't allowed, wasn't right. There was a lot Gracie didn't understand.

Storybook notions of good and evil were beginning to come to life for real – she sensed something very bad was happening.

The sad truth was that Gracie's Mam was beginning to sense the attention Joe was paying her daughter. Saw hunger in his eyes for her. How the violence in him brimmed up and spilled over time and time again, rage erupting at the slightest thing. Sometimes even without anything apparently causing the explosion. It was scaring her.

She had become accustomed to being beaten by him, and the look of disgust in his eyes he'd scarcely bother to hide when he looked at her. Paralysed with panic, she didn't know what to do. Would he lay a finger on Gracie? Would he dare? She took the beatings time and time again in a desperate hope that somehow she would be enough for him, enough to satiate that hunger for physical brutality he seemed to have. How had life come to this?

Once, Joe had been her big brother, her hero. It wasn't always like this, was it?

Memories of how he was floated into her consciousness. His smile, his charm. His persuasive boyishness. His green, sanguine eyes. That gorgeous voice. That commanding profile. His confidence. His charisma.

She sighed. The knack he had of getting his own way, no matter what.

Then she remembered it wasn't all that long before the hero big brother had shown a darker side. She saw with her own eyes how he began to take pleasure in ripping wings off insects and drowning mice. She wasn't sure if that menacing undercurrent had always been there or not. He either hid it well, or something had happened to provoke it. But once it started, it was as if he wouldn't, or couldn't, stop.

He told her that once, he'd tried to drown a cat but had to abort the mission because he was interrupted. And then she started hearing whisperings in the neighbourhood. About her own brother. There were rumours about a boy Joe had beaten so severely that he broke his jaw, his nose and his collar bone. That poor boy couldn't speak or eat solids for months.

Later, as other men were preparing for war, Joe was fighting his own battles – most involving alcohol. It wasn't long before he was sent to prison, where he'd been for the last few years until he showed up that night when Gracie was five.

Nobody seemed to know why he'd been locked up – and nobody dared ask. But that was the problem with Joe – nobody dared challenge him on anything, anything at all. He always found a way of threatening people, to hurt the thing most precious to them.

So Gracie's mother knew she had no choice. She felt she had to sacrifice herself to try to save her little girl. And to try to keep her mother safe. But if he wanted Gracie, she would do what she could to stall it. But she didn't know if she would be able to stop it.

Going to the police seemed futile as he would find a way to explain things, like he always did. And there was always that threat in the air, that he would find a way to punish her in ways she could not imagine.

That time when Mr Harper had tried to step in and stop him, Joe had broken his arm and told him he would break every bone in his children's bodies if he didn't stop interfering. Mr Harper was about as tough and capable as they come. Seen horrors beyond mention in the War. Witnessed the extremes human beings can go to. Experienced the worst of man. But there was something about Joe that stirred in his nightmares. An evil that seemed to reek from him like a bitter odour. A jut-faced rage that would punch its way through anyone and any-thing.

It was obvious that Mr Harper could have fought him, if he'd wanted to. A muscular, brave man like that. But Mr Harper told her there was something else. Said that he had to protect his family, too. And had muttered something about Joe threatening not just his children but something else. Something else precious and important.

Gracie's Mam had a sense what that might be and wasn't sure what to say. She felt powerless if even big, strong Mr Harper had decided it was better not to confront him. So what could she do?

But by accepting Joe into their home, she was also accepting the vile, poisonous darkness he brought with him. By tacitly standing by, she was allowing an unknown horror to be unleashed on her family. By watching silently, she would put in motion whatever fate awaited them.

Masks

So you must not be frightened
If a sadness rises up before you
Larger than any you have ever seen.

Her eyes drifted back into focus and she realised she must have been daydreaming. The book was comfortable in her lap, where it had sat a thousand times before. Its faded old cover feeling familiar in her hands – she could trace the veins of the leather and smell the faint cinnamon ancientness of the pages.

She looked at the words, her eye drawn to the turning point in the verse. How many times had she read and reread this poem, seeking solace in its wisdom and comforting embrace . . .

She felt the sadness welling up inside her again, the familiar, gut-wrenching lurch that would overcome all other emotions throughout her life.

Sadness was a wretched, raw, overwhelming sensation that would drown her in its misery, suffocating her breath and smearing her eyes in its salty waters. It would constrict her heart, leave her skin cold and damp one moment, hot and sticky the next.

It made her head hurt. Swirling around in its bleating despair, carrying with it the beckoning of death, the joylessness of existence. It was as if the lights shone dimmer, the colours faded and the air grew airless.

Sometimes she could taste the physical presence of absence.

That loneliness would grip her – an isolation so deep and so true it tore into the core of her being. Sounds would become extinguished – as if life itself was shutting her out, cruelly. She would grow deaf and blind yet all her other senses would sharpen, agonisingly. Sheer pain would surge through her body – not just rising up before her, but rising up inside of her.

I wandered lonely as a cloud . . .

It was that inner feeling of contentment she was missing. She knew others her age did not face such struggle, such torment.

Of course, the picture she presented to the world was a mask. What choice did she have?

She had thought those thoughts more times than she cared to remember. The beginning, the middle and the end of the story. Her story.

She wondered whether life really was holding her in its hand, whether she was not forgotten. She looked around the dull lavender walls, eyes briefly alighting on the MDF dressing table with its distinctive perfume bottle, and the ceramic pot of dying freesias. Their scent still clung faintly.

She still had Billy. Dear, dear Billy. He visited when he could. She was always amazed by his sprightly manner and cheerful chatter. He looked so strong and solid. *Her* body felt frail – a mere husk. She found the efforts she made to wear her mask harder than ever these days. Especially as the physical pain that twisted inside her overwhelmed her, made her breathless.

But having Billy helped – knowing he was there for her, that he still cared, still forged a link for her to their shared past.

Billy had never married. She often wondered why – whether it was because of what had . . . happened? Or whether he simply hadn't found the right person? Or perhaps he was too busy with work – running your own business must be time-consuming at best and exhausting at worse – and the stress! She did wish, though, that he perhaps had someone special he could talk to – about the ups and downs of the day – and the fierce imaginings of his heart. What a pity that Billy Harper didn't have children. She couldn't think of anyone in the world who built better dens, came up with better games, or told better stories . . .

The day after Gracie found her mother bleeding in the moon-beams, she resolved to tell Billy about what life at home was really like these days. She wasn't quite sure how she would find the words, but she felt too scared and too young to do anything else. It wasn't as if Mam was doing anything.

She thought about her mother. So sweet smelling – she always used Lux soap and had a wonderful fresh almondness about her. Her hands were soft and her cheeks were powdered pink and pretty. She had lovely deep-green eyes which looked like ponds in a wood. Lately, they had lost their sheen, and her voice – which had once been bright and full of laughter – had gone quiet and tremulous.

Some things remained the same. Ma had one or two luxuries

that Gracie wasn't allowed to touch. She only once dared to dip into the magical Ponds Cold Cream and tried to copy what she had seen her mother do a hundred times, but it made her shudder with cold – it was icky and horrible and felt freezing cold on her skin. She had thought it would be an extraordinary feeling – something special and wondrous and grown-up. Instead it was shockingly cold and frankly, her mother was welcome to it.

The other luxury was a small bottle of a French fragrance – which of course had to be sophisticated purely and simply because it was French. Nina Ricci's L'Air du Temps sat prettily on the dressing table. It was a beautiful, delicate bottle, topped with two birds either kissing or pecking each other – Gracie could never be sure – as a stopper. It smelt like heaven, and as a special treat sometimes she would be allowed to have a very small dab on her wrist.

Gracie wasn't sure what her Ma did to get money, but she knew it was something to do with the buses. She thought maybe a conductress? She certainly came back most days with stories of all the different passengers and had lots of stories of the Yanks on the buses during the War. One time one of those Yanks had a pack of peanuts – monkey nuts all in the shell. Gracie's Ma told him they were her favourite food – but she hadn't had them since before the War. To her complete surprise, he gave her the whole bag! It was things like this that made working on the buses such fun – she could meet people and natter. But she was only small so she had to come across as important or she wouldn't be able to do her job properly. She would tell Gracie how she used to love standing up to the rowdy lads and putting them in their places – a weensy five footer like her.

Gracie observed that she wasn't much good at standing up to Uncle Joe. She may well be able to tackle a bunch of misfits on a bus, but she didn't seem to know where to begin about her own brother.

Gracie wondered about Joe. Why hadn't her mother ever mentioned him before? Where had he been all these years? Why was he living with them now? What did *he* do to get money?

She preferred it when Billy's Da used to come around and help fix things and sort things out. He was really nice to her, and really nice to her Ma, too. She would wish she and her Ma could be part of Billy's family. Everyone got on with each other and were the best of friends. Even the grown-ups. Although Mrs Harper was always too busy doing her own chores to come over much. But Mr Harper often did, mending things that broke and doing painting and things. Sometimes Gracie would catch sight of him giving her Ma a little tickle to cheer her up. He was so, so nice. Once, she even saw him give her Ma a kiss on the cheek.

'Can I go out and play, Mam?' Gracie had said.

The two adults jumped slightly – they seemed to have forgotten she was there.

'Of course, pet, be good,' her Ma had murmured.

Gracie had skipped out to join Billy.

Hours later when she came home exhausted, after building dens which turned into castles and squealing with delight when Billy kept catching her in tag, she found Mr Harper was still there. He must have got very hot with all that plumbing, because he was just pulling up the braces of his dungarees as he was coming down the stairs.

'Bye then, little one,' he said to Gracie, patting her on the head, 'the pipes are all sorted now,' he added, glancing backwards as Gracie's mother came down the stairs after him.

'Bye you,' he said to Gracie's Ma.

Creatures

The lavender could be oppressive after a while. Fleeting scents of a past life would wash over her, at times soft and sweet, at others fugging and constricting in her throat. And the walls would smother her with their neat rigidness. So sterile, so clinical. A memory would swell up inside her – something to do with a small, tight room where all around were the silhouettes of pencils. But that was another time, another place.

Here, today, the detergent acidity of freshly mopped floors and a lingering odour of old skin in the corridors wafted into the lavender room. There was scant comfort outside today. Breezes of apple blossom discarded their snows across the lawn. Pretty, delicate, reminiscent of a fragility she had inside. For some reason the petal snowflakes conjured up a darker, more brutal thought. She let her eyelids droop slightly and allowed the focus of her watery irises grow to fuzz. The seas of snow blurred against the window pane and a misty whiteness caressed her to sleep.

The door slammed open and the fierce light flooded in. Gracie, startled into alertness, hovered at the top of the stairwell to see what was happening.

A stumbling Joe crashed into the hallway and smashed the console to the ground. A yellow china vase splintered across the floor, a trickle of water seeping slowly out, bleeding quietly onto the lino. A single white rose scattered its petals in a slow motion flurry through the air and suddenly – he stopped, as if he felt someone's presence.

She could smell him from up here. That familiar treaclish odour revolted her – ash mixed with a sour sweatiness, reeking into the air around him.

A cold clamminess gripped her. She could see he couldn't steady himself, and that frightened her. The orange walls downstairs had never looked so sickly. The incongruous, floral backdrop of a mad man. A nightmare unfolding before her very eyes.

Beneath the dark, intense brows, his eyes stilled and settled. As if he had found his quarry, the predator savoured the moment. He found himself compelled by an overwhelming need to penetrate her gaze.

He could see her lashes, fronding her languid eyes, and kiss curls of blondness framing her sweet, angel face. Her rose-cheeked softness and milky skin called to him, barely perceptibly. That citrus, lemony scent lingered in the air between them, teasing him. She was begging him to go to her, he could see that. She had a look of yearning in her, and he could tell that her heart was beating in anticipation, like a small, woodland creature. If he stilled to a perfect pause, he could see the urgent rise and fall of her breathing beneath her cotton dress. A still boyish chest with the trace of pink nipples poking softly under the whiteness of the fabric. The faint outline of her waist . . . He allowed himself a glance at those tawny, sun-kissed legs. A downy velvetness catching the light, waiting for his touch. He felt the moment and let it hang in the air. Aware of a primal deepening of his own core, he relished knowing what was to come next.

As a boy, the instants that stayed with him were the transitory moments between recognition and fear, desire and relent. When the fly would give up the struggle and relax into defeat. One wing, two. Crushed and squidged between chubby, toddler hands. But nothing as satisfying as that moment just before – when the prey would collapse into submission, seemingly aware that resistance was futile. The moment the tiny insect would stop and sigh – preparing itself for the agonies to come. The moment it relented and, tacitly, acknowledged this was what *it* wanted, too.

The moment an earthworm would give up wriggling its puny fight in the face of the bigger, stronger force, a knife-wielding boy. Seconds away from slicing its body, delighting in the visible tension and helplessness of his pathetic plaything, he would smirk a scornful smile and harden his eyes in a glassy stare, his whole body savouring the thrill – *la petite mort*.

The moment a mouse would cease to quiver as it submitted to its fate. Drowned noisily, thrashingly, sucking its last breath through bubbles of hate-stirred water.

Creatures were there to be played with, ripped apart, experimented on and forced to suffer. Why let a spider have eight legs when there was so much delight to be had slowly and carefully dismembering them, bit by bit. Why let a bunny rabbit keep its tail – or its life – when a few bloody tugs of a rusty knife would relieve it of its fluffy white pom-pom, and its last breath – far better the boy adds to his collection of death tales.

Of course the cat incident wasn't his finest hour. Couldn't believe it when bloody Finnegan bleated on about sparing the kitty-catty. Crap to that. Whine, whine, whine – it was bad enough dealing with the squeals of the creature without the blethering whining of a lily-livered bastard. So – a choice then. *The cat or you? Ha! Thought so, you weak little toad. I'm coming for you instead . . .*

Ahhh, that delicious moment when Finnegan stopped in his tracks and looked at him in horror. *You wouldn't! Surely you wouldn't! I damn well would. No, Joe, no! You've gone too far . . .*

The small boy's all too human face was frozen in a kind of rigor mortis, colour absent and eyes fixed with fear. Joe raised his fist and held the moment, just a little, breathing in the panic and anxiety he was inspiring in his friend.

And that was the moment he realised that playing with creatures had been his dress rehearsal. Playing with people could be far more intoxicating.

He watched and waited as Finnegan's shaking body, cowered backwards, then stopped. That waxen face with the hunted eyes begged Joe to stop, to think, to stop.

But Joe didn't stop. He lashed into his playmate and felt the judder of a collapsing jaw. Scarlet spurted from the slash that had once been Finnegan's mouth. His eyeballs rolled back and his whole body followed. A slow thud broke the silence as Finnegan landed in the hedge. Small green leaves scattered around him, splashed with syrupy red ribbons. A lump of red squishy something landed half a second after him, on his thigh. He brushed it away only to realise that it had once been part of his face.

Joe looked at his handiwork. Nice! Finnegan was laid, sprawled in a sticky mess half in and half out of a hedge. A stillness hung in the air.

Joe thought back to the moments before and felt the deep rush of blood through his own body as the moment of impact hovered in his clenched fist. To his surprise, he found the stirrings he usually felt when he tortured creatures had strengthened into something preternaturally pleasurable. His cock had hardened and was straining at his trousers.

He was familiar with this feeling, of course. Ever since he was little he'd enjoyed stroking his private place, and he'd experienced a groaning dart of *something* every time he killed or warped a creature. This time was different. The sheer animal energy he'd used to pound his friend had released something deep in his core.

He undid his belt and pulled the evidence out, admiring himself. He glanced over at Finnegan, still passed out on the floor, and began to stroke himself, softly. Then harder, harder, feeling the tension build and strengthen, an almost unbearable twinge of pain-pleasure as he gripped himself with both hands, thrusting with jerks and pulls. He felt the veins coursing with his own blood and virility, and never had he felt more of a man.

Twelve-year-old Joe continued to tug, hard, for just another few moments then felt the release of something immensely satisfying. His back and thighs stiffened and he found himself howling inwardly, allowing just a long, low groan to escape his lips.

The smirk that spread over his face was dark and slow. He had driplets of sweat on his brow and his heart was pounding with a new and delicious pleasure.

Finnegan, blinking back to consciousness, looked at Joe for half a second, his eyes blackening shadows.

Joe wiped his hands on his trousers.

He didn't know then that he would be arrested later that night, slammed in a cell for his first spell inside. He didn't know then that he would end up spending a few months in a correction house, a residential institution for young offenders. He didn't know then that this would turn out to be a pivotal night in his methodology, how being caught would teach him to learn from his mistakes, and would help him hone his craft. How he would get better at covering his tracks and hiding in plain sight.

'You tell a soul about this and your Ma's dead.'

Finnegan then slipped out of consciousness, and Joe stomped homewards, without a backward glance. As he sauntered away, he heard the faint mewling of a stray cat, picking its way through a thicket.

A few minutes later, the sound of a dog yelping out of someone's way was the only noise punctuating an otherwise peaceful summer night. An hour or so later, Finnegan stirred and began his own slow crawl back home.

Stitches

Gracie was beginning to succumb to the nausea of memory. Joe's thick, bitter essence was creating a wall of stench that permeated upstairs like a physical force, and she could feel it.

She could also feel the urgency in his black stare, and to her horror saw him begin to caress his belt buckle.

She felt rigid with fear, feet leaden, throat tightened, heart beating so fast she thought she might just die there and then. His long, dark coat had a sheen like armour. His hands looked like talons with thick, dirty nails and his hard, stern face made her think a monster had crossed the threshold.

She knew her Ma had popped out – Mr Harper had offered to drive her to a hardware store to get some supplies for some jobs that needed doing. They were going to be a couple of hours, they said, because the shop was a bit of a way away. A fleeting thought popped into Gracie's mind when Mam told her they were going out, but she wasn't quite sure what it was. She vaguely thought of the new scent bottle that had appeared on her Ma's dressing table – a glass sculpture of two birds intertwined for a stopper. Fancy French words on the front. A gift from someone special, her Ma had said, dabbing her wrists with the fragrance and, smiling, breathing in.

As usual, no one knew when Joe was next going to show up but it had been months since he'd fled that dreadful night, and life had begun to feel slightly happier again. Gracie knew the baby was living in Heaven now and all that mattered was that she had Billy, Billy had her, and everything was beginning to be better for Mam.

Billy was supposed to be calling on her soon – they had arranged another playtime around at the Harpers' but Gracie first had to finish up a sewing project she had to do for school the next day. She was embroidering a flower onto a piece of calico. It was a little bit rough round the edges but the colours were pretty – she had picked spring-like yellows and pinks. She was finishing up the word 'Mam' across the bottom because she hoped a little present might make her smile.

She had just begun working on the second 'm' – when the door blasted open.

Embroidery cast to the floor, all Gracie could do was look at the scene unfolding below. That familiar feeling of the air being squeezed out of her chest and a sense of foreboding, which seemed to be red-black in her eyes, was swamping her very being. She couldn't move, that was for sure, and she couldn't speak. Like a fly caught in a web, she stood, trapped, quivering, waiting.

Shoes

The white rose lay lifeless at his feet. Petals mostly scattered across the floor, now just a stem with thorns. Gracie tried to focus on the detritus on the floor to try to avoid seeing what Joe was doing now.

She became aware of the heavy sound of his breathing and drew a glance at his face. Eyes blacker than viridian black, and the sound of metal thudding against leather.

He took a step towards the stairwell, smiling at her but saying nothing. Menace hung in the air. The wall of stench overwhelmed her and she found herself beginning to retch. It was the trigger that broke the spell – that guttural wrench helped her uproot herself and run madly for the bathroom, where at least she knew there was a lock. Her heart carried her into the familiar space and she slammed the door behind her. She fiddled with the lock, trying to make it work, then realised to her dismay that the key wasn't there.

Behind her, thumping shoes pounded the steps, two at a time, and moments later the door was thrust open behind her, fierce light flooding in. He eyed her with his usual sneer, something like mild amusement playing across his face.

'What's wrong with you?' he asked. 'Run a bath, go on bairn. What's keeping you?'

Gracie had no idea what to do. The only other time they had been together, the two of them, was here in this bathroom. She remembered the sense of not knowing, and it felt the same today.

He was standing there, belt removed, waiting. He looked strong and tall. But he wasn't steady on his feet – the drink will get him one of these days, her Ma always said. Could this be the day the drink got him? *Can I run past him, can I escape?*

Mustering all her courage, she put the plug in the bath and began to run the water.

'Don't forget the bubbles,' he said, eyes glinting like coal.

She reached for the bottle of lemon liquid soap and poured some in. The froth began to dance in the light. Light and airy and free. Everything she was not.

She glanced around the room, urgently. Could she slip past him? Could she?

Only one way to find out. She picked her moment carefully – he was half-lidded, gazing at her, but looked less alert than before. She dashed forwards and ducked under his left arm. Hot breath, fire in her heart, legs soft and useless.

'Not so fast, bairn.' He seized her, hard, and forced her back into the room. He closed the door, carefully, slowly, and fished a key from his pocket. He held it up for her to look at.

He turned the lock and smiled at her. A trace of something lingered in the air.

He gestured to the bath, which by now was filled with the

familiar soft, white mounds. It seemed he had decided that was enough conversation for one day.

He gestured again, indicating she should get in.

Gracie once more felt herself thinking about God. What would God want her to do? But why was he putting her in this position in the first place? Was it a test? That was it! A test! If she passed it, perhaps Joe would leave her and Mam alone forever, and maybe they really could have home together, something warm and inviting, safe and cosy. Hearth and heart, home, sweet home.

She stood there in silence. She was already barefoot but wearing her pretty white tunic dress with the pale blue bow around the waist.

She stepped into the bath without removing the dress. It was the only thing she could think of to do.

'Are you stupid or something?'

His voice broke the silence. She always remembered her Ma would say what a gorgeous voice he had. It didn't sound very gorgeous now. More like the kraaa of a raven, it was deep and guttural and wasn't taking no for an answer.

She looked at him, apprehension hanging in the space between them. Of course she wasn't stupid, but after all he hadn't specifically said she had to take off her clothes. *Come on God*, she pleaded inside, *tell me what to do.*

Puddles

It was days like this that the lavender walls crowded in. Her mind was aching with forgotten memories. But part of her wondered how much she had forgotten and how much she had suppressed. She simply wasn't sure anymore.

She glanced around her. The comfort of books, of course, would bring her what little joy she could feel these days until she breathed her last breath. She suspected that wasn't too far away. There was a birthday card from Billy. A picture of daffodils in a white, china vase in a sunny, happy kitchen. She seemed to remember there was a place like that, once. A thought passed mistily through her consciousness.

Ten thousand saw I at a glance,
Tossing their heads in sprightly dance.

A piece of embroidery had been framed and placed carefully on the bookcase alongside a photograph of a little girl. The little girl had soft, blonde curls swirling around her face and she was laughing, prettily. There was such innocence and joy in that face, such young, vital energy and such hope. She must have been about five or six.

She pulled the pale blue cardigan around her, tightly. There was a slight chill in the air, and for some reason the photo made her feel uneasy. *Once beautiful and brave.* That was the girl in the photo, once beautiful and brave. A brave, beautiful princess.

The line lingered in her thoughts for a few moments, and she returned to the subject that most occupied and disturbed her. *Has life forgotten me?* she wondered. *Do I deserve life? My husk of a body, being kept alive with chemicals – for what? Do I have some other purpose I haven't discovered yet? At what point are you going to reveal it, if there is one? And if not, can I please just whisper into dust. It's just too hard, too hard . . .*

And she thought of the other line . . . *If a restiveness like light and cloud shadows, passes over your hands and over all you do . . .*

Yes, yes, she thought, *shadows dance in and out of my thoughts all day every day, obscuring my memories and diminishing my sense of self. I feel regret, and sorrow, and profound sadness. I'm not always sure what stirs my emotions but I know they run deep, and they run true.*

All I have is the books . . .

And that piece of embroidery, which ached for her and at her.

She bent down, slowly, and placed her fingertips carefully around the frame. Her old, gnarled hands were bent out of shape with raised veins pulsing bluely, criss-crossing the surface. She pulled the frame out and peered at it intently.

Outside, the rain had started again, intermingling with the apple blossom so it looked like a blizzard of white. The soft pounding of the water against the glass felt like a familiar refrain. Rivulets of water wound their way downwards, a slow inevitability of purpose. Puddles were collecting in patches across the lawn. Beyond, petals blurred into flurries and twilight began to fall.

The door opened, brightly.

'Hello,' Billy said, in a jolly apple-cheeked way unique to the Harpers. She glanced up, distracted. He realised that in that instant, she was lost in a memory and took a moment to reorient herself with today, with reality.

'I brought you some of those chocolates you like, you know, those rose and violet creams. You always did like those, didn't you?'

She looked at him with a gentle, wise expression.

'Oh, Billy, you are so terribly kind. Thank you.'

She searched her memory for having ever tasted rose and violet creams before and honestly couldn't place them, but she appreciated the gesture and knew he meant well.

'So how have you been the last few days?' he asked with a broad smile twinkling across his eyes.

'Oh, you know, Billy, there's so much going on here, it's hard to keep up.'

He had become accustomed to her usual response and waited to see if there was anything more.

'But I do think my memory may be coming back a bit, at least in fits and starts . . .' He couldn't help but see that she was holding the framed embroidery. She handed it to him.

He took it, and exhaled deeply. Pinpricks of tears stung the back of his eyes as he looked at the old piece of calico, lovingly made by a child's hand. Yellow and pink springtime flowers and the word 'Ma' untidily worked beneath.

It had been a while since he had allowed himself to look at this, let alone hold it. The memories it brought back for him were heart-wrenching.

He looked at the old woman in front of him and wondered how much she could really remember. He hardly dared ask her.

Billy glanced at the picture of the blonde child and a surge of warmth and happiness washed through him. His Gracie, his perfect, lovely Gracie. A world apart from here and now.

Then his eyes alighted on another photo, a quaint, old-fashioned picture of a little toddler girl grasping trustingly the chubby little hands of her slightly older friend, a boy. The photo was taken from behind them, and they were wombling away from view, into a pale clearing. There were leaves and trees framing the pair, and light was flooding the pathway and beyond. The little girl was wearing a smock dress and the little boy was striding manfully along, feeling important with his charge. They were walking onwards, purposefully, for a life of adventure and fun. Dragons and Princesses.

Billy looked at the old woman and felt hot tears begin to flood down his cheeks.

He looked again at the little girl and the little boy, and found himself drifting back to another time.

He came over, as always, and as it often was, the door was already open. 'Gracie?' he called. Was she already outside, he wondered, had he missed her? 'Gracie?' No sign. He pushed into the hallway and saw the console knocked over, the yellow china vase smashed onto the floor and the lonely, broken rose laying on its side.

'Gracie? Princess?' He wasn't sure whether to go back home and grab his Ma or to try to find out what was happening. Instinct kicked in and all he could think of was to find Gracie, his little Gracie.

He saw a belt lying on the ground at the foot of the stairwell and wondered, helplessly, whether this meant Joe was back. Gracie had explained that Joe frightened her, and that he would hit her Ma. Joe was a bad man and no one knew why Gracie's Ma put up with him. But they say blood is thicker than water and everyone knew Joe was Gracie's uncle and that there was nothing anyone could do about it. Billy secretly hoped that one day Joe may go back to jail, where he belonged, and out of harm's way.

He listened on the staircase, but couldn't hear a thing. He looked outside again – nothing.

There was little else he could do. So he began to slowly climb up to the landing, listening attentively in case there was any sign of his lovely friend.

He knew his Da and Gracie's Ma were off running important errands so wouldn't be back for a while. He also knew that his Ma had organised they would have a play together when Gracie had finished her embroidery. He also knew – and this was important – that Gracie never forgot plans to play with him and if she wasn't here, that meant something was wrong. She didn't normally stay in the house on her own – this was a special exception because they'd promised it would only be until tea time. Billy began to feel sick.

He remembered the last time he'd lost her. The two of them had gone into the woods for one of his special imaginary games and he had been so pleased with himself that he had planned the clever transformation of dragon to prince. He'd put together a royal posy to present to her and couldn't wait to see her face. He just loved making her light up. Gracie was so much fun to be with – she had the sunniest smile and the brightest, forest-green eyes. She really was a princess, beautiful and brave.

On that occasion, something had clearly scared the life out of her. She had thought she had been away, or dreaming, for days, whereas it had only been a matter of minutes. It was horribly scary for the both of them.

They had cut a rather tragic pair coming home, none of the robust cheeriness peppering their talk as it had on the way there.

Billy had taken it upon himself to take her out again for another game of Dragons and Princesses as soon as possible. Three days later, he seemed to recall.

He thought it better to help Gracie confront whatever it was that frightened her, and to help her confront it together. He thought it was like one of his bad dreams, which he knew in his heart of hearts was about fear of the unknown and fear or what *might* happen rather than what necessarily is real or true.

He thought maybe Gracie had seen a horrible shadow and mistaken it for something like a witch. After all, they often played witches and evil wizards and goblins and things. It wasn't that hard to imagine a dark patch taking on the form of something scary in the mind of someone already playing magic games in the land of make-believe.

So they went back out again, this time hand firmly in hand. Such a picture of innocence, and so happy, too. Back in those days you wouldn't think twice about children going off on their own and playing. They were more carefree, more gentle times. Safer, warmer, cosier.

Only they weren't, were they . . .

On that occasion Gracie and Billy had had a splashingly good time, creating a fairy tale world out of leaves and twigs. No one could make a den like Billy could.

It had rained the night before so there were puddles everywhere and they had enormous fun splish sploshing in and out of them, pretending they were pools of liquid gold and if only they managed to splatter into all of them, the wealth of the kingdom would be theirs and they would get married and rule the land in peace and all live happily ever after.

At one point, Gracie had a wobble, when she spotted the branch that the raven had been perched on. She pointed it out to Billy. 'There . . .' she said, 'that's where he was watching me from. And I knew he wanted to eat me, dig his claws into me, and hurt me. He really did, Billy, I could even smell him, it was bitter and sour and horrible. And it was like he had armour on, shiny and black. And his eyes were fierce and hard and like shining metal. Billy, his claws were so mean. He scared me and made my heart beat so fast I thought I was going to die . . .'

At the memory of it, she couldn't help but have a little sob. Billy smiled at her in sympathy and pointed out kindly that the raven appeared to be gone and that he had clearly decided to have something yummier than a Gracie for his supper.

This made her giggle. 'I don't think I would be very yummy anyway, do you?'

'I don't know – let me have a munch, I'm the magic munch-monster!' said Billy, and began chasing after her.

She squealed in delight and ran into the clearing, letting him catch her.

They both collapsed into uncontrollable giggles, the kind you just can't squish down because they burple up and pop inside you. Then they tickled each other to make each other laugh even more and ended up getting lots of muddy splashes all over their clothes.

It was a good day.

Bells

'Gracie? Are you there?'

Billy heard his own voice echo in the hallway. He glanced again at the belt on the floor and slowly followed the steps upwards. For some reason he particularly took in the orange gaudiness of the wallpaper. What a peculiar thing to be thinking about when he had an important mission to pursue. Not just the quests of fairy tales, this one was real. He had to find Gracie. And that was that.

He hadn't put much thought yet into what he would do if he found her, or how he could possibly confront a real baddie, whether they were human or goblin or whatever. He just knew that he had to find her. Had to save her . . .

And then he saw the embroidery, discarded on the floor.

He became aware of a slight sloshing of water and a profound sense of relief washed over him. *Oh thank goodness, she's just washing after finishing her homework!* he thought. But at the same time, the picture of the belt and the chaos downstairs was lingering in his mind and preventing the relief from taking hold.

He crept upstairs and cried out once more, softly and cautiously this time: 'Gracie?'

Still no reply, but a pause in the sloshing of the water.

He inched along the corridor and made out that the bathroom door was closed. *That's a bit odd*, he thought to himself. 'Gracie?' he asked, once again . . .

He paused outside the bathroom door and tried to peer in, but the key was in the lock and you couldn't see anything.

He listened carefully.

His heart was pounding harder than he'd ever felt it pound before. It made his own nightmares pale into insignificance. All he could think was that Gracie was either playing silly games, or was in trouble. The silly games thing was perfectly normal but usually it only took a matter of minutes for her to burst into giggles and reveal her hide-and-seek location or show what she was up to. She couldn't keep a secret to save her life.

He became aware of the scent of lemons, and thought that was how Gracie always smelled. Pretty and sweet and lovely and not normal. He didn't mean 'not normal' in a bad way, but he had never smelt that fragrance on other people. It was Gracie's scent and it would always be Gracie's scent.

He pondered what to do. Should he break the spell and reveal he'd found her and hopefully get to the point of the game and get on with playing properly? Or should he trust his instincts, the broken vase, the belt on the floor, the console lying on the ground, and worry that something bad was happening?

In the end, he decided to go back home and fetch his Ma. That's all he could do. He wanted to be big and strong like his Da and John and Simon, but he was only little and he decided if Joe was to blame for the mess at the bottom of the house, and if Joe had anything to do with the bathroom being closed and Gracie not answering the door, then Billy wouldn't be able to help much. Fetching Ma was the best thing to do. Mas always know what's best. Especially his Ma.

He thought for a moment about his parents. His Da was one of the only men in May Close to have survived the War. His Ma and Da were strong and good – and his two brothers were annoying at times but they were all fit and healthy and enjoying life. Poor Gracie didn't know her father, her Ma was all on her own, and the little brother or sister she was supposed to have decided not to come into the world after all.

He was like Gracie in some ways, though. Like her, he didn't really have all that many friends at school. He wasn't sure why, but he knew that he was a bit – well – different. He really did like playing make-believe, and he really did think Gracie was his best friend in the whole world. He liked helping his Ma with the cooking and stuff, and it was Billy who had given Gracie a helping hand starting her off on that embroidery. She had found it terribly difficult, having to hold the needle, so delicate and tiny. And didn't know where to begin threading it. She also had no clue about the different stitches you needed to know. So patiently, one day after school, Billy had spent a couple of hours showing her how to create some of the simple stitches other people seemed to find so easy to do.

Spelling and embroidery. Not Gracie's strong suits. But he couldn't understand why she didn't have loads of friends. She was just about the most special, lovely, sweet person he had ever met and he wanted them to stay friends forever.

He rushed outside without closing the door behind him. Scarpered around the corner and blurted out to his Ma: 'I can't find Gracie, Ma, I can't find her, but the bathroom door is locked and her Ma's not back yet and there's furniture all over the hallway and a belt on the floor . . .'

He puffed out the words in rambling breaths and Mrs Harper looked at him, concerned.

'Well, unfortunately your Da's not home yet so we need to think about what we need to do. I'll see if Mrs Armstrong's in and we'll go round to Gracie's together. You, Billy, stay here.' Billy got the impression that his Ma had no need of further explanations. She seemed to understand how serious the whole thing was.

Mrs Harper grabbed the poker from the fireplace and dashed out to number 12. She and Mrs Armstrong made their way over to Gracie's. Billy knew he'd been told to stay at home, but how could he let his Gracie be on her own if she was in trouble? So slowly, he followed his mother and their neighbour, and watched and waited. The women reached the front door and peeked inside. They murmured to each other and Mrs Harper called 'Gracie, dear, Gracie darling, where are you, pet?' There was silence. More murmuring. The suspense was killing him.

Billy waited in the shadows, desperate to find out what was going on.

Then, the sound of a Ford Transit van. It was Da and Gracie's Ma back from their trip. There was the sound of laughter, trilling in the air, before they turned the corner and up the drive. They sounded like bells, Billy thought, how funny, their laughter sounds like bells.

The moment they circled into view, it was clear something

was wrong. The front door was open. Billy was hiding (not very well, it turned out) in the bushes outside, and Mrs Harper and Mrs Armstrong were huddled together, nervously.

The bells in the car stopped pealing and Da and Gracie's Ma got out. 'What is it, Billy?' she asked.

'Why the hell have you been this long?' asked Mrs Harper.

Billy glanced from his Da to Gracie's Ma and ran to them, explaining what he had found.

Mr Harper seized control of the situation and told the ladies to wait downstairs and look after Billy. Mrs Harper shot her son a look of annoyance, quickly followed by tenderness, as if she had just remembered how awful this must be for him.

They waited outside. And waited. Nothing.

The silence was unbearable.

'Peter?' Mrs Harper called up. 'Are you alright?'

Billy scanned Gracie's Ma's face as it paled white and quiet. She wasn't calling out for Gracie, all she could do was hug herself tight and watch and wait with the others.

A stillness crept over her and the familiar greyness of the pallor he had seen in her face so often before slowly seeped back into her skin. In a heartbeat, the lightness and brightness of eyes and smiles were engulfed in shadows. It was as if he could suddenly see the ghostly traces of all the bruises and cuts she had suffered in the last few years. Her face seemed to shrink into itself, and an emotion Billy couldn't yet discern ebbed into her being.

The stillness continued. Then, a quiet dullness.

His Da came down the stairs and called Gracie's Ma over.

They murmured together for a moment, and Billy craned for a better view.

At the foot of the stairs was Gracie, wrapped in a towel, a hollow look in her eyes, staring vacantly, into the nothingness of beyond.

Gracie's Ma rushed in and smothered her with cuddles and kisses. Billy and his parents left, together with Mrs Armstrong.

Gracie would continue to stare into the nothingness for a very long time.

Blessings

Billy became aware of how hot and wet his cheeks were and wiped the dampness away, gently. He was still holding the embroidery but his eyes had been facing the photo of the sweet twosome, pottering off into a land of leaves, trees and adventure.

He felt a bit embarrassed, but frankly, it wasn't the first time she had seen him cry and he felt no shame in mourning what was lost.

A lifetime of love and joy had slowly begun to decay that day. He hated to admit it, but things did change after that.

Gracie, who had been so thrilled to learn a few basic stitching skills, never went back to finish her embroidery. The half-finished 'Ma' of 'Mam' became the final product. The freesias were pretty but unknotted and unfinished. Something very dark had happened in that house that day, and only Gracie knew what.

The foam was beginning to froth up and its lovely scent wafted into the air.

Slowly, she stepped out of her dress. She was standing there, self-conscious, just in her panties. She trembled with goose pimples and clasped herself tightly.

Joe grunted. He indicated she needed to remove her underwear. A tightening inside as her heart played drums inside and her blood rushed around her body made the dizziness she felt a light and welcome relief. Perhaps if she passed out, she thought, like last time, then it will all be bearable.

What 'all' was, of course, was completely unknown to her. She had absolutely no idea why Joe would have locked her in the bathroom, absolutely no idea why he would ask her to run a bath and absolutely no idea why he would want her to remove her clothing.

She thought about her mother. A lovely, slim but curvaceous woman with a beautiful figure, a warm, rounded hip and the sort of waist you had to wrap an apron around twice. She had a placid, lovely face with full lips and the sort of eyes you could wallow in whether you were feeling happy or sad.

She thought about her own body. A bit scrawny, but that was okay. Still hadn't quite reached the exciting times her Ma had told her about when hair would sprout and breasts would grow.

The only thing she had felt was that her nipples had begun to get a bit larger and harden. They were like small, rosebud points which reached out and tickled her clothing.

Well, she was 13 now so it wasn't that surprising.

But she still felt a little girl inside and didn't feel grown up yet.

Something told her whatever happened to her today would force her to grow up, fast.

*

She looked at Billy, cheeks still damp and a flustered expression on his face. She took the embroidery back from him and remembered that day, herself. The belt tossed aside among the yellow china splinters; the calico discarded by childish hands on the landing upstairs. The white rose half-forgotten on the floor downstairs.

Billy had remembered the rose, as well. After seeing Gracie cold and shivering in the half light, wrapped in her towel, he had taken in the full impact of the scene in front of him.

Ushered home by his parents, the three of them walking back in silence, he couldn't help but wonder what had happened to his friend. And couldn't help but take in the purity and light of the bursting blooms of the white rose bushes that populated the family garden at the front of the house.

His Da explained that Gracie had been alone when he found her, upstairs and cold. No one else was there. He said he would go back to check whether Gracie and her Ma needed anything.

Mother and daughter were locked in a tight embrace. Gracie shivering and sobbing, quietly. There was a tap-tap on the door, and they were relieved to see it was nothing more sinister than Mr Harper.

He said he hadn't been sure whether to disturb them or not – do you need help clearing things up?

'Thank you for everything, Peter,' Gracie's Ma said. Gracie still didn't say anything. 'It looks like he left by the back door,' she continued. 'It was open.'

The adults looked at each other as if they had a quiet

understanding of something important. They didn't say another word.

Mr Harper worked swiftly and efficiently, putting things back in order. He exchanged glances with Gracie's Ma, but the two of them seemed to not need to speak. Gracie sat, numbly, unwilling to move or go to bed.

When Mr Harper had finished sorting everything, he moved closer to Gracie's Ma as if to start to embrace her, but was quietly brushed away.

Gracie looked up and tried to make sense of the silent communion. Another time, Peter, her Mam seemed to be saying with her eyes. Such lovely, pond-green eyes.

The calico had been abandoned upstairs and Gracie could never bring herself to tackle it again. Too many painful memories. It would have to do, just as it was.

The next day her Ma said she didn't have to go to school if she didn't want to. 'It's okay, Ma, I'd rather pretend everything's normal I think. That way maybe it really *will* be normal again one day.'

Her mother winced and Gracie realised she might have said something wrong. 'I didn't mean . . .' she started . . . 'It's okay, pet, you're right. You're right to want things to be normal again.'

'Does that mean . . . *he* won't be allowed to come and live with us anymore, Ma? Does it? Can we make him go away?'

Her mother fell silent and looked down at her lap. She seemed to have forgotten a question had been asked. Just sat there, staring into nothingness.

'Ma? Please?'

Still silence, and still no breaking the spell of her reverie.

'Mam?'

'It isn't easy, pet. Your uncle isn't well. I'm his family. He's got nowhere else to go, pet. He's a brute and a bully and his temper is like nothing else. But we've got to be strong, pet. I want things to be normal, too. Sweet Jesus knows how much I wish things were normal.'

She glanced at Gracie and immediately dropped her eyes down again.

Gracie looked at her with puzzles and questions and a million wonderings whirling around her head.

'Do you think . . .' she began, pondering whether or not to raise an idea she'd had. 'Do you think maybe I should tell Mr Hall at school? Maybe he could . . .'

Before she was able to finish her sentence, her mother interrupted, sharply.

'No, Gracie. No. This is family, pet, we mustn't involve other people.'

'But what about Billy, and Mr and Mrs Harper?'

'It's not the same, pet. The Harpers help us because they're our neighbours. But we don't talk about things like this outside of the home. You don't understand, Gracie, and why would you? You're just a little girl. There's so much I wish I could talk to you about, pet, and one day you'll understand. For now, we have to make do, and I promise . . .'

At this, she trembled slightly and stifled a sob. She mumbled something quietly to herself. 'We are bonded, you and I, we are blood.'

110

Then louder, to Gracie, 'I promise I will do everything I can to make sure he doesn't scare you again.'

She began to look a little wistful, as the tears moistened her cheeks.

'He used to be so handsome, Gracie, and he had such a gorgeous voice. You would have loved him, back then.'

But 'back then' was a long time ago. Gracie wondered what her Ma and Joe had been like, before things went wrong in Joe's head. Or whether, deep down, he had always been cruel. Always been dark and hard and . . . she struggled to think of the word . . . evil?

The thought hung heavily, wordlessly, and she sighed, a shudder of memory coursing through her veins.

There was no use trying to understand it – there must be things her mother was protecting her from to allow this monstrous man into their home. The world shouldn't know.

Not for first time, she reflected on the strange cleanness of their house in contrast with the vileness of what happened inside.

Over time, she began to associate that smell of cleanness with his attacks. For every time he lashed out and destroyed something, hit something, broke something, Ma would recover herself and set to with the Jeyes and Harpic. Scrubbing, scrubbing, scrubbing. Until surfaces gleamed and a chemical odour pervaded the atmosphere. Spotless, like one of those dream homes you saw in pictures. Only this house was a dream that never was.

So back to school then. Gracie decided all she could do was get through things day by day . . . Even Tish and Jo and their pathetic bullying would seem child's play in comparison to . . . yesterday.

She felt convinced what happened had been some sort of test. And she was desperate to work out if she had passed it. For now, she was going to get ready for a different sort of test, a far less scary one. To her surprise, she found herself chuckling inside at the absurdity of it. Somehow a school spelling test seemed to fade into insignificance. How things change in a day! Last week the idea of learning how to spell 'rhododendron' and 'separate' and the other stupid words on the list felt like a horrible kind of torture. Today, it felt like something she welcomed, to take her mind off . . . other things.

School had a rhythm and a normality that felt safe and nice. Lessons came and went, breaks and lunchtimes were packed with routine activities like singing and extra PE and home economics. She was getting really good at cooking. Although the grown-ups always talked about the restrictions of rations, there were loads of things you could do with powdered eggs and powdered milk. She thought for a moment about the things she liked making. Eggless cakes were a specialty of hers. She could whip up a Mock Fishcake (the name made her giggle) using anchovy sauce for the fish flavour. She wasn't completely sure whether she had ever tasted fish, but she liked the saltiness of the Mock ones. Her absolute favourite recipe was for Potato Floddies with their yummy dripping-crunchy edges.

Cooking aside, her main hobby was reading. And that fledgling passion, embroidery, was something she never went back to.

It came up that first day back.

'You haven't finished this off, Gracie,' said Mrs Peston. 'Can you offer me any explanation or would you like to take two detentions this week to make time to do it?' Gracie ummed. She wasn't sure what to say. So she said a version of the truth.

'I'm really sorry you don't like it, Mrs Peston, but I made it for my Ma and she thought it was lovely. I'm not very good at embroidery, Mrs Peston, and I spent hours on this one. I even got my friend B . . .' she stopped herself blurting out the name because she realised it wouldn't help Billy's credibility for the whole school to find out he knew how to embroider. 'I even got my friend to help show me what to do, but this is as good as I could make it. But I love knitting and stuff. Could I make another project for you, a knitting project? I promise to try ever so hard.'

Mrs Peston looked at the curious earnestness of the young girl before her and paused for thought. It wasn't like Gracie not to try her best, and it wasn't like Gracie not to finish something off beautifully. Perhaps embroidery really was something she couldn't do. Gracie had never let her down before, so she resolved to make an exception.

'Okay, pet, you've talked me around. You can leave the embroidery and give it to your Ma as it is. But I want you knitting your first jumper within a month, within a month, you hear me?'

Later, her own words echoed back at her. 'Could I make another project for you, Mrs Peston? Could I fetch your bags, Mrs Peston, could I kiss your arse, Mrs Peston?' sang Tish and Jo together.

'God, you are such a little creep, Pastie Gracie. Teacher's pet! Teacher's pet! Teacher's pet!'

Gracie let the chants wash over her and realised they didn't hurt nearly as much as they used to. For the second time that day, Gracie found herself surprised. She realised she actually felt sorry for those two.

In the past, she had always tried to reason with them, explain stuff, get defensive.

This time, she sighed theatrically loudly and sauntered off, without so much as a glance.

'Teacher's pet! Pastie Gracie!'

The two kept it up for a moment or two but then stopped and turned to each other, chattering about whatever it is people like that chatter about.

Gracie found a tree to sit under and pulled her spelling list out of her satchel, contemplating the unexpected blessings of the day.

'R. . .h. . .o. . .d. . .o. . .d. . .e. . .n. . .d. . .r. . .o. . .n.' She repeated it over and over until she got it. The bell went before she had time to realise the whole of lunchtime had passed and she hadn't even eaten her sandwiches.

Secrets

It was nearly time for Billy to go. The room was beginning to feel constricting, not enough air, and there had been more than enough emotion that day.

'Would you like me to read to you this evening?' he asked, half-hoping that just this once he could make an early retreat. Of course, he felt terribly guilty about feeling this way. After all, he felt sorry for her. He had his health and his fitness and his business. He'd even managed to find love, belatedly, although he hadn't been able to tell anyone about it. Not even her.

She would be shocked, he was sure of it. And his brothers would tease him mercilessly – yes, they still counted him as the runt of the litter all these years on . . . His father had died many years before . . . and his Ma was too old and frail. She would be devastated. He couldn't put her through that.

But he smiled softly to himself, thinking of the worn, crinkly face of the lovely man who had shown him light and comfort over the last 15 years. Aidan worked at a bank, nice respectable job, but he cut a dash every day with flamboyant pinstripes and natty cravats. He was immaculately groomed, and he was gentle and kind.

They would sit in companionable silence together in the

evenings, Billy poring over his log books and dreaming up eso-
teric new designs – delving into the depths of that famous imagination to see if he could come up with something that rivalled
– or even eclipsed – his brilliant invention, the engineering com-
ponent he had lovingly crafted as a young man.

Thirty years on and he never had.

Aidan would sit on his favourite armchair, still perfectly
suited and booted, immersed in whatever book had caught
his eye from reviews in the *Observer* and the *Times Literary
Supplement*.

They would most often have music on in the background.
Bach, usually, or perhaps a touch of Mahler. Aidan had intro-
duced him to all that stuff. Personally, Billy was happy with a
bit of Sinatra, or even, for a more modern twist, a touch of
Enya, or even a dash of Pet Shop Boys – but he felt warm and
cosy with Aidan there, and the old-fashioned notes were perfectly inoffensive.

They would take turns cooking for each other, and natter
about their respective days. Billy always had some adventures
to relay – even the journey into work could be spun into an
adventure in Billy's world . . . a tale from the lunch queue, a
funny conversation overheard and taken out of context. He was
still the mad inventor of joyous stories which endlessly enter-
tained his companion. Dragons and princesses tended not to
feature these days, but there was no end of laughter and fun.
The companion may have changed but there was still love and
laughter in his life.

Aidan was quieter, calmer, but in that Jeeves and Wooster

way he had he would bellyache with the best of them when something tickled him. Then he would roar with laughter.

They were good together. It wasn't a particularly conventional coupling, and neither shared their happy secret with family members, but they had a small group of friends for wine and supper. It was a most satisfactory arrangement.

And through Aidan, Billy had been able to grow to appreciate the poetry that had meant so much to Gracie. He learned to hear the cadence and rhythm of the words, to spot the themes interweaving like spun silk, not just through individual poems but through swathes of letters and works. The spark of light poets like Byron and Wordsworth ignited in every syllable meant each and every word was illuminated in a new, unexpected relief. Poets could weave words together with such beauty, such magic, like a word puppeteer – making them dance and sing and move seemingly without effort. Their phrases could inspire tears of sadness and lift the spirits with a burst of joy – all within a stanza.

Billy couldn't quite understand *how* those poets worked their magic – hardly anyone could, to be fair – but he had grown, in time, to feel the beauty of their work in the depth of his being.

At first, he had read the words as if they were merely a collection of – well – words. But with Aidan's expert guidance (he really was rather brilliant at things like that), he developed a personal understanding and could feel an emotional connection.

But today, he wouldn't be reading. 'It's alright, thanks, dear Billy. I'm a little tired today and feel I need to rest.'

Billy smiled kindly at the worn, ill shell of a woman and

wondered how long she had left. She had been so weak and debilitated for such a long time. He shook himself and forced an inward apology on himself. Gosh, how terrible to think that, he chastised, silently.

He bade her farewell and kissed her lightly on her forehead. She reached up and touched where he had placed his lips.

'Dear Billy,' she said, barely audibly, and smiled with her watery eyes.

The weeks were passing with a pleasant monotony at school. Gracie grew to enjoy the regularity of it, the timetable. Sometimes she would spend hours drawing up the latest schedule of lessons, colouring them in pretty colours and – of course – colour coding all the different subjects.

She discovered she was particularly good at English – everything about it, really. She particularly loved reading, she realised. When you read, you could be whisked away into your imagination and escape whatever realness was around you. If it was a good book, you'd be lost for hours, living the story with the characters, feeling their feelings, a silent witness to their lives. There was something deliciously intoxicating about squirreling yourself away for a while and letting your thoughts take flight. The author would be there to guide you gently, maybe hold your hand now and then, but you were doing the hard work of bringing the stories to life.

She felt the same about reading poetry. But poems were more magical somehow (well, good ones were), and they needed you to concentrate really, really hard. Not to get the top layer, of course, it was easy enough with Shakespeare and Wordsworth and Byron and that modern poet John Betjeman to skim the surface and get the gist. And even the surface layer would take you off to new places, new ideas. But to really *feel* a poem, you needed to learn how to peel back its layers, like a rose, and examine each petal in detail to reveal its secrets. You would peel and peel and peel away and – phish – another lunchtime would be over, another bedtime would come.

Of course the trick was to get so used to the peeling process that it would become automatic, so that even when you started reading a poem for the first time, the organic whole would separate out and reconstitute itself *as you were reading*. This was the really magic bit. The bit Gracie wallowed in and loved. The rose would peel back its own layers all by itself, and slowly fold back into itself, all the while under your touch. A bit like you were a conductor of an orchestra, playing a soft and gentle tune. Hardly without anyone realising, you were encouraging it along, teasing out its melody and its tones. Shaping it. Moulding it.

So you would see the threads and the themes, observe the colours and the sounds and the scents, hear the syllables of emphasis and sense their meaning by their weight. By reading out loud, you would hear new secrets revealed, as you listened out for repetitions and sounds and echoes, sometimes softly rippling beneath the surface, other times crashing rhythmically from line to line. It was only by reading aloud that you could spot lovely tricks the poet would hide from view if you scanned it on a page.

Gracie had no idea where her passion for literature came from. It's not as if her Ma was a voracious reader, although she seemed to like dipping into old favourites like Brontë and Austen and Thackeray from time to time. And on a good day, they would find bits and pieces to read out loud to each other. Those precious, special times were all too rare these days. But when they did happen, they were cherished by both of them. And they would wonder why they didn't do it more often. But then life would get in the way and the weeks and months would drift by without another reading session.

As for Billy – well he certainly didn't spend hours with his nose in a book. The very idea made her chuckle. He wasn't the kind of person that liked to 'waste time' as he called it, when there was so much playing and inventing to be done. Dear Billy, she thought, he really was the tenderest, sweetest person she could ever hope to meet.

A few days after ... *it* happened, Billy came round for Gracie.

'Gracie!' her Ma called, 'Billy's here. Do you want to go for a walk?'

She heard her mother call up, and she looked up from her book. She was buried in *Great Expectations* and was wallowing in Pip's latest exploits. Pip was helping her escape, and a very good job he was making of it, too. She wasn't sure how long she had been adventuring with him, but she realised shadows were casting across the room and it was late afternoon.

She pottered downstairs, deciding it was time to talk about it. But she wasn't prepared for the overwhelming rush of emotion that would descend on her at the sight of Billy.

She had been so good, so strong, refusing to let school or her

Ma or the memory distract her from her mission of pretending everything was alright.

But one look at Billy and she collapsed into tears.

He rushed over towards her and stood, awkwardly, not quite sure whether he should touch her or wait for her to recover. He put one arm around her, tentatively. She wrapped both arms around his waist, clasping him hard. So he hugged her back, not even quite knowing what was wrong yet, but sensing the enormity of what was to come.

The jagged tears came fierce and hard, soaking his shirt. He didn't mind but didn't know what to do, other than stand there in the hallway, patting her gently. She let out little gulps of breath and sounded like a wounded animal that had been pricked by a thorn.

As her small body convulsed in tears, he caught sight of a shadow on the floor, and realised it was the silhouetted remnants of what was once a flower, scarcely more than a thorny stem – its petals thrown roughly aside. It brought into sharp relief the violence and the destruction of that day. He hugged her tightly.

Gracie's Ma let out a slow groan of despair. Billy looked at her, noticing how overcome she seemed by the raw emotion she was witnessing in her daughter. It's true that until this moment, Gracie had been so composed, so very grown-up about what had happened. Of course, she hadn't told either of them the details of what *had* happened, not yet, at any rate.

Billy had felt so proud of the way she had bravely coped these last few days and couldn't help but feel her Ma was thinking the same.

But deep down, he wondered whether seeing her now,

quivering with heart-wrenching tears in his arms, the scale of the hurt little Gracie must be feeling would start to affect her. Affect her enough to do something about the dreadful situation they were in. How could she put her own daughter through something like this? Why wasn't she doing anything?

Billy secretly believed Gracie's Ma was wanting Gracie to be able to cope, to pretend everything was okay, because if *she* pretended, it meant they could live in a bubble of silent conspiracy with each other. Then, when the time came, they would be able to cope, together, with whatever Joe did next. That was what he thought she wanted to happen. He got carried away with the idea. Maybe she wanted that bubble to scoop them both up and protect them with strength and silence. Maybe she wanted to be able to put all this behind them, forget it ever happened. Billy thought if Gracie's Ma had her way, she'd want to slam the door shut on it, forever. And carry on as if nothing out of the ordinary has taken place.

'Oh Gracie,' he murmured, her convulsions subsiding. Then to himself, 'How am I going to help you if your own Ma won't?'

Gracie and Billy walked outside, hand in hand. She was 14 now, he almost 16, but there was still something charming and innocent about the picture they made together. Gracie's Ma glanced at the black-and-white photograph on the mantelpiece. She didn't have many photos, but that one of the two of them had pride of place. They were much younger then, and were setting out together on one of their adventures. Today, they were walking away with a heaviness in their hearts. Back then, there was only joy and expectation.

In the photograph, they were stepping into a clearing in the trees. One of the places they went to play – well, whatever it was they used to play.

These days they didn't play so much, but they talked in hushed tones, telling each other stories, she supposed, sharing secrets and being there for each other. And they would make each other laugh! How they would make each other laugh . . .

She mused on this now, comparing the dwindling silhouette of the two in the distance with the two in the frame.

How innocence so easily morphs into experience, she thought to herself. *You blink and suddenly your little girl is growing up. Your turn your head and she is becoming a woman. You go out for a drive with . . . with . . . well, the man you adore . . . and your little girl changes, forever.*

Rosebuds

Gracie looked at him and realised she had no choice. She waited, momentarily, to see if God would do another miracle for her, like he did when she was locked in the cupboard all those years ago.

She searched her mind for an explanation. The regular anxious refrain tormented her. Was it a test? Or had she done something wrong? Had she hurt someone by accident? Had she forgotten some of her chores? Was she a bad person, but just didn't know it?

So many questions and not a single answer. And all the while standing there in her nix, as she called them. She was horribly, painfully aware of her body under his fierce gaze.

She wasn't sure what exactly he was looking at, but she could hear his breath intensifying. A slow smile seeped over his face, and his tar-like eyes glinted. She thought of that beady eye in the leaves all those years back. It was the same intent. She was under no illusion this time either, he wanted to devour her. Hurt her, tear her apart.

'Get them off,' he commanded, in a low whisper.

*

He knew she was just teasing him, look at her, the little slut. She was always prancing about in her thin cotton dresses, taunting him with the silhouette of her shape and the tawniness of her legs. Her eyes were wide and dark, pupils dilated with desire for him. He knew it. He could sense the magical combination she was feeling of fear and trepidation mixed with an acknowledgement of the submission that was to come.

He felt the slow pulsing of blood coursing into hardness in his trousers. He luxuriated in the familiar hotness, the pain-pleasure urgency that was building there. Aching inside, aching for her, aching for those deer-like eyes to give up their fight, to relent, to submit to their desire.

He slowly let his gaze wander over her skin. God, he could breathe in her almond milkiness from her. Soft, pale shoulders crowned in a froth of yellow hair. Those budding nipples, straining in aching need for his touch. God, they were just about the prettiest things he had ever seen.

They were the dusky colour of rosebuds about to open on a spring morning. Perfect little circles of lusciousness, waiting to be licked and sucked and bitten. They were raised into little points in the centre. God, it was fucking good to see them. They had been tantalising him beneath her dresses for months, and now they were his.

He looked at them, letting their rosebud pinkness tempt him. He could tell they were softly fleshy around the outside and hard as fuck in the middle. He was going to get his teeth around those. Jesus.

He was aware of his own hardness intensifying to a glorious sting of need. He felt it pressing against the fabric, fiercely.

He looked down at her small stomach. Flat as a boy's with a cute, yes, he chuckled to himself, cute little belly button which just cried out to be tasted.

And those legs were something else. She had sprouted up several inches in the last few years and her long limbs were elegant, beautifully shaped, perfect. There was a downy softness to them as little hairs caught the light that was wafting in from the window.

He saw she was still wearing her underwear and issued the command.

Slowly, she began to remove them.

Aha, this one likes a striptease, does she? He chuckled to himself, watching her bend over in front of him. Now *that* was a view he liked, he chuckled some more. *We'll be having some of that later.*

He stared at her awkward frame and ordered her to get into the bath.

The water was about halfway up and the bubbles were landscaped into snowy peaks across the surface.

The girl cowered in front of him. This he liked very, very much. That exquisite communion of fear and submission. She was going to do everything he wanted, everything. He felt the excitement mount in his trousers and let himself groan in pleasure of the anticipation.

For Joe, it was always the waiting and the watching. The more he waited, and the more he watched, the more devastatingly fucking powerful his release would be.

He had learned to watch and wait for hours. God, it wasn't easy. Like anyone else, when he was on the point of being ready, his body naturally wanted to give in to that wave of pleasure spasms. But he'd learned with practice that he could intensify his own climax beyond the hopes of any man by lingering in an almost pleasure-pain for as long as possible. Then, my friend, the impact of that wave of spasms would be blow-your-fucking-mind extreme.

Of course, he'd learned this self-awareness over time, and over time took the liberty of practising with many, many victims. He didn't like to think of them as victims, naturally, he would think of them merely as accomplices to his own will. After all, they always submitted in the end, when that desire-relent moment hovered between them, like a bubble waiting to be burst.

Finnegan was the first of many. Joe had realised that day that violence towards people did something more exquisite for him than torturing creatures.

Shame, in a way, because he'd always got a lot of thrills from thinking up new and exciting ways to taunt and execute God's furry, spiky, slimy, pathetic little friends.

Ha! So the Lord God made them all, did he. Well he would show Him! If the Lord God made them all, it was down to Joe to, well, kill them all.

And so he did. Scores of them. Foxes, badgers, snakes. Cats and dogs, after a while. Nothing was too much of a challenge.

But people were something else. There was something about the emotion you could see in the beating heart of another human being, the expression in their eyes, the thrill you would feel when they reached that sweet point when they knew there was no way out.

God's creatures were great and all – but nothing compared to the fleshly humanness of his own kind.

After Finnegan, there was that hiatus in his progress. Being locked up for a few months did two things. First, it forced him to rethink how to carry out his business more discreetly. Second, it meant his Ma and his sister were told what he'd done. He'd need to win them round again and explain it was self-defence. He knew he could do it.

After he'd been released, he allowed himself less than a day before striking again. That feeling of wretched, gut-tearing, ball-breaking pleasure-pain had so overwhelmed him, so exhilarated him, that he needed to find out whether he could replicate it.

So at dusk the following day, he went out for a walk. His Ma's voice ringing in his ears 'If you're not back in half an hour, we're not waiting and your tea will go in the bin'.

He knew she was lying. There was no way Ma would actually discard food. They were too poor for that. It would be neatly wrapped up, or kept hot for him, or put somewhere to cool, depending on what it was. He was always his Ma's favourite, despite everything. Despite even Finnegan. She'd bought the story about Finnegan attacking him and Joe needing to defend himself. She had to believe in him, she had to. She *needed* to. He was convinced he was still her favourite. Well, why wouldn't he be? Those beautiful, leaf-green eyes, the black eyelashes fronding them, a strong jaw and one of those noses a Roman emperor would have had. Powerful, beautiful.

He tanned at the slightest hint of the sun so was walnut brown throughout the year. And he was blessed with genes which made him strong and muscular with very little effort. He had a defined stomach and arm muscles before he was out of junior school.

And as he entered his teens, he had that gorgeous muscle line only very well-toned men develop, at the base of the abdominals and leading down . . .

His thighs were toned and strong but not thickset like some boys get. He was lithe and muscular, dark and dashing, with the flashing whites of his eyes contrasting glintingly with the dark-green pools of his irises.

All the girls admired his physique, and unquestionably his own mother believed her son to be utterly lovely. His beauty helped him disguise the ugliness of his nature. Even after the Finnegan incident, people struggled to pin the blame of tortured animals, broken wings, drowned cats, on Joe.

It was one of the reasons he had had to react the way he did when Finnegan stepped in and tried to stop him. For the first time in his life, someone had witnessed that wicked sneer, that evil glint, that full-body, muscular grip of power. So he had to do something about it. Even if it led to consequences for him, too.

It was true that even in the throes of his violence, there was something warrior-like, attractive even, about him. Finnegan saw it that day. A strength and a sense of knowing that would make grown men nervous. Even in the depths of his evil, Joe had the looks of a storybook hero.

His sister hadn't been so lucky in the genes department. She had a quiet, placid face . . . somewhat pale and uninteresting to look at.

But still, her bird-like fragility fascinated him, and he pledged himself that at some point he would taste her moment of submission, too.

Now, before him, a young girl was clambering into the bath. He watched as the foam snows caressed her form. He smelt the air, smelt her skin, became aware of the lemony sweetness engulfing the room.

Her knees were raised slightly, because of the smallness of the bath. She was eyeing him in trepidation. The desire she had for him was wallowing in those eyes, peering out from under her lashes with the look of an Old Testament temptress.

He looked at her parted knees and followed the line of her thighs down as far as he could see.

White, fluffy soap suds gathered across her navel and between her legs.

It took him straight back to that first time, when he had had that first tantalising glimpse of the gap between her legs.

Not that he could see anything then, and not that he could see anything now.

But he knew what was there. And his body groaned and strained for it, wanted to see it, wanted to touch it.

Watch and wait, Joe. Watch and wait . . .

He felt the hardness swell between his own legs. Slowly, exquisitely.

Her rosy sweetness, softly sheening in the water now as the hotness flushed her, begged to be touched.

Her shoulders had white bubbles glinting on them, and her perfect little nipples were hazed in whiteness.

His attention was caught again by the gap between her legs.

He groped inside his trousers for one, hard, torturous squeeze. *God, that felt good . . .*

And he watched the bubbles sparkle and play, prickling against each other.

He pulled his hand out and hovered it above her, above that private place only her Ma and Billy had ever seen before.

He imagined its taste. Sweet, young, juicy. He imagined the feeling he would have when he touched it. He knew how soft and yielding it would be.

Even now, he could sense how desperate she was for him to do it.

But I'll make you wait, you little bitch, he thought, like you've made me wait all this time.

And his thoughts drifted back to what it would feel like to touch it, to part the soft folds, pinkly warm because of the water. He could imagine the small, perfect roundness of her pleasure point and felt – urgently – that he needed to see it, now.

But he watched, and he waited.

Daffodils

Sun dappled through the trees and speckled onto the school lawn. She didn't know it yet, but today was going to be one of the most important days of her life.

It had begun ordinarily enough. Pulled on her grey pinafore, popped on her beret and yanked up her scratchy grey socks, tying them up with those garters that left horrid red marks around her legs. Forced down her spoonful of malt and cod liver oil – revolting – the daily ritual her Ma imposed on her which was supposed to keep her fit and healthy.

Skipped down the road to school, contemplating the day ahead and looking forward in particular to the times tables test as she had learned them all off by heart now and was feeling rather pleased with herself.

Tish and Jo could be as mean as they liked. They couldn't take away the happy feelings she got at doing well at something.

As expected, times tables went well and it wasn't long until before lunchtime. Gracie sneaked into her favourite haunt, the library, picked out a storybook from the shelves and settled herself down.

Yellow sunshine streamed in through the windows and cast

its glow in columns of fairy twinkles, each dust particle brightly kinetic with energy and light. She started humming to herself, quietly.

The door opened behind her and she realised Mr Hall had come into the room. Lost in thought, he tapped on the spines of several books in a corner section of the library Gracie hadn't investigated much and landed on a dark blue cloth-bound book with beautiful gold embossing down the edge.

Still standing, he opened its leaves and looked intently at the pages. Gracie wasn't sure whether she should make her presence known or not. She didn't want to be spying or anything. So she did a little cough.

Mr Hall looked up and smiled broadly.

'Hello Gracie, how are you today?'

'Very well thank you, Mr Hall. How are you?'

Mr Hall wandered over, the blue book still clasped in his hands.

'What are you reading today, Gracie?'

'Oh, it's a lovely story about a young boy who travels through space and meets an airline pilot and a whole series of other grown-ups. He's a very lonely boy and he loves a rose that he discovered growing on his planet. But he feels upset because of some things the rose did and said, so he leaves her. But then he starts missing her, and he realises he loves her. And he meets all these people and ends up feeling he doesn't really understand grown-ups.'

'*The Little Prince?*' asked Mr Hall.

'Yes!' Gracie gulped, delighted he knew the story.

'What is it you like about the story?'

'Well, in a funny kind of way what I like about it is that I want to be the Little Prince's friend, and cheer him up and make him see things will be alright. I feel sorry for him and I think I understand some of the feelings he has.'

'So you're experiencing what we might call "empathy". It's when something we hear about resonates with us and we feel completely in tune with a feeling or a thought. If you're feeling sorry for him, it's possible it might be reminding you of times you have also been sad, or treated badly by people.'

Gracie listened intently.

'The wonderful thing about literature is that it helps bring us closer to our own emotions, and helps us process and understand what we are going through ourselves. If something is written beautifully, it can spark something special in us, make us feel a little bit more alive.'

At this, Gracie was a little surprised, but thought about it and mentally ticked off a number of stories that had made her laugh or cry, or feel sorry for someone or feel angry at someone. She realised he was probably right.

'Do you mean, like if I read something that makes me sad, that I am feeling something really powerfully because it reminds me of something myself?'

'Yes, that's the sort of thing I mean. When you're older I'll teach you about transference and counter-transference but that's something for another day. For now, let's just think about how literature can help you feel closer to your own emotions. Closer to your own imagination.'

Gracie thought about the Little Prince and how brave he was, setting out on his own. And also how lonely he was. And

how what the grown-ups said really didn't make sense sometimes . . .

'How much poetry have you read, Gracie?' Mr Hall suddenly
asked.

'Not loads, sir, mostly stories really. Oh, and hymns. "All
Things Bright and Beautiful" is a poem, isn't it?'

'Yes, that's right, Gracie. Lots of songs are poems, not just
hymns.'

He paused a moment.

'I think you're exactly the kind of girl who might like poems.
You are thoughtful and patient and you take your time to enjoy
words.'

And then he said it. That one little phrase that had stuck with
her ever since.

'Poetry is the most marvellous Secret Key to escaping real life
and disappearing into a world of your own. It's your very own
Castle of Make-Believe.'

'I'm not sure I understand, sir . . .'

'Well, Gracie, the clever thing about poetry is that each and
every person will read a poem in their own way, bringing with
them their own experiences and perceptions and opinions and
prejudices. Each and every person will see different things in
different ways. An interpretation of understanding here, a shade
of emotion there. And the layers! You would be amazed all the
hidden layers there are in poetry – but unlike in maths, there's
no "right" or "wrong" answer. All that matters is how it makes
you feel, and what it makes you think.

'There are word patterns and sounds; clever loops and references and what we call sonic echoes, where the sounds words

and syllables make reflect each other and echo each other. Some people will spot some things, other people will spot others. Some people will hear things, some people won't. That's the beauty of it, Gracie.'

Gracie was thinking it sounded very confusing.

'Of course there will be similarities, there's bound to be over-laps. But there's an art to reading poetry and if you discover it, I promise you, you will never regret it. It's the best way to escape the drudgery and difficulty of real life. It lifts you and guides you, it inspires you, it helps you. When you are lost in your imagination, building mind shapes and orchestrating your own Castle of Make-Believe, you have the Secret Key to life. Let me show you what I mean . . .'

He opened up the blue cloth bound book and showed her it was an anthology of verse. He flicked through the pages and hovered over this one, then that one, then another.

'I think we'll start with Wordsworth, Gracie.'

He began by asking her to read a poem out loud. It was called: 'I wandered lonely as a cloud' – a lovely title, she thought.

She started with some hesitation and stumbled a few times over the words, but got through to the end.

> I wandered lonely as a cloud
> That floats on high o'er vales and hills,
> When all at once I saw a crowd,
> A host, of golden daffodils;
> Beside the lake, beneath the trees,
> Fluttering and dancing in the breeze.

Daffodils

Continuous as the stars that shine
And twinkle on the Milky Way,
They stretched in never-ending line
Along the margin of a bay:
Ten thousand saw I at a glance,
Tossing their heads in sprightly dance.

The waves beside them danced; but they
Out-did the sparkling waves in glee:
A poet could not but be gay,
In such a jocund company:
I gazed—and gazed—but little thought
What wealth the show to me had brought:

For oft, when on my couch I lie
In vacant or in pensive mood,
They flash upon that inward eye
Which is the bliss of solitude;
And then my heart with pleasure fills,
And dances with the daffodils.

She finished and looked up from the page.

'First of all, Gracie, what are you thinking, right now?'

'Well, I feel a bit embarrassed about mucking up my reading in a few places and I feel slightly out of breath because I forgot to breathe in and I spoke too fast.'

'Okay, Gracie, very good – but I mean what are you thinking, right now, about the poem?'

Oh. She paused, and reflected.

'It made me see pictures in my mind – I was imagining the poor lonely cloud floating about in the sky feeling all lost, then feeling all happy when it suddenly came upon all those daffodils. It was like all that yellow felt real to me, I could really imagine what it all looked like. It was really easy to think about it in my mind.'

'What else, Gracie? What did the choice of flowers do in the poem? How different would it have been if, say, it was a host of dark purple flowers instead of a host of golden daffodils?'

'Well – the colour golden makes you think of bright, happy things, and – sorry I don't know if this sounds silly, sir, but daffodils are quite a funny shape with their big trumpet middles sticking out like jolly tongues poking into the air. So they seem like cheery flowers. And because they're yellow, you can't help thinking there's like a warmth and happiness about them.'

'Very good. You see how your mind's eye can join the dots and make pictures come to life in your head? And how what the words make you imagine start creating an emotional reaction in you? You don't just *observe* their colour and their shape – the *fact* of their colour and the *fact* of their shape influences how you, Gracie, respond.

'The funny thing about poetry is that when you start peeling back the layers, you realise lots of the time it has an effect on you in unexpected ways. You are reminded of a fragrance, a sound, a physical touch. All five of your senses start coming alive when you start joining the dots in poems and let your inward eye do the work.

'The trick is to let it wash over you to a certain extent, and to start rereading and noticing what the words and phrases and sounds do to you. Let the power of the poet do its work. Let yourself feel things. Experience how it impacts on your senses, how the sounds come together and echo each other and immerse you.'

Gracie glanced back down at the page and skimmed the words.

'I really like the way the poor, sad poet ends up being able to cheer himself by just thinking back to his happy memory. And words like "twinkle" and "sparkling" remind me of light reflections on the sea; and words like "dance" and "sprightly" seem full of movement and joy! And isn't it funny how the poet uses the word "golden" and then also "wealth" so you get the sense that the experience is rich. And isn't it nice that he's using words like "glee" and "gay". And isn't it wonderful how in just a few lines he moved from something so sad and lonely to something which is filled with "pleasure" and "bliss".'

Mr Hall smiled at her. He had had a feeling young Gracie would get the hang of it.

'Exactly, Gracie. Next term we're starting to study the wonderful art of poetry, and you'll discover the power of words like you've never done before. Why don't you borrow this book and start seeing what you think?

'Poetry, if you let it, will help you make sense of the world. It can be your solace and your friend, even in the loneliest of times. Your escape. Your Secret Key.'

Words

The rain was lashing down that day. Rivers of wetness, sloshing into the tops of trees, crashing against window panes and drenching anyone who had the misfortune to be out in it.

You know the kind of rain where it's almost as if God was emptying great big baths of water everywhere? Well, that's what Gracie was thinking. The heavens were opening that day.

She was coming to the end of morning lessons on a Tuesday. Maths. Bit boring really. They were having to work out how long it would take to get to Margate from Bury St Edmunds if you were travelling at 30 miles per hour. Why did maths questions always seem to have Bury St Edmunds in them? Was it even a real place? And why did it matter how long it would take? And didn't the route you took affect the answer? Why did they always want to pin you down to one fact when there were thousands to take into consideration?

Her mind was drifting to loftier places, the soundtrack of the tropical rainstorm playing rhythmically in the background, beating down in slow symphony with her heart. She had been trying to memorise the Byron poem Mr Hall had set for her as a bit of extra English homework. Ever since that unexpected lesson in the library, he'd been giving her suggestions of poems to read and learn. Some of them she found easier than others. Sometimes the vocabulary was just a bit too difficult and if you got more than one hard word in a row it made it tricky to make sense of the whole thing.

She was particularly fond of poets that wrote using simple language but with vivid 'imagery'. Mr Hall had taught her all about imagery recently and she loved conjuring the pictures in her head. Letting the emotions wash into her.

This new Byron poem was absolutely wonderful. As she read it, the phrases danced in her thoughts, and a calmness settled in her.

The words hovered in the air before her, enticing her to create mind shapes . . .

> *She walks in beauty, like the night*
> *Of cloudless climes and starry skies;*
> *And all that's best of dark and bright*
> *Meet in her aspect and her eyes . . .*

Gracie was floating, luxuriating in the sounds and images playing together. A shape was being created in her mind, connecting the dots of the meaning of the words to the dots of the forms of the words to the dots of the sounds of the words. Like a spider's web spinning outwards and back in on itself, the poem was taking form, coming to life in revelation. She was the invisible conductor and her mind was spinning the web of layers, conjuring an extraordinary sense of the poem's inner being.

'Gracie, come on.'

Her reverie was broken and she found herself rudely brought back into the classroom. She became aware of the hardness of her wooden chair, the roughness of the old school desk in front of her, etched with a thousand half-legible messages from times gone by. Outside, the rain was beating down.

She peered into the words marking the desktop – carved she supposed by compasses. There seemed to be girls' names, boy's names, secret love messages and one or two phrases about teachers long gone.

'Gracie, I said come on!'

She looked up and understood she was the only person left in the room. She wondered how long she had been caught up in her mind shapes. She had been on the cusp of teasing apart the opposing forces of darkness and light in the poem, exposing its themes into naked being. She loved the contrast between the beautiful lady's raven tresses and the soft light on her face . . .

In the doorway, Mrs Spindler was chiding her. 'Come along, it's lunchtime.'

Something as mundane as lunch felt so unimportant to Gracie these days. She was still in her spell, and wanted to play with her flights of fancy some more.

She wandered off to the library so she could sit quietly and contemplate the poem further. It was as if the beauty was somehow above her, a benign, beautiful presence which was too spiritual for this earth. And innocence was at the heart of her, and of the poem itself. Purity, love, goodness and light. Gracie hugged herself with the joy of seeing and understanding. She listened to the sounds it made, softly reciting it aloud so she could bathe in the richness of its watery depths . . . cloudless,

tress, less, express, nameless, goodness . . . the 'ess' rhyme un-
dulated up and down through the river of the poem, echoing
backwards and forwards with the other words. The glow below,
the light denies. The clever way he used day and night as inter-
locking themes, knitting the words together with fairy thread. It
was just so very, very . . . beautiful.

> *She walks in beauty, like the night*
> *Of cloudless climes and starry skies;*
> *And all that's best of dark and bright*
> *Meet in her aspect and her eyes:*
> *Thus mellow'd to that tender light*
> *Which heaven to gaudy day denies.*
> *One shade the more, one ray the less,*
> *Had half impair'd the nameless grace*
> *Which waves in every raven tress,*
> *Or softly lightens o'er her face;*
> *Where thoughts serenely sweet express*
> *How pure, how dear their dwelling-place.*
>
> *And on that cheek, and o'er that brow,*
> *So soft, so calm, yet eloquent,*
> *The smiles that win, the tints that glow,*
> *But tell of days in goodness spent,*
> *A mind at peace with all below,*
> *A heart whose love is innocent!*

The peace and calm in the poem lulled her into a serenity she
craved these days. If she let herself drift too far into her own

thoughts, memories of what happened in the bathroom would jaggedly overtake everything else. So it was words she turned to, to escape.

She had come to the poetry section of the library, the place where Mr Hall had pulled out that blue-spined poetry anthology the day of the 'poetry lesson'. Well, there were three shelves in the whole library with poetry on but it was a start.

She glanced outside the window and took pleasure in seeing the raindrops gathering pace, chasing each other as they snaked down each pane of glass. Round, wormy droplets which seemed to absorb the greyness of the day in their fatness.

The bell startled her. She realised she had had no time to properly select a book, so she grabbed one with 'rain' in the title. It seemed appropriate enough.

She stuffed it into her satchel and dashed off to double art.

Billy looked at her with a tenderness she could scarcely bear.

'Oh Billy,' she said, softly, her voice so low you could hardly hear her.

A thousand thoughts were whirring around inside Billy's head. He'd decided not to mention what he had realised about the white rose having come from his garden. He couldn't understand why his Da would have brought a flower to Gracie's Ma so decided it couldn't have been important. He'd also decided not to ask too many questions. It was up to Gracie to explain what happened, in her own words and in her own way.

They were walking side by side, back to the clearing they had played in so many times when they were younger.

The memories of those happier, innocent play days seized them both at the same time. They exchanged glances, neither needing to say it out loud.

Billy was remembering building dens which were really castles, and making secret dark green holes which were dragons' lairs. He had loved inventing worlds for her to discover, populated by fairies and goblins and princes and demons and witches. Dragons and princesses.

Gracie was thinking about how much they had enjoyed chasing each other, pretending to be otherworldly creatures from storybooks. She thought back to how she would join the dots of the characters and the places he created to understand the world he was making – ahhh, so I'm a princess, so this lump of stones and moss and leaves must be my castle. Ahhh, so I'm a fairy, so this clearing of twigs and branches must be my fairy palace. And this puddle must be my fairy pond.

Without thinking, they pottered over to the tree stumps where they had often started their games as children. They sat down, silently.

Gracie looked at Billy, and wondered how on earth she could put it into words? It was so much more than words – it was *feelings* of darkness and fear and terror. She wished she could join the dots for him so he could see what she felt, so she wouldn't have to describe.

But she knew she had to say something . . .

'Billy, I was frightened. It was awful. Joe is . . . he's an evil man. This is going to sound strange, I know, but it's like there's something not right about him, Billy. I don't think he's got any niceness in him. He is the cruellest person I have ever met. And scary, too. He scares me like the birds do, Billy. And I mean really, really frightens me. Like he's going to hurt people. Hurt me.'

Billy understood what she meant, and nodded.

'It's as if there's blackness in his eyes, like that raven Billy, you know . . .'

How could he forget.

'He looked at me in the same way. As if he was . . . hungry. As if he wanted to devour every bit of me, Billy.'

Again, Billy wasn't sure what to make of this. He knew what a cannibal was and felt pretty certain Joe wasn't one of those. He had the feeling Gracie was trying to break what happened to him gently, either to protect him or to protect herself, he wasn't quite sure which.

'He made me take my clothes off and run a bath.'

Now this was beginning to sound weird. Why would her uncle make her run a bath? He knew about men and their urges, of course. In fact he'd experienced the odd twinge himself even as a fairly young boy, but he had the feeling he was built differently to other boys. Not on the outside, on the inside. Where the other boys were running around chasing girls' pigtails and trying to glance up their skirts, he had no sense that there was any point to it at all. He had his Gracie and that was that. And he certainly didn't want to make her run a bath.

He wondered whether to ask why Joe had wanted her to run a bath but thought better of it.

'He just kept staring at me, Billy. Everywhere. You know . . . everywhere.'

Billy looked at her. A shadow had crossed her face, darkly.

That beautiful, innocent face. She had rounded cheeks like rosy apples and dark eyebrows which contrasted prettily with her yellow hair. She had such a sweet, sad expression. So soft, so calm. Even now, telling him this, her calmness moved him.

She was just so . . . lovely. He hoped that whatever Joe did to her he wouldn't take that away from her. It was the very essence of Gracie-ness and he loved her for it.

'I have asked Ma to stop him ever coming back.'

'Do you think she will?'

'I don't know.'

Milestones

She thumbed the old pages carefully, letting the dusky paper fall through her fingers. She could feel the weight of the leather and the heaviness of the spine. Her fingertips traced the embossed lettering, as if conjuring a memory and willing the book to come alive.

The scent of old books was reminiscent of cinnamon somehow. Their dustiness and mustiness would tingle in the air and settle in anticipation of the pleasure to be had when words mingled with imagination.

The old poetry book was her dearest treasure. She looked at the book plate: 'Harwood High School 1947', it read in royal blue ink. The library stamps decorated the first two or three pages – red and black seals with dates ranging from September 1947 through to July 1952.

She thought back to those times. How very different they were. You'd have blancmange and jelly for a treat. Hardly anyone had a television. The wallpaper could be shocking . . . she remembered that orange floral paper with a shudder.

People spent their time talking, reading. Being together. People spent a lot of time at home. These days, there was lots more going out. Lots more external distractions. That was it –

back in her day, folk were happy with hearth and home. Family. Ahhh, family . . .

Now it was much more usual for daughters and sons to live miles away. Sad, that . . . families were fragmenting and dissipating. Back in her day the family unit stuck together, and that was that. Helped each other. Supported each other. Stood by each other. Even in the worst of times . . .

She had a clawing sense of regret and guilt but could never place it. Only the words of the poems helped her feel light and free these days – mostly because of the memories she had of that mother–daughter togetherness, when they read out loud to each other. She could reach back and touch that lightness, that sense of communion, that special bond they'd had.

But those moments were fleeting, and even when they surfaced, she soon lost track of what she was thinking.

There's so much going on.

Even Billy's visits were becoming more strained, she felt. She got the impression he wished they could be speeded up. Bless him, he was her only visitor. She wasn't quite sure when she stopped having friends, or even whether she had friends. She paused a moment. *I must have done!* She thought to herself, *I must have done.*

She racked her memory and all she could think about was how the world was apparently getting more connected as she was slowly withdrawing. You could see it on the television. The gadgets of today seemed to have swelled in proliferation. In her day, every new invention seemed to come along with years and years in between. Computers then were the size of buildings. It's extraordinary to think a tiny microchip today can do ten times the things one of those great big machines could do then. Not that she had had personal experience of all those things, of course, but Billy brought her the paper from time to time and she hadn't lost her marbles, yet. Just her strength. And some of her memories.

She turned to another of the books on the shelf, placing the poetry anthology to one side. This other one was dark blue hardback and had childish, spidery handwriting throughout. Black ink. She always wrote in black.

She turned to the inside cover: 'Gracie Scott. Aged 14.'

She had spent many an hour whiling away the time, flicking through old memories. The diary had chronicled lots of childhood recollections tracing back to the start of everything. And then there were day-to-day notes and scribbles. As if somehow Gracie Scott, aged 14, felt the need to tell her story.

And it was the beginning, the middle and the end of the story, really, wasn't it. Some of it was too hard to read. Some of it she refused to read. Some of it she reread a hundred times, with a smile in her heart.

Blowing bubbles with her mother in the garden. Sunny, carefree days. Playing in the clearing with young Billy. Princesses and fairies.

Little Gracie had carefully mapped out all the key milestones of her young life. It was almost as if she knew . . .

There were lots of references to Billy, to how he was the best friend in the world ever.

Lots of story snapshots of games they played, chats they had.

She had also recorded little notes of memories from her much younger childhood, carefully marking them 'Memories From

When I was Little'. Like that secret moment of swapping peeks into each other's private bits in their 'jammies'.

All sweet and innocent games.

She also wrote down all the different foods she had to eat, as if it was a mission to capture the time and place it in aspic, to be remembered forever.

Minced beef and dumplings. Hotpot. Stotty cake. Pease pudding and pork sandwiches. Crumble. She really liked her crumble.

And at the back of the diary she had made lots and lots of lists, as if she wanted to help historians of the future. She had put prices of tin cans, household goods, sweeties and furniture. With careful descriptions about everything, meticulously written up:

'Lollipops, 3d for a bag the size of your fist! These take forever to eat! They're enormous and they last for hours, But you can forget talking or playing or doing anything else. They're so big! They taste sweet. They come in different colours. My favourite is yellow.

'I also like boiled sweets (which are clear and fruity) and nougat sticks. I don't much like liquorice strips because they make your teeth go all black.

'But the yummiest is either toffee apples or chocolate, I can't decide. Sweet rationing stopped in 1953 and since then everybody eats chocolate. You buy it in 2lb boxes!

'And talking of black things, you can also get biscuits called Garibaldis which look like they've got squashed flies squidged inside! But they're really currants and actually quite delicious.'

She had also noted down all the vagaries of currency and

weights ('we have something called the Imperial system, I think because in the past we in Britain were very Imperial. But we don't have an Emperor, like they do in places like China') and there was a line each for every member of the Royal Family ('I particularly like the Queen. She is so beautiful and young and gracious. She is married to a stern man called Prince Philip who I think is very handsome but looks a bit serious.')

She had crafted a precise sense of time and space, with florid descriptions of everything from how houses are decorated to what the streets and landscape looked like.

She painted word pictures and when you read her lists, written as they were, punctuated by exclamation marks and childish chatter, you could hear her voice and imagine her there, explaining excitedly everything you could possibly want to know about life in fifties Britain. Or more specifically, life in early fifties north Tyneside. But for Gracie, that was just about the same thing.

She talked about the big foghorn they tested all the time – so loud and noisy. And she talked about the weather ('I mostly like it when the sun shines and it's warm and fine. But quite often it rains. It rains a lot actually but I try to make it fun by thinking up clever ideas about what the rain drops look like, as if I'm a poet.')

And she wrote about her school lessons, her struggles with spelling and her annoyances with various teachers. There were descriptions of all the school buildings and lots of her class-mates, their clothes and their personalities. There's a special section all about Tish and Jo with a typically Gracie take on their childish bullying:

'Tish is quite tall and built very solidly. She has short brown, mousey hair and a babyish voice. She isn't very good at sport and so far doesn't seem to be very good at lessons, either. I can't understand it myself but she seems so confident and strong, as if she doesn't have a care in the world on the outside. But I think she seems bitter and unhappy and always looks as if she has been sucking on something sour (like maybe those sour sweets you can get). So I'm not sure if she really is confident or whether she is putting on an act.

'Jo is short and – well, I'll say it! – dumpy. But she has very nice fluffy pale blonde hair. She's quite good at running but like Tish isn't very good at lessons. Jo is one of those people who looks really sweet, she has pink round cheeks and her Ma buys her lovely clothes. But she can say the most horrible things to people (well, to me). I don't really understand why she wants to be mean to people, but she does. Apart from Tish, neither of them are friends with anyone else. But those two are thick as robbers (is that the expression?).

'The pair of them go round together all the time and call me Pastie Gracie because I have fairly pale skin. I don't particularly mind having fairly pale skin but I mind being teased about it. Or rather, I *did* mind. I think after what happened, happened . . . that first time . . . well, it helped me put their girly teasing into proportion. And it occurred to me that maybe they're not very happy either.

'The main thing is, I've got Billy, and Billy's got me. We look after each other. And we always will.'

Dragons

She got home from school that day and emptied her satchel onto the bed. Out fell her notebook and some pencils. And the book from the library.

She looked at it properly for the first time.

'Rainer Maria Rilke' it said on the front cover. In her haste, she had thought it was a poetry book – something about 'rain' – now she realised the rain bit was just part of someone's name.

She didn't have a clue who this might be, but she was intrigued. He hadn't come up in English yet. She scanned the opening pages. He'd lived from 1875 to 1926 and wrote in the German language. Luckily, this book was an English translation. German was something you associated with the War, not with poetry and beauty, she thought. She read the introduction carefully. It turned out Rilke was born in Prague and had lived through a difficult childhood but went on to become a world famous poet. She felt excited at the discovery, as if she had snuck upon a secret place only she knew about. She couldn't wait to see what his writing was like.

She turned the pages and began to read.

She saw to her surprise that he had composed his own epitaph. She'd only recently learned that word but was amazed that someone had the forethought to write the words that would mark their own grave. She contemplated whether she should make an attempt at writing her own one of these days. She read . . .

Rose, oh pure contradiction, delight
of being no one's sleep under so
many lids.

She let the words float into her and felt their gentle power begin to take shape in her mind.

She couldn't be sure what the epitaph meant, but it intrigued her. She wondered if he'd hoped that instead of dying, which would have a forced finality to it, he wanted to fall into an everlasting sleep. She imagined the scented folds of a rose embracing each other, with every petal nestled into fragrant hugs with the next. Joined together at the base, strong and bonded but frail and prone to separation at the gust of a fierce wind or at the mercy of intense rain. The human hand could cherish it or tear it apart.

She thought of the physicality of sleeping. Eyes closed, heavy-lidded with tiredness. The depths of slumber gently rocking you to bliss.

She couldn't think what 'pure contradiction' meant but the mind shape she conjured revealed the petals of the rose as eye-lids, softly closed and asleep.

Then suddenly, she remembered the scattered white roses on the floor of the clearing that day when the raven wanted to attack her. When she had fallen into a kind of sleep. She shuddered. At the time the sight of them hadn't registered but thinking about them now, they had been collected together like a little posy. The shudder brought about by the raven was quickly replaced by the warm, safe glow of thinking about Billy.

And now back to her other new friend. Someone to love alongside Billy and Wordsworth. Rilke.

To be honest, some of the collection was quite hard to get your head around and Gracie was beginning to feel tired. She caressed the pages of the book tenderly and leafed through a few more, thinking to herself it must be nearly time to go and help Mam with the tea.

Then something happened. The words 'dragons' and 'princesses' seemed to dance off the page towards her. She peered down at page 27.

It was the first time she had ever seen the poem that would become the talisman of her life. She slowly read the opening phrase and an overwhelming sense of coming home engulfed her.

How should we be able to forget those ancient myths
That are at the beginning of all peoples.
The myths about dragons . . .
That at the last moment turn into princesses.
Perhaps all the dragons of our lives are princesses . . .
Who are only wanting to see us
Once beautiful and brave.

She put the book down and gazed into space.

A chord struck deep in her core and she felt she was at the edge of discovering something profound about life.

She thought of the raven. She thought of Tish and Jo. She thought of her Ma on a bad day. And she thought of Joe.

The dragons of her own life.

She pondered what this could mean.

Perhaps everything terrible is in its deepest being . . .
Something helpless, that wants help from us.

She was transported back to three-year-old Gracie and thought of the grass that bit her. The wasp, the grown-ups said.

She thought of the dead bird, chasing her in the hands of a taunting boy.

And she thought of the raven. Eyes locked on her, hungry. Wanting to devour her.

She looked at the raven's beak, its talons, its shiny, menacing blackness and Joe's stern, dark face loomed into view. Eyes locked on her, hungry. Wanting to devour her.

In the way that children often can, she began to speculate about the fate that brought her to this book. Is it possible that this was a special message, just for her? Was she supposed to understand something important about the nature of *things*? Had she been suffering so many punishments for so long for a reason?

She had searched long and hard over the years for an explanation of the persecution she endured. She had always drawn the conclusion that somehow God had wanted her to suffer because she had done something wrong. She had never been quite sure what it was, but she had utter conviction that somehow it was all her fault.

Now a new sense of understanding was dawning within her.

So, even evil had something weak and helpless at its heart? So there's no such thing as pure evil, there's no such thing as a man without a soul.

It didn't make sense, it didn't. But then maybe it did . . .

Another thought drifted into her mind. The familiar refrain of her favourite song began to play in her head, quietly.

> *All things bright and beautiful,*
> *All creatures great and small,*
> *All things wise and wonderful,*
> *The Lord God made them all.*

The Lord God made them all. Perhaps everything terrible is in its deepest being something helpless after all.

'Gracie! Gracie, pet!' Her Ma's voice stirred her out of her drowsy thinking and popped the bubbles of her mind shapes.

'Coming!' she cried back, slowly closing the pages of the book together and placing it onto the small white table in her bedroom. She had found a new friend, and she was looking forward to getting to know him better.

Bruises

At home with Aidan, Billy was getting comfortable on the big leather sofa. They'd not long ago savoured a sumptuous chicken risotto – one of Aidan's specialities, and the cello chords of Bach were wafting thoughtfully in the background.

They'd just opened a bottle of red and were settling down for the evening. It had been a couple of days since Billy's last visit to the hospice.

The clock on the mantelpiece tick-tocked comfortingly and the warm cream walls were tastefully decorated with a swirling cream art deco pattern, something a bit William Morris but all monochrome. A modern take on an old theme.

There were two oil paintings on the wall. The first had a deep azure foreground with cream and white dapples. Perhaps an ocean, or a sky. The second was vivid magenta with cream swirls and azure flashes. A sunset, perhaps.

The floor was hardwood, beautifully sanded and varnished, with a plush cream rug knotted with Damascene silk. You could see why they weren't keen on children visiting.

On the table – a dark teak piece apparently heft from an ancient fallen branch – sat a sculpture of marble. Reminiscent of Rodin, two hands entwining. And alongside the sculpture was a carved fruit bowl, scooped out of fossilised volcanic rock.

There was a vase of irises and cornflowers on the mantelpiece, picking up the azure depths of the first oil painting, and in a short black vase on the table squatted some magenta orchids, reflecting the tones of the second painting.

Aidan's favourite was the large, deep brown armchair fashioned with a footstool and headrest – a reworking of a Tom Dixon he had once had the pleasure to sit in at a hotel while away on business.

Billy favoured the old chesterfield. Buttons smart as a pin and leather lovingly restored – it was an ancient piece but good as new – since the restoration – and comfy beyond compare. Especially with those big squishy pillows. Azure and magenta, of course.

The room was an object lesson in tone and taste. It could easily have featured in one of those homes magazines which left people sighing with envy.

'I can't stop thinking of the child she used to be,' he pondered, 'so calm and placid, but with a wise and clever head on those shoulders. I wished you could have met her then.'

Aidan didn't need to ask who he was talking about.

Over the years, this was a subject he returned to endlessly. It was as if by talking about it, he could somehow recreate the person she was and breathe life back into her innocence.

'Tell me a bit about what happened,' Aidan encouraged. He'd heard it a thousand times before, but he knew that it would help his partner to go over it again. He was sure there wasn't anything new to say – God knows it had happened so long ago

– but if it helped Billy, it helped Billy. They were there for each other, to love and to hold, through good times and bad. He could tell Billy had been having a bad few days.

'The worst thing is, I think it could have been prevented . . .' Billy mused.

'Gracie's mother was a lost soul, I think, and didn't know what to do with herself when Joe turned up. I think at first, from what Gracie told me, that she might have been pleased to see him. But if she was, that turned sour fairly quickly when he started beating her.

'And of course it seems that he had been taken by young Gracie from the very first time he set eyes on her. Gracie had always said he looked at her strangely, with a kind of fierce intent. Surely her Ma would have been worried about that? Wouldn't any parent? And it turns out there had been a previous occasion when he had stalked into the bathroom unannounced, intimidating her. Gracie had let her Ma know, but she had brushed it aside as one of those things. She had developed an unnatural tolerance for Joe and his ways.

'Sometimes, we children from the Close saw that she had bruises and cuts. She had tried to cover them up, but it wasn't hard to see that Joe was being very rough.

'Everyone knew he had been in jail but no one really knew what for, other than it involved violence. Some said he had even murdered someone. But no one knew for sure.

'There were rumours swirling around him but there was an aura of untouchability he emitted, as if nothing and no one could get in his way.

'I heard from Mam years later that Da had been threatened

by him once when he'd tried to confront him. Apparently Joe had said he would break every bone in all us children's bodies if he ever interfered again. Now you know Da had seen action in the War and been to hell and back from what we learned much, much later. But there was something about what Joe said that made him take it very, very seriously. Mam thought it all a bit odd, given Da was a soldier and should have been able to take him on. But apparently he was adamant.

'There are times I think I will never forgive him for not stepping in and doing something. What were they thinking, Da and Gracie's Ma – just standing by and letting him do what he did? Why didn't they report him? Why didn't they get the police round? Why?

'But as I've got older I think I am coming round to understanding a little better what they went through, how terrified they must have been. Da must have been scared witless not to do anything. He must have genuinely believed our lives were in danger. How could he risk sacrificing us to that monster?

'And I don't know the full story with Gracie's Ma, other than what Gracie told me herself. That family was everything. That you stood by family. That nothing mattered more.

'And Gracie thought that Joe at some point had threatened her Ma about doing something horrible to *their* mother. The grandmother she had never been allowed to meet . . .

'Maybe also, especially in those days, it was easier to turn a blind eye. Pretend it wasn't happening. Put on the mask of civility and go through the motions of a life better lived.

'The first time I saw his violence with my own eyes was just over a year after he had arrived. He always stank of Guinness or some other black stout, and he smoked endlessly so there was the stale stench of ash clinging to his clothes, his hair and his skin. You could smell him before you could see him!

'On this occasion, I was about eight so I'm guessing Gracie was six. She looked like an angel, all blonde curls, big emerald deep eyes and rosy cheeks and lips. She could have been a human doll, she was that pretty.

'She was wearing a white dress with white roses embroidered onto the bodice. I'm not sure why I remember that bit, other than perhaps I've always associated white roses with Gracie. I think she used to like them.

'We'd been playing in her sitting room, building blocks and using old scraps of fabric to evoke a fairy-tale land of some sort. Maybe Hansel and Gretel's house – you get the gist.

'We were both hiding – maybe we were pretending to be sneaking away from the wicked witch – and cowering up together behind the sofa. We were still as statues and even quieter. Even though we could hardly contain our giggles – that always happened whenever we were trying to be quiet, we were silent and serious in our mission to escape the witch.

'Suddenly, the door rammed open and in strode Joe. He was staggering and seemed to have blood on his face, a cut lip, and a ripped shirt sleeve. The smell of him was overpowering, just revolting. Can you imagine?'

Billy glanced at Aidan, who nodded in collusion.

'He stormed through the sitting room, straight to the kitchen, where Gracie's Ma was preparing tea. I think it was pease pudding and pork that night. I'd been asked to stay to tea, which was always exciting. Other people's mums always made tastier food than your own Ma.

'We stayed deadly silent, looking at each other. The giggles we had been trying to swallow faded away and were replaced with worried little frowns. Gracie had told me all about Joe's habit of turning up after a fight, clothes torn up, blood everywhere, and a treacherous mood to boot. She had told me he had the scariest temper, and would smash furniture, walls, doors, anything that stood in his way. People, sometimes.

'There was a yelp and a suppressed scream. It sounded like Gracie's Ma had been hit then stifled. Then we heard it. "Come on, you know what to do," he snarled at her. Another yelp, a pleading noise, "Please, Joe, the children . . ."

'"I don't give a fuck about the children." We heard him swear. I'd never heard a grown-up swear before, only youngsters at school who were trying to be hard.

'"But they're in the house, Joe," we heard her beg.

'Then, thwack. Thwack again. Then thump, thump, thump.

'An "ow", softly, then another thwack.

'Silence for a bit. Then what sounded like a belt unbuckle. The kitchen was just a few paces away from where we were crouching.

'"Agggh! Joe, Agggh!' A thwack of the belt against her skin. Once. And again. And again.

'Gracie was white, the look of a haunted animal across her face. Neither of us dared move.

'Then as soon as it started, it was over. Joe marched out. Peering from behind our hiding place we couldn't see much, only hear the steps stomping down the driveway.

'He didn't bother closing the door.

'Minutes later, we relaxed, convinced he wasn't coming back, and ran into the kitchen. Gracie's Ma was collapsed on the floor, blood on her blouse and a rip in her skirt.

'She had cuts and bumps on her face and her right arm. A bracelet was twisted and broken on the floor.

'A plastic bowl with flour and some liquid had been smashed down the side of a cupboard.

'She lifted her head, hardly able to look us in the eye. "It's okay, children, I just took a fall. Why don't you go and have tea round at Billy's this evening, pet? I need to take a bath and get myself feeling better."

'We were so shocked all we could do was concur. Gracie had seen the cuts and bruises come and go over the past year – we all had – but this was the first time I had witnessed what Joe did. Thank heavens we didn't actually see what he did – but what we heard was brutal and vicious.

'Gracie's Ma looked at us pleadingly then quickly looked away. A second first for us both that evening. An expression on her face we couldn't quite place. And something we both grew to recognise. Shame.

'It was to be a look we would both grow familiar with as the years passed and nothing was done. For some reason, Gracie's Ma decided it was acceptable to welcome Uncle Joe into her home. With everything that would come to mean for their family.

'Neither of us could imagine that the damage was going to get far, far worse.

'We looked over at Gracie's Ma. She was still sitting on the floor, nursing her arm and looking frail.

'Purple bruises were already beginning to show.'

Poplars

It wasn't long before Joe started to get addicted to the high he would feel when he performed what was now becoming a ritual. He would stalk out his prey and pick his moment. There would be a long, drawn-out period where his accomplice would play the game along with him, resisting, withdrawing, attempting to escape. There would be animalistic fear in the victim. And animalistic urges in him.

The enduring torture would last as long as he could force it.

As part of the stalking process, he would identify the perfect place to commit the contract. That's how he liked to think of it, a contract between him and his accomplice. Their tacit understanding and acquiescence binding them together.

So the person and the place would be set. But he never planned in advance what form of dance he would conduct. Some accomplices, he found, responded exquisitely to physical pain. The terror in their eyes would be a thing of beauty to behold, especially when that perfect moment came when they both recognised that submission would come.

Others put on a bravura performance when he played with their minds. Hardly laying a hand on them, hardly saying a word. The occasional smirk shadowing across his face, a raised eyebrow, a look of intent.

In some ways this was a more refined art and Joe felt intense pleasure in playing with people's minds. Letting the threat of some unimaginable terror hang in the air and suffocate them. He admired the brain's workmanship, its ability to think the worst beyond any menace he may enact.

He would look into their eyes and savour their helplessness. Pupils would dilate in desire to be put out of misery.

Shudders of nervousness would be morphed into waves of nausea and uncontrollable shaking. Some would vomit from fear. Others would loosen their bowels. There was no denying this feral creature had the capacity to terrify his fellow man without so much as touching him. And that's what he thrived on . . .

Some would attempt to plead with him, reason with him. These were the ones that irritated him the most.

You bastard, he would rage. *If you think I'm the sort of person who would be open to your petty cries and stupid whimperings, do you really think I would have brought you here in the first place? Do you honestly think you're going to make me change my mind by blethering on about your child, your wife, your work? Ignorant fucker.*

He would feel incensed that they would insult him with the proposition of defeat. *How dare they suggest I don't go through with it.* And it would strengthen his resolve and encourage him to be even more brutal when he meted out his punishment.

He remembered one occasion with particular fondness. It was maybe number thirty-two or thirty-three after Finnegan.

He was perhaps 14 by now. Had mastered the craft of concealment. Developed a physique that made people look twice. So had to be extra careful about hiding the evidence of his conquests.

Strong, far advanced through puberty and imbued with a sense of his own exquisite virility. Beautiful.

His voice had dropped an octave and he'd developed a baritone beauty which softly emanated from his larynx. He hardly ever raised his voice. He hardly ever needed to. He spoke slowly and intently. In another life, in another world, he could have used his voice for art. Everyone who heard him speak was struck by it. Like the low cello notes of a Bach concerto.

Such beauty in such corrupt misuse was only the beginning of the tragedy.

The 'performances' *he* delivered were paced and practised but anything but art.

Spellbinding, maybe, but spellbinding in the way the spider tantalises the fly, caught in the web.

It was a warm, summer's day and the sunshine dappled in the trees. He had left school by now and did odd jobs and labouring on construction sites. In-between grafting, he would watch the people walking by and see if anyone caught his eye.

He didn't have a preference for man or woman, young or old. What he was looking for was a sense of fight barely perceptible under a veil of vulnerability.

It was the veneer of niceness and decency he craved, but not someone who would immediately back down into submission. Where would the fun be in that?

But someone nice and decent would always deliver impeccable

performances for him. They would hesitate to confront him, they would be trusting and naïve at first. They would be deliciously disappointed first, horrified later, when they realised they had been duped and there was no way back.

He was finishing up early today. A Thursday afternoon. He'd worked hard all week to ensure he could leave when he needed to. It had to be a Thursday because on Friday the man may change his routine, go out to a pub or start the weekend some other way.

For about a fortnight, he had made eye contact and exchanged smiles with a businessman who made polite conversation with him and some of the other lads as he made his way to and from work.

He was wearing a wedding ring and carried an old battered briefcase. His shoes were worn leather and his suit looked well lived-in. He wore wire framed spectacles and had neat, short back and sides. He had a jaunty gait and always seemed to be – irritatingly – in a good mood.

I'd like to wipe that smug, self-satisfied smile off that fucker's face, Joe thought to himself.

Well today, if everything worked to plan, it would be step one to making that happen.

Joe had a lean, muscular body and with his height and strength could easily pass for sixteen years old. He had black hair razored tight to his head on the sides, but a disarming, floppy mop of black hair which fringed his face like one of those lads in advertising posters. His fierce eyes shone out of his face in dark-green-black pools. He was striking by anybody's standards and had cultivated a patina of politeness and normalcy so no one would begin to suspect such a nice, moral, good looking lad would be anything other than exactly that.

He lived at home with his Ma and sister. Got fed and watered there but that was about it. He was a loner. Didn't need friends. His own sense of sexual adventure was all the intimacy he needed. He wanted to be able to select his accomplices and adopt – and discard – his temporary playthings at will.

Having to hang out in gangs like most of the other lads didn't appeal to him at all. He would pass the time on his own, mapping out new lairs for attacks, devising new ways to thrill his accomplices with fear, and perfecting his new craft of watching and waiting.

It was only a matter of time before he started his other lonely pursuit. Drinking. He learned to love the sickly bitter-blackness of stout, loved the surges of extra confidence that propelled through his body when he'd had a few.

But drinking, like his planning, was something he preferred to do alone.

He could put on the act, of course, be one of the boys when he needed to. Especially if it helped him design a strategy of stalk and attack. But it was always an act and the minute he could, he retreated into himself to experiment more with the physical awakening that stirred in his core.

So, Thursday, leaving work early. He placed himself a short walk away around the corner of the site and found a suitable spot. Then he watched, and waited.

Around six-ish the businessman was one of dozens who spilled out of their offices and onto the sunny streets. There was lively chatter in the air, the buzz of traffic and seemingly a spring in the step of the collective crowd as it welcomed the still sunshiny warmness of the early evening.

Joe watched and waited. When he laid eyes on him, he fell into step with the other pedestrians thronging the pavement. He slowly meandered through the people-treacle until he was on the point of overtaking the businessman.

'Oh hello, young man!' he heard that voice he was expecting. He turned slightly, in mock surprise, and took his cap off.

'Hello, sir,' he said, warmly.

'It's you from the building site, isn't it? You lads are doing a fine job, that great big shop you're working on is going up in no time.'

'Yes, sir, it is that.'

'A lovely day, isn't it. So lucky the sun's still out after a hard day's graft, eh?'

Joe looked at his eager, friendly face, puppy-dog-like in its enthusiasm. He felt nothing but revulsion for this preppy blaggard.

'Yes, lovely,' he said, softly.

'So what's the shop going to be?'

'I'm not quite sure, sir, but they say it might be a new grocer's which will have a butchers, bakers, fishmongers and greengrocers all in the same store. Not sure if that's right, but that's what they say.'

'Oh that sounds interesting, my wife will be most interested to hear about that.'

So he was right, Joe smiled inside to himself, there was a wife.

Now all we need to do is follow this bastard home and plan step two. He could already feel the stirrings of anticipation deep in his body.

'Well, I'm taking a right here. You take good care, now,' he said, 'and enjoy this lovely evening.'

'I will, sir, I will.' Joe smiled again, allowing his eyes and cheeks to light up in what he knew looked to be an entirely authentic grin.

Joe dropped back and started following the businessman, too far behind him to be seen but not too far away that he couldn't keep up.

Big poplar trees lined the streets, their bright green leaves rustling in the breeze. You could hear children playing, chasing balls and flicking marbles. In the distance, the faint tinkle of an ice cream van catching the evening air.

You could see parents bustling home – armfuls of shopping for some, briefcases for others. Labourers and factory workers, shop assistants and market traders all wending their way home. And still that interminable cheery chatter as people savoured the delights of a sunny Tyneside night.

The businessman maintained his jaunty walk for the next 10 minutes or so. Joe was taking care to stay well back and yet note where he was going. Every detail mattered.

He'd been planning this ever since he first eyed the businessman. He was perfect, he'd thought. The right side of chipper. A wedding ring. A face that needed punching and a smile that needed wiping away.

He arranged the schedule meticulously so that Thursday would be his last night on the site. He would make contact that night and identify the real accomplice, the businessman's wife. It was with her the contract would be done.

He would monitor her schedule and select the perfect time to strike a week or so from now.

By then all minor connection or association with the construction site worker would be a forgotten, irrelevant detail for the businessman. He would have other things to worry about.

Joe's imaginings pulled hard at his groin when he thought of this. That stab of pleasure-pain darted through him, and he felt himself harden.

Watching and waiting was a game of chess, a patient man's game. But it was worth it, more worth it than anything you could possibly imagine. He let his eyes roll back as the ache of desire felt hot and pulsing inside him. He allowed himself a slight pause, keeping the businessman in his sights all the while, and pressed his fist against his crotch, then allowed his hand to grasp himself through the fabric, hard. One luscious squeeze and the pulsing intensified.

The groan escaped his lips and he smiled, resuming his walk stiffly.

At number 38 Poplar Avenue, the businessman unlocked the door.

'Daddy! Daddy!' Joe heard a child's voice and saw a toddler in dungarees scurry up to the door, swiftly followed by a slim woman with neat brown hair in a bun. She was wearing a pale green apron around her waist and a white sundress splashed with poppies. She raised her face to his and they exchanged a kiss.

The businessman bent down and scooped up the little boy

and momentarily, the three of them embraced at the doorway. Then their voices dropped to a murmur, and the door closed behind them.

So that's where you live, Mr and Mrs Businessman.

Another squeeze, hardening inside. Pleasure-pain. Groaning.

He lurked in the shadows for about half an hour, enjoying the sense of quarry marked.

He would be back, and back again, and it wouldn't be long before that blissful release would be his.

Metaphors

Gracie had had the Rilke book for about a week now. The epitaph had moved her deeply, and she had been interested to read about the story connecting Rilke to a rose in his death. They said he had died because of the prick of a thorn.

She wondered if he had known a rose would seal his fate when he wrote the epitaph, and she wondered how true the story was. And if the story was true, and if he hadn't known the role a rose was to play in his demise, then how very sad and ironic.

She wondered what she should write if she were to compose her own epitaph. She liked roses, too, she thought. White ones in particular. Maybe she could create a short poem inspired by Rilke's?

She burst into laughter at the idea. She was only a schoolgirl, for goodness's sake. How could she think about writing a proper poem?

She reached into her bookshelf and pulled out a small, dark green, hardback book punctuated by her own childish scrawl, and leafed through it in amusement.

She had written little rhymes and limericks on and off for a couple of years now. Very childish and silly, she was almost embarrassed to look at them.

> *Hound chases fox*
> *Fox chases shelter*
> *Hound barks*
> *Fox falls*
> *Hound runs*
> *Fox stalls*
> *Hound sinks teeth in*
> *Fox bites back*
> *Blood is swirling*
> *Fox sees black*

That was her most recent one, she had written it in English in the third year. She had quite liked the rhythm of it and there was something neat and simple about the imagery she'd created – but it was so straightforward and easy and she felt quietly ashamed at how thin and uninteresting it was in comparison to the complex beauty of Rilke's words.

But she remembered why she'd written it and what influenced her at the time. Mr Hall had asked the class to write a verse based on something from their own experience, but to use a metaphor. They had spent the previous few lessons looking at metaphor in the poetry of people like Marvell and Donne. It sort of meant a way of telling the story without actually telling the story.

In her case, she racked her memory for a suitable experience. She could think of plenty. Some of which all too easily. For her, the raven and Joe had almost taken on a dual identity. One was the other and the other was one. So a large part of her was already consumed in the power of metaphor.

For her, because Joe inspired the same fears and terrors in her that the raven did, she found herself intertwining them in her mind. Joe–raven. Raven–Joe. One and the same. The power of metaphor . . .

But she didn't want to write about that in English. Apart from anything else, it wouldn't help her special plan of pretending everything was alright to bring it out into the open, and anyway, she felt the deep, private aspects of the story were too – well private – to share. With anyone. Anyone except her diary, perhaps. She wouldn't even tell Billy the full extent of what had been happening. How it had been a slow, inexorable journey with signposts on the way. Signposts her mother preferred to ignore.

But the journey was set and the raven was clawing at her heart, tearing her apart in slow, defiant strikes. It was a course that was progressing slowly, but progressing it was, and for Gracie, there was no obvious end in sight.

Her home no longer felt like home. No safe refuge there. It had become a clean, chemical impression of hearth and heart. A game of make-believe. Of nightmares. And she was the animal being experimented upon.

So no, there was no shortage of metaphors cramping into her head. But what would she be prepared to share with the class, with Mr Hall?

She remembered being chased by that boy ramming a dead bird down her back when she was little. She wondered, briefly, whether that was her first encounter with the raven. Was it a raven? She knew the bird was black but couldn't be sure. She was too terrified to know, running away as fast as her little toddler legs would carry her.

But that feeling of being hunted quarry had stayed with her, and if that *was* her first meeting with the raven, he had done a fine job of scaring her half to death. Even through his own death he clawed at her heart.

She shuddered at the memory.

She decided she could use this story as the starting point for the exercise, and would be okay about telling everyone what had happened. What she wouldn't reveal is the sad continuation of the story. How the blood swirling and the fox seeing black was real, was her, and had happened more than once.

She had let her mind drift away, imagining the pacing of the chase and the emotion she wanted to convey. It was then that the idea of a fox hunt came to her. She had remembered learning about fox hunts a while ago. They had been mentioned in a book she had read, and she had asked her Ma about them. So she knew a bit about the general premise. A team of huntsmen on horses would use hounds to help them chase down a fox for the sheer sport of it. 'The thrill of the chase,' her Ma had said. So here, now, wondering what metaphor to use, the hunt seemed perfect. It was all about one small, harmless creature that hadn't done anything other than just to *be,* caught up in a game beyond its control. As far as Gracie could tell, there wouldn't be much fun for the poor fox, no thrills of the chase for the prey.

So she worked hard thinking up the hunt story she could use

to capture the feelings of her own experience. The words, the rhythm, the passion she wanted to invoke.

She wondered if that was the sort of thinking Wordsworth had done, and Rilke, when they were composing their poems.

She knew she wanted to share the panic of the fox and the single-mindedness of the hound. She also wanted to give a sense of finality to it, to leave people wondering if the fox had died but not actually saying so. It took ages to do but she had been happy with the simplicity of her effort, and hadn't minded sharing it with everyone.

Mr Hall had said it was 'promising' but that she could have worked harder making proper rhymes.

She thought that was a bit rich given that Wordsworth and Byron and Donne and even Shakespeare mucked around with rhymes all the time. She thought about her own attempt and wondered if it would have been much better if she had had pure rhymes throughout. The mind shapes took hold in her and the hunt came to life through the pulsing and the urgency of the rhythm and the staccato of the words. She felt the panic in the fox, sensed the bloody determination of the hound.

Nope, she decided, throwing in some extra perfect rhymes wouldn't necessarily have made it better than what it was.

Now, rereading it, she was convinced it wasn't purer rhyming that it needed but better thinking.

And with that, she turned to the thought she had about attempting a verse inspired by her new poet hero.

She let her mind float away into nothingness, waiting for something to coalesce. A stillness flowed into her and she found herself falling into a slumber. She vaguely thought about the idea of falling . . . what was that line again, about life not forgetting me? *It will not let you fall . . .*

Droplets

He was staring, hard, at that gap between her thighs.

The froth of the foam obscured the view, achingly teasing him with what lay beneath.

He could hardly bear the thought of it. His whole being was consumed with the surge of anticipation. His appetite needed to be slaked. The pulsing inside was rhythmic, totemic. As if an electrical current was ignited within, coursing through his veins with gripping, groaning power.

His hardness was almost at the point. But he needed to watch and wait some more, for this to reach perfection.

Her wide eyes were wearing the look of a creature caught in a trap. Eyelashes, dark, framing her angel pools of green loveliness.

Her creamy, sud-soaked skin was gleaming in the light, white peaks delicately frothing at her waist, a pile of snowy softness caressing her whole body.

She looked so small. Her scent a babyish almondness intermingling with the lemony tang in the air.

Her devastatingly pretty nipples, calling him to devour their budding roundness, suck their apple hard pointiness. He found himself gazing at them, mesmerised.

He stripped to the waist, exposing his own, sculptured torso, his nipples in communion with hers. His muscles flexed in spasms, his strong arms preparing for the task ahead.

Then he reached inside and allowed his aching, pulsing, secret self to stand proud, hard against his belly.

He reached down to under the softness below and began his slow stroking, careful not to squeeze and careful not to let go. He needed to let that surge ride inside for now.

He looked at the effect his stance was having on the girl. The frightened creature caught in a trap was shivering, quivering.

Her wet curls tangling around her shoulders, water droplets decorating that sweet skin. A slow trickle working its way down between those nipples and down to her stomach.

His attention was caught again with the idea of her warm, pink place.

Groaned aloud.

Then, a voice. A child's voice.

Fuck, this isn't in the plan, he snarled to himself. For it to be as it should be, there had to be no interruptions, no distractions. Just a perfect calm.

He heard the girl's name being called. Someone else calling his angel, his most perfect of accomplices.

He had watched and waited for years for this moment, had planned it with his usual meticulousness. It was the culmination of timeless longing which had developed into an urgent, brutal need that had to be satiated. And now the calm was being compromised . . .

'Gracie, Gracie!' the child was calling.

Then a soft thud, thud, thud up the stairs.

Gracie stiffened. 'Billy!' she whispered under her breath. It was the first word she had uttered and it punctured the silence.

Joe looked at her in disgust. *You stupid little slut, don't you go ruining this, don't you even think about it.*

If Gracie had thought for a moment that by yelling out she could save herself, she would have done, but she was gripped by those claws into constricting breathlessness. All she could do was sigh Billy's name in frail, hushed, futile tones.

They both listened out as Billy stopped at the door, waiting to hear if he could discern anything.

She could sense his fearful anxiety.

Billy, save me, she was thinking, hard. *God, help him hear my thoughts, I'm pushing them through the door to him, hear me, Billy, hear me. I'm trapped with this man who has been keeping me his wet prisoner, standing guard over me. Boring his black, black eyes into every part of me. This is bad, Billy, this is very, very bad.*

They heard the footsteps retreat and the thud, thud, thud going back downstairs.

Then, silence.

Joe looked at his damp angel and fixed his face into a sneer. She wondered what he was going to do, what he was going to say.

'This was the beginning of something very special between us, Gracie. Can you feel it?'

He looked at her intently, willing her to understand. For her to be this most perfect of accomplices she had to grasp her role in this.

He reached down to her and traced his fingers around the curve of her jaw.

'Pretty Gracie.'

His rough, dirty fingers slowly followed the length of her neck and he extended downwards, to have that first touch of her teasing right nipple.

Slowly circling around the edge, watching her shudder and hearing her squeal.

Perfect.

He gripped the centre with a tenderness that surprised him, and felt that electrical connection shoot through his hardness.

He held her, right there, squeezing the rosebud pinkness soft then hard, soft then hard. His left hand gripping himself with an agonising roughness.

He could see her looking down at what he was doing and sensed her ecstasy, admiring his hard, throbbing cock.

'This is just the start, Gracie, just the start. I've got to go for now but it won't be long before we are together again . . . I'll come back soon. Be ready for me.'

She watched him awkwardly stuff that revolting inflamed purple animal back into his trousers and unlock the door. He carefully removed the key, putting it into his pocket.

'Not long, not long,' he whispered in that baritone voice. 'Not long . . .'

And with that, he was gone.

Sandwiches

Aidan looked at his partner, the story having come to life with a vividness which pierced the space between them.

'What did you do?'

He knew the rest, but he could tell Billy had the appetite to go on. For some reason he had been particularly exercised about it all in the last couple of weeks. Aidan wondered if the conversation was getting particularly difficult at the hospice. He knew Billy struggled desperately with his visits there and really had to muster something deep within to keep going. Duty? Honour? Kindness? He wasn't sure what. Probably a combination of all three, he suspected. But they always exhausted him and left a shadow in his heart.

'Are you sure you don't mind me going through it again? I'm not sure why I feel the need to talk about it. I'm sorry, Aidan . . .'

'Honestly, I mean it, go on. I want to hear what happened next.'

Billy felt very fortunate to have this supportive man by his side. He took a small sip of wine, and continued . . .

'We clung to each other, frightened. It had happened just a

few steps away from us – every blow crashing down seized into us, too. The sound of it was – oh God – it was excruciating . . .

'Of course neither of us were strangers by then to her Ma's purple bruises. But this was something that would wrench us both out of sleep in the coming months. The realness of it seeped into every part of us, lodging firmly in place. Like a poison.

'Gracie told me later it had been the worst attack on her Ma since Joe had come back into their lives.

'We left her as she asked, both feeling guilty and awkward about doing so. But it was clear we had no choice in the matter. Gracie's Ma was a broken little bird on the floor, but her will couldn't be ignored. We owed her that dignity.

'We walked out of the house and pulled the door gently behind us.

'We looked at each other wordlessly. I remember shrugging my shoulders in helplessness. What should we do? I wondered, not sure whether to ask out loud.

'"I think it's best that we leave her, as she asked," Gracie suddenly said, looking out down the road. It occurred to me that she might be looking out for Joe.

'So we slowly made our way over to my house. It was twilight by then. I've just remembered for some reason the white rose bushes were looking lovely, it's funny the things you remember, isn't it? and I spotted the large, fragile heads of the flowers swaying in the breeze.

'The front door was open, as it often was at this time. We tiptoed inside.

'There was the raucous sound of John and Simon having some play fight about something or other.

'Everything looked neat and ordered.

'I could hear my Ma's voice tinkling over the sounds of the wireless and the odd monotone reply from my Da.

'We went into the kitchen.

'The moment they saw us, they stiffened. I could tell they were noticing something unusual about us.

'It's true, usually we would be giggling together, whispering conspiratorially and sharing secrets.

'Today we stood there, limply, not knowing what to do.

'Gracie's face was damp from the tears she had shed. I think I had gone a bit red from the awkwardness of the situation.

'"What is it, pet?" Ma looked at us, urgently.

'Neither of us spoke.

'"What's happened? Tell us?" she coaxed, gently. She was clearly sensing the reluctance we were both feeling to do or say the wrong thing.

'"That man . . . that man . . ." began Gracie, her voice trembling.

'She was struggling to get the words out so I pitched in to help her along.

'"We were playing dens in Gracie's front room and hiding behind the sofa when her uncle came in smelling of beer and ash. He didn't see us and we were quiet as mice.

'"But he was making a lot of noise, banging about and throwing things. Then he went through to the kitchen and started shouting at Gracie's Ma. She seemed very frightened and was begging him, telling him we were there. It was if she had hoped that whatever he was going to do would be stopped if he knew.

'"Then, we heard the sound of hitting. Over and over and over . . ."

'I felt the emotion choke inside my throat. Gracie looked at me gratefully. We exchanged looks and I gave her my best big brave smile.'

At that, Aidan twinkled at his companion warmly. He had always been such a lovely person, and he loved him for it.

'At first, my parents didn't know what to do or say. Then the questions came tumbling out. Was he still there? Had he hurt us? Where was Gracie's Ma? Did she need to see a doctor? What did you see exactly? Where did we think Joe had gone?

'We reassured them that we were both fine, other than shocked and appalled at what we had heard. And we told them we thought Joe had gone. Gracie explained that he would take off for long stints at a time. And she explained that her Ma often had unexplained bruises and cuts which she attempted to cover up. It was slowly dawning on all of us that Joe was a dangerous man who was repeatedly taking out his temper for some reason on his sister, Gracie's Ma.

'They were asking themselves if they should call the police and debating the merits of interfering or not. It seemed like hours but looking back now I'm fairly certain it was just a matter of moments. They wondered what, if anything, she had said to us.

'"She told us to come home here, to leave her alone. She wanted us to go away for a bit and was going to clear herself up," we babbled together.

'They both looked terribly worried and we heard them murmuring. "I knew something was wrong . . . she hasn't been her old self . . . she kept hurting herself, she would tell me she'd fallen over, had slipped . . . I never liked him, never . . ."

'And then, Da said he was going over to check on Gracie's Ma and find out if she needed medical attention. He said he would find out what to do about the police.

'Gracie smiled up at him gratefully, as if my dear old Da in his brown trousers and white shirtsleeves could make things better. She was beaming at him with such appreciation, he gently placed his hand on her shoulder.

'"Has he been frightening you, too?" he asked.

'At that, Gracie's face dropped from a smile to a frown and the darkness I'd seen before crept over her face.

'"I think he is a wicked man, like the wicked witch or the monster or the dragon," she said. She spoke so seriously I don't suppose either Ma and Da doubted her for a second.

'"Don't worry, Gracie, we will fix this."

'And again she gave him what I used to call her "sunshine smile" at him. She looked so relieved that at long last someone big and strong was going to deal with Joe and let her and Ma get on with their lovely happy lives.

'Later she told me that what she was hoping was for life to go back to normal again, with Joe gone. Forever. I remember her telling me that she was looking forward to it being just her and her Mam again. She talked about how nice it would be to just sit and read fairy tales together again. And that there would be days being outside blowing bubbles again. And carefree moments making tarts. And day trips to the estuary to fish for cockles.'

At this, Billy found his eyes moisten. He was describing the perfect life Gracie had imagined for herself. Aidan patted him gently on the arm.

'What happened next?' he said, encouragingly.

'Well, just as he said, Da marched out the door and we heard his footsteps gradually fade away.

'"Come on you two, you need something to eat. How does jam sandwiches sound?" Ma always knew how to make things seem alright. We both turned to her gratefully and took our places at the table.

'There was a blue and white gingham cloth draping down and blue napkins placed in a pile at the end. Ma began slicing into a large loaf of snowy white bread and delved into the larder for some butter and the jam pot. She handed everything to us and instructed us to make the best possible jam sandwiches that had ever been made.

'Happily busy with all this activity, Gracie and I got on with our new game, a sandwich competition where the best sandwiches would get served at the Royal Banquet. It was easier, somehow, to chatter in our play world rather than talk about what we'd heard. Gracie made a particular point of having a smear of butter but oodles of jam. "It's what the Queen would like," she explained.

'I preferred to get the butter–jam ratio exactly even.

'We tried each other's and both proclaimed the other the winner. And giggled together for the first time in several hours. It was a good feeling.

'Tucking into those sandwiches that day felt like a turning point in our lives. It was the moment we'd glimpsed the complexity of adult life. We had experienced the brutality of violence and seen the veil of shame. But rooted in it, no matter what, was our friendship.

'I remember thinking that something had changed. And I could feel it, viscerally, that Gracie seemed lighter and freer than I had seen her in ages. I remember realising how very much she was looking forward to Joe leaving their lives.

'If only it had turned out that way . . .'

He paused and looked at Aidan, tears welling up gently in his big brown eyes. He took a sip of red wine and looked away into the distance.

'Do you think it's the right thing, keeping going to see her at the home?' Aidan asked. He didn't want to influence Billy but at the same time was keen to help if he could.

'I think so. In fact, I know so. It's comforting in a sense for me to see some of her old things. Her poetry books, photos, things like that. But you're right, it's hard, and it's taking a toll on me. I never stop thinking "what if" and I never stop wishing things had turned out differently.

'But she doesn't have anyone else, and even though her memory is scarcely there these days, I think it brings her some small lift to see me. I take her the papers and we natter about inconsequential things, mostly. Sometimes we'll both get whisked away in a memory, and that can be painful. But if I didn't go, who would? It can't be right for someone to live out their last days completely on their own, can it?'

Billy was almost wondering out loud, but he knew his own answer. He was duty-bound to see her right, to do what little he could to soothe a balm over the past.

Dots

She had lost track of how long she had been staring out of the window. The rain had cleared up now and the garden had a freshly washed greenness about it. Yellow dandelions were popping up all over the lawn and the yellow and pink crocuses were dotted sprightly in bunches at the bases of the trees.

There was a white china vase on the windowsill, stuffed full with fresh new flowers.

Yellow daffodils, cheerfully sunning themselves in the light.

> *Continuous as the stars that shine*
> *And twinkle on the Milky Way . . .*

She loved daffodils. They must be the happiest flowers, she thought to herself, with those big golden trumpets thrusting out to embrace the day and egg-yolk-yellow petals radiating out like mini suns. She couldn't think why such optimistic flowers made her feel so sad. It was as if an uncomfortable memory were buried deep among the pollen, shying away from speaking up.

She dismissed that feeling as nonsense and went back to

admiring their bursting springness. Wondering who had brought them in for her.

She looked around the room and saw that a fresh bottle of water had also been brought in, together with a new glass. An old tea cup from this morning, she supposed, had been taken away. On the dressing table was a raggle-taggle collection of things. A box of rose and violet creams – oh how lovely! She did love those. She strained to think how they had got there but was met only by a blank fuzziness. Oh, what did it matter, how lovely.

Alongside the box was a hairbrush and a hand-held mirror, both with silver handles and mother of pearl gleaming on their backs. They were placed mirror and brush side down so the soft shininess of the shell gleamed prettily in the light. There was a small jewellery box, silver again, with some embossed swirls and the letters 'GS' engraved in a framed area at the top. She couldn't quite remember what was in the box, and reached towards it, elderly hands struggling to lift the lid.

Inside nestled a long string of pearls and a golden crucifix without a chain. There was also a locket. With some effort, she sprung the locket open and a curl of blonde hair fell onto the dressing table.

She looked at the curl for the longest time, her mind blankly joining indistinguishable dots. Nothing.

Then, a sense of knowing rose up in her, and to her surprise she felt the prickle of tears stinging the backs of her eyes.

The poetry of lost innocence, beauty and love floated in the back of her mind.

The dots were still indistinguishable but memories of a lost world fleetingly took shape. A gorgeous little girl. A sweet smile. A veil of shame.

As swiftly as the memories appeared, they faded and the curl retained its mystique for another day.

She clumsily attempted to twist it back into the locket but was unable to do so. She thought she would ask someone next time she had a visitor.

Her gaze wandered over the other bits and bobs on the dresser. An ancient bottle of L'Air du Temps with their lovebirds entwined together at the top. A small black and white photo in a silver, swirling frame. She examined this more closely to try to identify the picture.

A slim figure of a woman in her early thirties with dark hair and a placid face. She was sitting down on the ground, on a lawn perhaps, and had her legs tucked under her. She wore a serene look and was apparently distracted by something off into the distance. In her hands was a pure, white rose. A single stem.

She placed the frame back carefully and willed her mind to conjure up the sense of all these eclectic objects. Evidence of a life; mementoes of a past long gone.

She realised there was a book partly open on the bed and picked it up. It was the diary she had been leafing through earlier. It was open on a page which chronicled all the names of all the plants and flowers of May Close. What a funny little thing she'd been.

She flicked forward a few pages and alighted on a passage

which described the young girl's decision to write a poem inspired by Rilke's epitaph.

'I just want to try to create something complex and beautiful,' the childish hand had written, 'something to make people think. Something I can be proud of.'

A little further down, she was musing about the poet himself. 'I wonder if Rilke wrote for other people, or for himself? I think the best thing to do is write for myself, then when I'm an old lady (hahaha) at least I'll be my own fan.'

A few pages onwards, and there was a carefully scripted verse in beautiful handwriting. Just above the verse, there was a line of explanation: 'The original is in my poetry book of course but I thought I would share it with you, diary, as I've been talking about it for so long and I know you'll want to see what I came up with in the end.'

White petals folding in
A calmness resting
Quietly
Stillness in sorrow
Buried gently, softly,
The sweet, sweet calm of a new day.

Reading it now through old eyes – old, forgetful eyes – a connectedness and a profound sense of loss and sadness was rising up in her.

These days, she couldn't make sense of what the poem was supposed to mean, though she sensed a white rose played a starring role. The connectedness faded in and out like old memories.

An overwhelming sense of unhappiness wafted over her. It was at once complex and beautiful. The little girl had crafted something she had been proud of.

'So what do you think diary? It's not anywhere near as good as Rilke's of course but I'm pleased with it.'

Tears began to flow down old, papery cheeks. The sweet, sweet calm of a new day.

Routines

Number 38 Poplar Avenue. He let the words linger on his tongue, a tiny droplet of saliva escaping his mouth.

He had been back three separate times now. He needed to get a sense of her routine, needed to know the types of places she went, and when. He was the master of shadow lurking, blending into the background. For such a handsome, striking man he had a remarkable ability to shrink into the white noise of nothingness, unseen by anyone.

He'd learned that her name was Polly. They had just the one child, Charlie. She got up early every day and with a precision you could set your watch by, she went first to the butcher's, McKinsey's on Church Street; then the greengrocer's, the brightly coloured Apples and Pears on Market Street. She would always finish up with a dash into the baker's, a place a bit further up Market Street known locally as Stotties.

Armed with her supplies, she would march straight back home, presumably planning her menu for that night's supper. Charlie was a noisy child, clattering and chattering like toddlers do. He seemed happy enough, bumbling along with his mother every day.

The rest of the morning they seemed to spend together. There

199

was the odd boisterous sound of play and occasionally an indulgent 'Oh, Charlie' drifting out of the open window, 'what are you up to now?'

Quiet time seemed to happen straight after lunch. He got the impression that was when the child took a nap. She never left the house during these quiet times. From what he could see through the bunched white nets at front window, she used this time for knitting. If you stood at just the right angle off to the right-hand side of the house you could glimpse in through a gap in the curtains.

An hour or so would pass then the wail of a sleepy child would pierce the air.

The afternoon seemed to be devoted to chores – cleaning and dusting. That woman seemed to scrub the floors every single damn day.

Around four-ish there would be visitors – another mother with a child coming over to play, he presumed. He could just picture the two women gossiping, over coffee and cake, too distracted by their own nattering to pay attention to the children.

He had no idea what women found to talk about and didn't much care.

He was far more occupied by trying to identify a moment in the routine when he could do what he had to do.

He decided the only option would be to strike in that quiet moment after lunch. He would have to watch and wait for the child to go down.

Bide his time and pick the precise instant when there would be no chance of distraction and interruption. This was a critical part of the routine he had slowly established. He needed calm in the air so he could fully luxuriate in the sexual completeness of what he needed to do.

The slightest noise would spoil it, end it. He was playing a high-stakes game with a high-risk hand, but high rollers get their kicks by beating the odds. And that was how he could achieve the yearning, violent high he craved – beating the odds.

Today was the day.

He went through the start of the ritual, slowly. He washed himself, taking his time, feeling the groaning ache that had been growing inside him for the last two weeks. Release would come today, and it would be fucking immense.

He allowed himself some slow strokes, starting at the base of softness and working up to the hardening core. He closed his eyes, savouring that sweet, hurting ache.

He thought of her tiny waist and pictured the womanly curve of her hip. He knew she would want him, desire would be hers and submission would be his. There would be that delicious cunt, wet and wanting, parted just for him, inviting him in. It would be dusky pink and gleaming with evidence of her need.

But she would play the game, oh yes she would. She would make frightened animal eyes and squeal and make noises of protestation. She would resist and pretend this wasn't what she wanted at all. She would do a good job of trying to look convincingly scared. If he'd judged her right, she would have that beautiful combination of vulnerability and need. She would be angel made woman and good little housewife made slutty whore.

He gripped himself at the thought of it. He was going to

enjoy this. A surge of deliciousness shot through him and he felt his ache intensify.

Not long now, he promised himself, not long now.

He got dressed stiffly and checked his hair in the mirror in the bathroom. He flicked it back and inspected with disgust a small spot on his forehead. He sneered in repulsion and dealt with it, causing a little blood to seep out.

He waited for the bleeding to stop, just a moment or two, then let himself out of the door to begin the brisk walk to Poplar Avenue. To begin the brisk walk to Polly. Polly with the small waist and wet cunt. Nice.

It was a dull day – a slight breeze stirring in the air but no sign of sunshine. Greyness abounded – the walls of the buildings, the expressions of the people. There was no excited chatter in the air today, just people bustling about their business and getting on with life. Children playing in scattered clumps together – a group of boys kicking a ball around over here, a group of girls gathering to skip and play over there.

Nothing and no one interested him. All his focus was on the task ahead. He had worked out what he would do, carefully, weighing up the type of person he thought she was and what she may or may not respond to.

In no time at all, he had arrived. This was going to be the first time he had picked a place which was the home territory of the accomplice. So dangerous, even higher stakes. But he knew what that would mean, if he got it right . . .

He had already observed the architecture of the street. Having worked in construction for a while now, he could recognise the patterns of different types of houses and know exactly where back doors would be located, or how safe and secluded back gardens would be.

Poplar Avenue wasn't a wealthy street but it was a perfectly pleasant road. Good, solid houses. Some semi-detached and some detached. Mr and Mrs Businessman lived in a semi-detached house, which was better for external access. He knew he had to slip down the side of the house and let himself in the back door, or back window if needs be, all without being seen. All in broad daylight. And all very, very quickly. He would have to be in and out within an hour to ensure the child's wailing didn't come too soon.

He glanced up and down the road, and as always at lunch-time here it was pretty quiet. There was a young lad running around with a dog further up – but he'd left those other pockets of children behind when he'd turned into the avenue.

He heard the dog barking but otherwise the wind rustling in the leaves was the only sound.

He looked at his watch and then up at the house. He was about four houses down. All quiet.

And it was time.

He turned in silence and walked down the side passage of the fourth house down. He'd visited the area a few days before to plan everything out, and knew all he had to do was move swiftly but noiselessly and within a few paces he would be at the back of number 38.

He just had to hope that there would be no one out in the gardens. He doubted it, it was only housewives who were home in the daytime and they were normally getting on with lunch for their charges at this sort of time. If it had been a nice sunny day of course, it would have been a different story. But there was a reason he'd picked a grey day with a chill to the air.

He eyed up the back door and made his move.

He turned the handle downwards, quietly, praying that it wouldn't be locked.

The latch lifted and the door opened outwards. He let himself in.

This was the kitchen, a small room with a small table. A pile of sixpences nestled in a saucer. Washing up plates were stacked up on the side of the sink, drying off gradually in the cool air. A stack of melamine bowls nestled into a corner. The smell of Harpic and Jeyes fluid hanging in the air.

There was no sound of Charlie. Good. He'd counted on the boy being tucked up somewhere upstairs, and he was right.

He moved soundlessly from the kitchen to the front room. The hallway was painted white and there were some cheap Spanish-style paintings hanging on the wall. A wooden coat stand was bursting with the paraphernalia of a normal life in a normal home on a normal day.

A twisted smile played on his lips as he contemplated the idea that nothing much would feel normal after he'd done what he'd come for.

He heard the clackety-clack, clackety-clack of knitting needles, and the soft hum of a vaguely familiar tune. A tick-tock of a clock. A distant barking. Otherwise, silence.

He glanced at his watch. Half past one. Good.

On the red sofa with her back to him sat the humming, knitting object of his violent lust. His accomplice. Dear, sweet Polly.

With a stealth surprising in someone as physically imposing as him, he secretly approached her, two paces, three, four.

Then, a pause to breathe in the scene. Her soft scent, floral, caught in his nostrils and he watched her shoulders gently moving, swaddled in a pale pink woollen cardigan. A white dress peeped out below and kicked out over her knees.

He could just see the pert outline of her right breast. He knew already that her nipples would be darkly dusky and hard, engorged with desire for him.

The blood in turn flowed through him.

He saw the white nets at the window, reassuringly gathered to prevent sight of whatever was about to happen. You would have to really strain to find the one or two spots where slight gaps would allow a peek. Like he did, the other day.

He reached down behind her and pulled his hand over her face, locking her mouth into silence.

She wriggled and attempted to hit out, mouthing a scream which just muffled into groans.

He allowed her to see him, swinging himself around in front of her and pinning her down into the redness of the sofa.

Knitting needles fell helplessly into the floor and a ball of dark blue wool rolled into the hallway.

Sheer terror gripped her heart, crippling her into spasms of resistance.

His excitement mounted, feeling her twitching like a creature caught in a huntsman's trap. Her eyes were breathtakingly blue, paler than any he had seen. He was momentarily caught off guard by their transparency.

'Don't say a word,' he murmured, breathing hard onto her neck.

She spasmed again, fear locking her into paralysis.

He reached under the white dress and felt her warm legs, shivering slightly. His other hand was gripping across her face, squeezing her clamped shut.

Her eyes searched his for some kind of meaning, an explanation.

He wasn't about to offer one up.

He was enjoying the sense of control within him and the powerlessness within her. It was more perfect than he could have imagined.

His hardness was at the point of desperation. But he wanted to watch and wait some more.

Seeing her terror was the most exquisite aphrodisiac. He pushed his right hand slowly up her thighs, noticing the soft roundness despite her lean slimness.

He reached up further and pulled her underwear away between his finger and thumb. Then, with agonising slowness, using his third finger, he softly, softly began to stroke the folds buried deep between her legs.

He watched her face, taking in every sign of resistance, and waiting for the moment of submission.

She raised her eyebrows questioningly, still unable to speak. She was achingly perfect, the accomplice of his dreams.

He pulled his hand away from under the dress and moved instead to her right breast. He pulled apart the finely spun cardigan and allowed himself to look. The gentle rise of her breasts asked him to touch her. *Come inside, feel me.*

He obeyed his accomplice, hungrily, tearing slightly the white cotton of her bodice. But he was curiously tender in his touch as he started down the curve of her breast and reached the nipple. Palming it softly, he massaged hard on her, rubbing its pointiness so it couldn't help but grow harder under his touch.

Satisfied with her response, he looked down once more at her eyes, pleading with him.

She looked on the point of collapsing with fear. Or with desire?

Perfect.

So this was when he withdrew from touching her and pulled himself up, releasing her face.

'Not a word . . .' he whispered, smiling darkly. He reached inside his trousers and let his hands work up and down, pulling it out and admiring its strength.

What Polly did not know was that Joe had never consummated any sexual encounter. For him, desire and release was all about the imagining, the anticipation, the watching and the waiting. For him, the thrill came through the forensic workings of his frenzied mind, picturing the fear in his accomplice, imagining their terror-struck physicality and making their response a reality. The meticulous planning and the mapping out of detail unlocked a passion which took him on a journey that would end in ecstasy of his own doing.

The faces of his accomplices danced before him, first Finnegan, then another boy, Taylor, then an old woman called Iris. There had been another, a pathetic creature whose whining had cost him dear, irritating the hell out of Joe with his mewlings.

So he had smashed his head into a wall, leaving him brain damaged, unable to speak ever again.

And now Polly, pinned by her own fear to the recesses of the sofa, and watching him tug at himself ferociously, groaning. An expression of violent agony gripped his face, his eyes rolling back.

It wasn't long before that sweet pleasure-pain exploded through him, and all over the white dress.

He raised an eyebrow at her, knowing her desire for him was consuming every cell of her being.

That fear-submission look was all too familiar to him now.

He thought back to the feel of her hardening nipple and the softness of her folds, and he knew he would leave her desperate for her own release.

His green-black eyes bored out at her from beneath his eyebrows. He rearranged himself and straightened up.

'Good girl, good girl,' he said, and he sauntered into the hallway.

Pulled the front door open, and walked out into the cool breeze.

Without so much as a backward glance, he walked out of her life, safe in the knowledge that he had destroyed something today. Mr and Mrs Businessman would never be the same again.

Letters

There was a knock on the door, slight pause, then a bright swing inwards.

Billy stepped in, smiles dancing around his mouth but sadness buried deep in his eyes.

It had been almost a week since he'd last visited, but he'd had that cathartic chat with Aidan and was feeling more resigned about it all.

'Hello,' he said, peering at the back of the seated figure. A wisp of long, pale hair was tied into a pony tail at the back, a few straggles dangling down either side. She was on the bed, facing towards the window.

She didn't stir.

He walked around the bed to say hello properly. Perhaps she hadn't heard him. As he came around in front of her, blocking the light with his stocky frame, she startled.

She looked up at him, recognition dawning.

Thank goodness for that, he thought to himself, *she's having one of her good days.*

He wrapped her shawl more tightly around her shoulders and asked if she was alright, whether there was anything he could get her.

'It's alright, Billy dearest, I'm quite alright.'

'How have you been?' he asked, routinely. Waited for the familiar reply.

'Well, it's hard to keep up, you know, so much going on . . .', she began. He smiled, encouragingly. 'I've been thinking a lot, you see, trying to join the dots of my memories. But it isn't easy, Billy. Things go a bit hazy after a while. I find myself wondering whether I had friends. I find myself trying to work out the gaps and plot the story.'

She looked tired, frustrated.

'I'm trying so hard but so much is missing. I remember things, fleetingly, and when they are there, they crystallise, and I feel alive. But they fade again just as quickly, first into black and white and then into a grey nothingness. At times I have a warm glow inside, as if I'd just remembered something precious. At others I feel gripped by a coldness, as if some dark memory is casting my heart in stone.

'And I wonder about love, Billy. Have I been loved? Have I loved?'

It wasn't the first time she had asked him about love.

It was as if, deep in her subconscious, she knew.

'Of course you have had love, of course,' he said, soothingly, reluctant to go into all the details with her again. She would only forget them, again.

'Do you remember what our lives were like, when we were in May Close?' he asked. He found it was a good technique, getting her to natter about the things that she could remember well.

She would perk up and chatter away, her mind whisking back to sunny skies and bubbles.

Her face would grow animated and a light would catch in her eyes. It was nice seeing her like this. The veil would lift and a glimpse of the person she had once been would emerge.

He sometimes wondered whether he did this selfishly, because to hear her recount excitedly this or that recreated a sunnier time for him, too. But he remembered that the carer at the hospice had advised that Alzheimer's patients tended to respond well to childhood memories – and young adulthood through to the mid thirties. The earlier the better – as of somehow the first couple decades of life had been hardwired into your psyche, indelibly.

So yes, it felt somewhat selfish, but also he knew that he was helping her do some good to herself. And there was something rather lovely about seeing her eyes come to life. It didn't happen often enough.

Of course, this was partly because she was suffering so much pain. Despite the drugs they were pumping into her, traces of agony would sometimes wince across her face.

And she had grown terribly thin, especially in the last couple of months.

He could feel every bone in her spine when he embraced her, and her clothes were beginning to hang limply off her.

At one point, he had made the mistake of bringing his ancient Polaroid camera in and taking a couple of snaps for her. He thought she would marvel at the machine and be impressed by how clever it was. Instead, her first reaction was one of puzzlement. 'Who is that?' she asked, peering down at the picture.

There she was, captured on film, a shaky smile. A pale blue cardie wrapped around and a yellow dress underneath, flecked with sprigs of violets.

She'd looked down at herself, noting the dress and the cardigan.

'But who is that, and why are they wearing my things?' she asked, in exasperation.

'But it's you, silly thing!' he exclaimed, laughing.

But his laughter was soon cut short when he realised she genuinely hadn't recognised herself.

'But that's an old woman, and she's thin, look how thin she is . . .' she had trailed off.

Shocked, Billy realised that she hadn't quite grasped the brutal physical decline she had endured and resolved never to confuse her like that again.

It also reminded him how very much she had changed, and he thought about that, wistfully.

And with that, the chatter dried up and she was staring at her dressing table.

It was nice that this establishment let people bring in some of their own things, little mementoes to cheer the place up. It wasn't too bad, he supposed, but pale purple walls were a bit sickly for his liking – how they expected people to feel better when that nauseous colour was staring back at them from all sides he didn't know. But they'd made an effort with the faux impressionistic art. She had three paintings hanging higgledy-piggledy on the wall above her bed.

They were a bit of a theme throughout the hospice. In the common seating area, there were several more, and dotted throughout the corridors they were pale, inoffensive splashes of colour which at least made the walls a little less bland.

He looked over and followed her stare. There was that old bottle of perfume and the paraphernalia of all women's dressing tables – brush set, jewellery casket, usual stuff.

But then he alighted upon something he hadn't seen before.

A golden skein of silk was illuminated from a dapple of sunlight poking through the leaves on the trees outside.

He went to examine it, wondering if it was something from an old sewing kit. Briefly, he remembered having helped Gracie with her embroidery. She never had got the hand of that sort of thing.

As he neared it, he realised he had been wrong. This was no skein of silk – it was a curl of hair. Yellow blonde hair.

'Oh God!' he muffled into his hand.

Gingerly, he reached to pick the curl up. It looked so pretty in the light. The colour hair Rapunzel would have had. The colour hair Gracie would have had. Back then.

He looked at her, sitting on the bed, quietly. Her eyes were staring but unseeing. She was having one of her moments where her mind drifts off.

Billy didn't mind. It gave him time to look properly at the curl, and wonder at its provenance.

He noticed the open locket discarded next to the jewellery box and understood that this had been the hiding place of this treasure all that time.

Tenderly, he curled it up and placed it back inside the locket.

At that moment, the lump in his throat burst into sorrow and he found himself crying long, wretched rivers of tears.

Like an old cine film, his mind played back a thousand memories, skipping through the seasons, scratchy and obscure in places, shiningly bright in others.

'Let's play in the snow! Let's build a snowman! Let's build a garden of flowers with icicles for him!'

'Can we go fishing for cockles? Can we take a picnic?'

'I'd love to blow bubbles today, wouldn't you, Billy? We can pretend that bubbles are the magic potion to restore the life back to the sleeping princess. All we have to do is blow them over her and ta-dah! She will open her eyes and smile and kiss the prince.'

Fortunately, she was still gazing into space, locked in a reverie that even his jagged, throaty tears couldn't stir.

He calmed himself. That bubble game had been a favourite of hers. She always liked taking fairy stories and adapting them for Billy and Gracie land. He thought back how many years must have passed since they last played together. Then he remembered how it was that even when they grew older and stopped playing childish games together, they would still talk, still share secrets and still rely on each other for everything.

He picked up the locket and began to close it. But he thought there was something under the curl, so he carefully unlooped it again and looked beneath.

The letters PH were engraved inside, and there was an inscription. 'Forever yours,' it read.

He looped the curl back inside and fastened the oval tightly shut.

'PH?' He wondered who that had been, then a flicker of acknowledgement helped him see. Peter Harper? He wondered, out loud. Had Gracie's Ma been given this trinket by his own father? Did it mean what he had, deep inside, always suspected?

He thought back to that important day when he and Gracie had shared that dreadful experience of hiding and hearing the beating.

Going back to his home and spilling out everything that had happened to his Ma and his Da.

Taking comfort in the ordinariness of jam sandwiches.

Seeing his Da stand tall, to go to Gracie's Ma, to look after her, to protect her.

A knight in shining armour dashing down the road to save the maiden.

Billy tried to collect his thoughts but they tumbled one after the other. The amount of time his Da would help Gracie's Ma with fixing things. 'She's all on her own, she needs the help of a good man,' he would joke to Billy's Ma.

Billy's Ma would watch him disappear, again, while her own window latch went unmended, the kitchen counter went unsanded and the stool in John and Simon's room stayed leaning against the wall, two legs missing their third, broken, brother.

He remembered the increasing number of drives he would take her on, to go and purchase various things that needed buying. 'She hasn't got a car, dear, she needs me to help her out,' he would say. And Billy's Ma would sigh to herself.

Billy speculated now whether she was wondering what happened to the day trips they had used to make together, Mary and Peter.

And he thought about that single white rose that he'd found on the floor that day. He remembered noticing it, and vaguely being aware that it was a rose from his own family's garden.

And then he remembered that day was, horrifically, the day this had all started. He asked himself whether it could have all been prevented if only Peter Harper had stayed home with his own family that day. How could he? Off instead with Gracie's Mother. Leaving Gracie all on her own.

Then, another terrible thought struck him.

What about Gracie's little baby brother or sister who had decided to go straight to Heaven? Now he knew about these things, it wasn't that hard to piece the remaining elements of the jigsaw together.

He felt slightly sick.

And he thought of his Ma now, frail and old. He wondered if she had known.

Accomplices

Sauntering through the twilight, Joe allowed himself a moment to play over in his mind again what had just happened. He smiled with a surge of pleasure-pain. The look on her face! Her pleading eyes . . . the feel of her body tensing up as he touched her, nipples hard and ready. Playing with him, teasing him, provoking him.

Walking along, he liked the feeling that he was hiding in plain sight. He liked knowing he could have extinguished her life, just like that. He liked knowing he could have slit the child's throat, if he'd wanted.

He liked walking away, safe in the knowledge no one knew who he was or what he had done.

Spotting a boisterous pair of boys ribbing each other and joshing on the street, a memory of his own childhood fleetingly caught his attention. As a boy, he didn't have friends. Didn't need them. Preferred doing his own thing. Always far more interested in doing his little experiments.

He scorned children of his own age, playing together and running around laughing and joking. He had no time for such stupidity when there were insects to crush and creatures to maim.

The fleeting memory began to take on substance as details started coalescing together.

He remembered how he'd discovered early on that enjoyment for him came in different forms. He developed a knack for finding ways to inflict cruelty, pain and fear. And he developed a taste for masochism. He liked nothing more than savouring the moment when an animal was close to breathing its last breath. That helplessness, that submission to the inevitable. It made him wretched with agony, dying as he was to just stamp out whatever pathetic life was quivering before him. But he learned his own pleasure intensified immeasurably if he could push through the pain barrier and wait. Watch and wait.

He prided himself on his restraint. Others, he felt sure, would simply smash the life out of something. He, on the other hand, would hold back. Let the moment linger. Refuse to put any living thing out of its misery. He rationalised it to himself as evidence of his superiority as a human being.

He remembered coming across his Ma in the early days. Weeping to herself, a large white handkerchief sodden wet. Mumbling to herself about Jack. Whoever Jack was.

Occasionally he would catch a word or two between the tears.

'Prison', 'life', 'murder' and 'bastard' seemed to be the ones she said the most.

Growing up with just a Ma and no Da was just normal for Joe and his sister. It wasn't till he was 10 that their Ma had sat them down and told them the story of their father. How he'd been a bad man. How he'd hurt people. How he wasn't right in the head.

218

She said he was somewhere safe now, where he couldn't do harm to anyone anymore.

Joe had found the story moderately interesting but to his surprise his sister started crying alongside his Ma. What is it with these crybaby girls? But he was smart enough not to mock. He did his usual thing and acted his little heart out, giving them both the biggest hug he could muster.

Ma smiled at him with that lopsided smile she did sometimes when she was happy about something one of her children did. And there she was, little Sweetie, looking at him too with that tearful half-smile; was she trying to be all grown-up and okay even though she was upset?

God, he hated the pair of them.

Wandering down the street now, he mused on what he would think of his father, if he'd ever met him. Fuck him. Bastard.

His Ma had told him more of the details as he got older and he found himself hungry for the details of what he'd done. She never told him enough, always kept him hanging. He wanted to know more about the victims, who they were, where they lived, how old they were.

Once, she was telling him what Jack had been like when she first met him. Joe was patiently waiting for her to meander through the boring bits, aching to hear more about the times she'd realised her husband had had secrets.

She never told him very much, but as he got into his teens, occasionally there was a detail about a rope or a knife. Fire. Even these little snippets riveted Joe, captivating his imagination. He found himself wishing he could have seen what his father had done. Tasted it.

And he started feeling twinges of raw, animal arousal when he pictured what might have happened.

He liked it.

He liked knowing he was getting hard right there in front of his Ma as she started crying again. Occasionally, when she sank into her hanky with deep, jagged tears, he would touch himself, pinching hard through his trousers to heighten his desire. He didn't care she was so close, might see. His obsession, his need for that physical force pressing against his cock took over everything.

He mastered the art of waiting. And as the years went by, decided this would be his signature. He vowed to restrain himself from release for as long as humanly possible, and resist the temptation of consummation.

He would taste the fear in his accomplices, knowing that they didn't know his signature. Knowing they didn't know he would prolong the moment. Knowing they didn't know he didn't care.

Petals

It was another rainy lunchtime and she couldn't wait to race to the library and reread the poem she had found last night. Sitting there on her bed, dusky twilight making shadow shapes on the walls, stillness and magic were in the air, and words were dancing in front of her, captivating her.

Her new friend was unlocking new worlds and helping her uncover new truths about life, and about herself.

This one was about a little girl. Naturally, she indulged the urge to place herself in the story, hearing it speak to her.

The bell went after a dreary double maths and Gracie swiftly packed her things up into her satchel.

She had brought sandwiches from home today. Nothing special, just some spam and pickle. And there was a red apple for afters.

Ignoring the throng of youth pushing behind and in front of her, she found her own calmness and wordlessly moved to the quiet place where she could be alone.

She pulled open the heavy, wooden door and felt the warmness and stillness wash over her. Heading over to her favourite spot in the corner under a small window with a small stained glass pane at the top, she settled down eagerly.

Splashes of green, blue, red and yellow illuminated the table from the light behind the window. There must be a sunny lull in the rain, she thought to herself.

Satchel down, book pulled out, sandwiches abandoned – for now – in the bottom of the old leather folds, she opened up the pages and flickered through until she alighted on the right spot.

At first, she read the poem all the way through again, slowly taking in the word shapes and soundscapes as she went. The imagery coming to life with a lightness that came naturally to her.

And layered beneath the imagery was a rich depth of meaning you could glimpse from the surface but would need time and thought properly to uncover.

She felt a slow burning of pleasure as she glowed in her endeavour.

The phrases each earned their place – there was both not too much and not too little. So a brevity, then, but nothing stilted or staccato. The pacing seemed to vary like different footsteps across different areas of the poem, perhaps mirroring the journey of the girl. Her journey that day as well as her life journey. Skipping along one moment and taking her time the next. Stopping completely when she felt like it.

And there was something profoundly comforting about the core of the poem. Something reassuring and calming and embracing.

She set about reading it a second time, savouring each line carefully and allowing the mind shapes to subliminally guide her.

Sometimes she walks through the village in her
little red dress
all absorbed in restraining herself,
and yet, despite herself, she seems to move
according to the rhythm of her life to come.

She runs a bit, hesitates, stops,
half-turns around . . .
and, all while dreaming, shakes her head
for or against.

Then she dances a few steps
that she invents and forgets,
no doubt finding out that life
moves on too fast.

It's not so much that she steps out
of the small body enclosing her,
but that all she carries in herself
frolics and ferments.

It's this dress that she'll remember
later in a sweet surrender;
when her whole life is full of risks,
the little red dress will always seem right.

There was something about the way Rilke wrote that called out to her, spoke to her. She realised that she probably only half understood the many textures and intricacies that lay within his words. But like a puzzle that needed solving, the verse asked her to delve deeper, to discover what she could.

She pondered the dream-like state of the girl, and the inventions and fictions of her movements. The rhythms rising and falling; racing and rushing here, hesitating and stopping there; moments of bravery and openness and others of tight closing in.

There was a sense of daring and discovery but also a reticence and a knowingness about some distant truth.

It lingered on today but it spoke of a whole life to be lived.

Gracie paused on the phrase 'sweet surrender' and wondered what that part could mean. Sweet suggested something nice and tender. But surrender was about giving up. Submission perhaps.

And the girl's future seemed to take shape as a thorny road, bristling with spikes and traps and horrors and risks. It seemed curiously at odds with the carefree frolicking of her childhood. But on rereading from the top once more, she saw that even through the girl's frolics there were restraints and halts and ferments.

The red dress seemed to be the anchor and the link. The comfort and the memory. The talisman. The Secret Key of her life.

Gracie's eyes were staring into space, past the stained glass colour sploshes and into her own world of memory.

The last stanza's emphasis on memory: 'It's this dress that she'll remember,' echoed that wonderful last stanza in the Wordsworth one.

For oft, when on my couch I lie
In vacant or in pensive mood,

Petals

They flash upon that inward eye
Which is the bliss of solitude;
And then my heart with pleasure fills,
And dances with the daffodils.

She wondered what the equivalent of the red dress, or the daffodils, would be for her. She didn't really have an item of clothing that carried memories or comfort like the dress in the poem, and at home she had very few possessions. She thought about her bedroom. There was a bookshelf stuffed with books. There was baby Victoria. There was an old, much loved knitted rabbit wearing a pale blue jacket, its long, floppy ears rather grubby round the tips; its fluffy bobtail somewhat scruffy and worn over the years. Samson, she had called him, when she was little.

There was a small box where she kept secrets. But none of the secrets were all that special at first glance. Or at least, she didn't think anyone else would think they were special.

There was a particularly shiny black stone that she had found in the woods once. It had a white, zigzag stripe across its back and it gleamed prettily in the light.

There was a funny little twig object Billy had given her a couple of years ago. He had fashioned it into a childish sculpture, mounting a teak-coloured acorn on the end of the twig. It was hardly a thing of beauty, but it meant something to her because he had made it for her.

There was also a gold crucifix with a long, fine chain that had once belonged to her mother. It was crafted from very thin gold and had an engraved, slightly raised flourish around the

225

edges, a medieval-style decoration which made it look old fashioned, like something out of a fairy tale. But the chain was far too long for Gracie so she had never worn it. Plus, she had been worried about what would happen if the chain broke or if she lost it.

Nestled against these small mementoes were a couple of curls of rose petals. They were rather brown and wrinkly now, but you could still smell the musty rosiness if you breathed in deeply. She didn't know why she didn't just throw them away, it seemed so pointless keeping them! But they took her back to a special day when she was just five.

Thinking about it now, it must have been just a short time before *he* entered their lives.

It had been a perfect spring day. Sunshine and smiles. The laughter of a mother and child at play.

It was one of Gracie's first precious memories, what happened that day.

She recalled it had been at the end of a joyous afternoon of running around and inventing stories. They had made pictures in the dirt with a pointy branch. Created a den in the woods with leaves for a canopy. Pretended she was a princess who had to go to sleep for a thousand years (the beautiful queen would come and rouse her with soft stroke of her forehead and a heavenly kiss on her cheek). Played at making cakes and holding a tea party for invisible friends.

One of those perfect, perfect days.

An exhausted Gracie was going to sleep well that night, her head filled with dreams of cakes and princesses.

As they packed up in the woods, her Ma pointed out the

white rose bushes that populated the edges of the clearing. They were in full bloom, heavy scented heads bobbing about in the breeze.

Bumble bees and butterflies were hovering around them, diving into their centres to play.

The flowers looked like neat little pompoms and had a delicious, musky scent.

'Those roses always remind me of you, pet,' she said, softly, eyes smiling.

'Why?' Gracie was puzzled, but quite pleased at the same time. The logic of childhood didn't pause long to ponder such things.

'Well, they've got a special name, they're called Little White Pet. And that's how I think of you, Gracie, you're my Little White Pet.'

And she had collected a pool of petals into her hands and given them to Gracie to hold. The chubby little fingers took them eagerly, and she stroked them softly. In the late afternoon light she looked like an angel. Golden, silky curls collecting on her shoulders and pale milky skin whitely reflecting the powder creaminess of the flowers around her. The lovely scent hovered between them in the magic moment before dusk settled.

Then they had walked back home together, contented.

So the worn, papery shards were fragile browned wisps of memory. An afternoon of happiness captured in a couple of curls of muskiness.

But not quite the stuff of a talisman.

It occurred to her that perhaps her talisman wasn't a thing as such, but a moment of awakening.

She refocused on the book and flickered back to an earlier page. The extract which explored the fear of the inexplicable, taken from a letter Rilke had written.

She scanned the words, settling on the last few phrases:

So you must not be frightened
If a sadness rises up before you
Larger than any you have ever seen.
If a restiveness like light and cloud shadows
Passes over your hands and over all you do
You must think that something is happening with you,
That life has not forgotten you,
That it holds you in its hand;
It will not let you fall.

This was it! She cried out in delight, momentarily forgetting the pious setting of her exclamation. Fortunately, as always, she was the only pupil in the library, so there was no danger of disturbing anyone else. Just Miss Weaver, the old librarian, a bird-like, skinny woman whose voice rasped and whose bustling busybodyness pecked and scratched around the piles of books hardly anyone bothered to read.

'It will not let you fall,' Gracie murmured the last line, beaming to herself.

She decided that this piece of writing would be the talisman of *her* life. Her Secret Key. Her red dress. Her daffodils.

Politics

The accomplices began to add up over time, and he understood that the violent lust that ached in him varied in potency depending on how long he spent watching and waiting.

It was always about intimidating his victim, breathing in their fear, their incomprehension. In the case of a female accomplice, he had the added frisson of sexual discovery, the anticipation of what she looked like weighing down like a physical pull in his crotch. It added a layer of thrill that he didn't experience with the males.

But with the men, he had the added frisson of feeling bounteous in his virility, impressively forcing them, however apparently strong, to cower and tremble in his presence. The fear he would provoke in them gave him a different edge to the sexual excitement.

Either way, it was immensely satisfying and he couldn't wait till the next high.

And then, something happened.

He reached an unwelcome hiatus in his activity.

He'd entrapped a particularly smug-looking political activist. The type with weedy hair and a whiny voice. Pockmarks of acne still denting his face, even though he was by now well into his twenties.

There was something so intensely, revoltingly smug about the little mongrel, Joe spent weeks planning his contract with him.

He'd first come across him in a pub. Joe had been sitting nursing some drinks on his own, smoke swirling around him and the bitterness of the ale doing its job, alcohol throbbing in his head.

Lost in his own silence, he suddenly became aware of the whinging mewlings of a hectoring new convert.

He looked up in the direction of the noise and saw a young man holding court over a group of older, working folk.

The young man was suited and booted in a cheap grey flannel. Tie skewed on, greasy face poking out of an outsize shirt collar.

He had slightly too-long hair and he was bleating on about workers' rights like a student on a rally.

He went on . . . and on . . . and on . . .

Joe's head began to hurt.

He tuned in now and then to catch phrases here and there . . . 'the power of the people' . . . 'harnessing the good of the common man' . . . 'standing up for what you believe in' . . . 'putting up a fight' . . .

He stared at him, coldly.

He would give him power. And he would give him fight. The fight of his puny little life.

At this, the smirk crept across his face and a dark pallor sank into quiet resolution, setting his jaw.

He established soon enough that the young politician would

come to this pub several times a week, canvassing support and meeting his would-be constituents.

He'd wander into shops, lurk in markets and pounce on housewives out doing their shops.

Sometimes, he would go directly to the estuary and talk to the fishermen, untroubled whether he was interrupting their work.

On other occasions, he would pick out three or four factories to target, and spend hours talking to people, handing out leaf-lets bearing a photo of his ugly mug.

He was possibly the vilest, most irritating person Joe had ever come across.

He would wipe that smile off his wretched face.

At the thought of it, a dart of pleasure-pain would push into his groin, forcing a stiffening of anticipation. He would feel his breath draw deeper, and he would picture the way the runty wretch would squeal like a girl when he finally made him his.

He would allow himself just one, urgent grip of his hand through his trousers, only to release slowly, tasting the fear on his tongue, feeling his need surge through his whole body.

After three weeks, the plan was set. He'd selected a good location – a quiet alleyway the politician would pass by on his way to and from the pub. Joe had decided to spring his surprise when he was on his way back. The downside was that he would have to listen to him drone on for a while. The upside was that it would be darker and the tyke would have had a few.

It was a Thursday night. The stage was set. The contract was issued. The accomplice would begin the slow journey to sub-mission.

Joe eyed his quarry in disgust. There he was as usual, twittering on to anyone who would listen. He generally held court with three or four votaries and tonight was no exception.

They would share a convivial pint and humour him, few having the inclination to actually take in what he was blethering on about and fewer still preparing to act on it.

Unlike the others, Joe *was* prepared to act. He would shut that whining up. For good.

He thought back to the smashed jaw laying in bloody spatters across Finnegan's thigh, and he remembered that other whinging piece of shit he'd dealt with. Brain damaged, they'd said. Good.

The memories pulsed through him, building on the electrical throbbing deep inside. Intensifying that pleasure-pain sweetness as the anticipation of this new contract entwined with the thoughts of what had gone before.

He took in the skinny wretch reaching for his coat and smiling jovially at the other drinkers.

He sipped one last sip and slipped out into the darkening evening behind his new accomplice.

Their footsteps quickened in unison, the politician blissfully unaware that he was in the sights of the other man.

Blissfully unaware of what was about to happen.

Joe watched him approach the entrance to the alley and made his move. By now he was just one pace behind him, so it was easy to swiftly move forward and pounce. Digging his claws in, rigidly.

Saying nothing, but shoving him into the blackness of the narrow street. Pushing him further down, preventing that whiny voice from making any sounds by clamping his mouth shut with a gnarled, dirty hand.

Feeling his arousal throbbing to distraction, coursing in excitement from that hot, damp place to the rest of his being.

He moved him to the perfect spot, roughly 70 feet down the alley. It was quiet and calm. And there was a soft pool of light, cast from a lamp on the next street.

In the background, the bustle of vehicles and people making their ways home. A murmur of burbling but nothing distinct.

The light allowed him to peer into the eyes of his prey.

Startled, angered, almost *indignant*, for fuck's sake, the acne-dappled bugger was cocking his head at him, a confidence and a swagger Joe hadn't expected.

He caught himself wondering what kind of person starts preaching to strangers about things like power and fighting and – that insult – the 'common man'.

Who did he think he was? And anyway, what kind of arrogant, no-hoper idiot would waste their time, day after day, trudging around factories and estuaries and streets trying to make an issue about rights. Pointless.

The young man was struggling, hard. He clearly knew his way around a wrestling match – wriggled here and tried to secure a grip there. He was one of those public school tossers who'd learned a few tricks but didn't know their arse from their elbow.

And this accomplice's eyes were aflame with anger.

Well, this was a first.

Usually, they were full of fear at this point, petrified, lacking any sense of comprehension. Terrified eyes begging him to explain.

This was usually the moment where he strung out the watching and waiting, amusement tickling around his lips, as the accomplice slowly conceded the situation, recognising there was no escape.

Usually, the struggling would subside, overtaken by that peculiar desire-submission where Joe would succumb to their silent, hot-eyed request for vanquishment.

From the victim's point of view, it may have been more like an urgent need to get whatever their fate was going to be over as quickly as possible, once they recognised that they were in the presence of a madman who had no intention of letting them go. It was human nature to fight as long as physically possible, but not to compromise one's possibility of survival.

That was what Joe counted on, although he didn't interpret it this way. From his point of view, time and time again, the accomplice would be begging him to conquer them. He knew only he could satisfy them, which is why the symphony harmonised so beautifully.

He thought back to Polly. Pure Polly, in her bright white dress and sugar pink cardie. He had felt how hot and wet she was. There was no doubting the swelling hardness of her nipple. That look in her eye, overcome by desire for him, needing him, wanting him.

It had given him perverse pleasure to leave her wanting more, satiating instead his own desperate impulse.

Of course, he couldn't see the truth, that this was a woman

at the point of collapse, fear stopping the blood to her brain, eyes sparkling into unseeingness from the horror of the moment.

What Joe saw was a woman, breathing hard for him, hankering for his touch, his roughness, his cock.

He knew her husband, Mr Businessman, would never have driven her to such passion. What a limp, pathetic bastard. He had stood there, proud, tugging himself, safe in the knowledge that all she wanted was him. And for the rest of her life she would long for him.

The reality may have been different.

Poor Polly had been left in disarray, navy wool straggling across the floor, hair straggling across her face. Splodges of semen dampening her dress. Her candyfloss cardigan sullied forever. Constrictions in her chest as she struggled to breathe. A sense of abject horror at the nightmare that had just unfolded in her house.

She struggled to rearrange herself, tidied her bodice and neatened up the knitting needles. Then, with a lioness roar, she suddenly thought of her son.

'Charlie!' she had called, dashing upstairs to the nursery. Gentle duck-egg-blue light pooling through the bottom of the door. She opened up, frantically, desperately, fearing the worst.

But to her joy and amazement, there he was, slumbering softly, buzzy light breathing filling the air in sniffles and snuffles.

She scooped him up and held him to her, tightly.

At least he was safe.

As Joe had sauntered out into the sunlight, he had been left with a different perspective. He knew that sweet, dear Polly had been wet and hard for him. Knew that she had at least 15 minutes before the boy would stir.

He had no doubt in his mind what she would be doing right now. There she would be, on the sofa where he had left her, coyly glancing at the nets on the windows to see if there was any possibility of anyone seeing in.

Satisfied that there was enough privacy, she would have pulled the fabric of her dress up her thighs, slowly, enjoying the sensation of slightly coarse linen playing at her skin.

She would have retraced where he had been touching, underwear discarded on the floor. And she would have reimagined every soft stroke, every intense exploration of his fingers.

She would have been thinking of that exquisite touch he had, and would be wishing, silently, that he would come back and finish what he had started.

She would picture him, standing over her, an imposing silhouette. Doing what he did, for her, because of her.

The idea of it would overwhelm her, and she would try to imagine what he was seeing – her, sat small but sprawling willingly beneath him.

Her right breast exposed, lusciously.

She took her left hand and slowly palmed her nipple, hard, like he did.

Hard, hard, hard. Then she took her thumb and fingers and squeezed it tightly, until she gasped. She rotated the pertness of it roundly, and couldn't resist looking at what she was doing, her own arousal washing over every part of her.

Her right hand was still slowly feeling the folds of her damp pinkness, tracing the wetness over the different aspects of her private place. It felt electric.

And then, something magical happened. Her finger alighted on a rigid, hard place which was bathed in hot wetness. He had caressed it earlier, and now she had found it again. The sensation flooded her inside, and she used her third finger, like he did, to trace its shape. It was agonising, and felt connected by a current to the nipple she was twisting, hard.

She resisted the urge to rub that aching place hard and instead slowly luxuriated in soft, aching strokes. Up and down, up and down, all the while wrenching her nipple into a pain she had never felt.

She would think of his face, contorted in desire, and she would think of his erection, pulsing before her. And she would bring herself to a pleasure point she had never before experienced, with him and for him. Spasms of ecstasy would flood her. And it would be because of him.

That's what Joe was thinking, as he sauntered off down the street, more pulses of arousal pushing through him as he made his way home. Once he got there, he locked himself in the bathroom and indulged in another round; the memory of what he had imagined her to have done, buzzing in his brain.

Today was different. Usually, he got his kicks with the men by beating them into weak submission, seeing their terror morph into acquiescence.

But this angry tyke was writhing and fighting and refusing to accept defeat.

This was not the plan.

And inevitably, this intensified the violent hatred he was already feeling. He roared in fury, incensed that this weasel could be refusing to comply.

And he landed a blow with his right hand which smashed into the side of his face, a loud crack singing out into the night air.

The politician collapsed onto the floor, and Joe pulled him up slightly, to tighten his grip around his neck and shoulders. Then he flung his head backwards, repeatedly, crashing the pock marked lumpiness down with dull thuds, again and again.

He watched as the lad's eyes rolled backwards and a froth of blood foamed at his mouth.

There was the slightest murmuring, followed by silence.

Joe's rage flooded through him, as he saw the prone shape on the floor. Completely still now, not even a breath escaping his scarlet, unnatural lips.

Slumped into awkwardness, the politician lay there, undignified, the distant glow of a light illuminating his silhouette.

Joe looked at him, satisfied, and the realisation dawned on him that this was the first human life he had extinguished.

Exaltation surged through him, and that familiar feeling pulsed deep in his core.

He allowed himself the rapture of release, there and then in the alley.

And Joe being Joe, had his wits about him and when it was all over, took care to rub the evidence into the ground with his shoe and kick leaves over it.

Then he turned his back on the lumpen outline and meandered, slowly, back onto the main street.

What he hadn't realised was that the bellowing roar he had howled in anger earlier had been heard by a number of people, who had raised the alarm. The police had been summoned, apparently, and three young bobbies were out looking for an explanation.

Joe emerged onto the main thoroughfare into a throng of activity and his senses immediately alerted him that something was wrong. He wondered if it was connected to what he had just been doing, or something else. He decided caution would be the best way forward.

So he continued his slow meander, through the people-treacle.

Then, a shout, a shriek.

'Look, he's covered in blood!' someone yelled, and someone else added, 'Catch him!'

He began to take off but had scarcely gone three paces before the crowd closed in.

'Where have you been?' a hefty, bearded man in dungarees demanded. 'What have you done? Why are you running? Why are you covered in blood?'

Others in the crowd weighed in, four or five of them baying for an answer.

At this stage, the bearded man was simply interrogating him, not sure if he was victim or witness or perpetrator.

But the mob has a will and when he refused to speak, they closed in further, jostling and pushing and forming a human chain which could not be broken.

It wasn't long before the police arrived.

The rest of the evening passed in a bit of a blur, but he woke up in a dark, dank cell. Just a piss bucket in the corner and the whole place stinking of shit.

His memory came flooding back, and all he could think of was that this had been the politician's fault. If only he had just played the game, given into desire and submission, allowed himself the fear.

Instead, he had fought back like a runty fox caught in a trap, desperate to escape and desperate to live.

Well, Joe put paid to *that* particular ambition.

Now he was alone in a cell, the blackness crowding in.

He wondered how much the coppers knew, wondered whether there was any chance the body hadn't been found, that they would think this was some terrible mistake.

For now, a sense of foreboding told him this was irrational. He'd only just stepped out from the alley, for fuck's sake, it was obvious that people would retrace his steps to find out where he had come from.

All he could think of was that he needed to come up with a plan. He would need to watch. And wait.

Surprises

Billy and Aidan had just finished up a delicious home-made lasagne. The béchamel sauce had been just so, and the bolognaise unctuous and rich.

Plates and dishes cleared into the dishwasher, they settled into their usual evening routine.

A bottle of red was slowly relieved of its cork with a satisfying 'pop'.

The wine glugged softly into two crystal glasses and clinked together in a warm toast.

'To the end of the week,' Aidan smiled at Billy. Billy winked back. 'Thank goodness,' he agreed.

They each took a sip and reached back into the squishiness of their chosen seating. Aidan on the Tom Dixon as normal and Billy sinking into the Chesterfield.

Mahler was playing gently in the background.

'I've decided to go and talk to Ma,' said Billy, seriously.

Aidan looked at him, thoughtfully.

'Are you going to tell her?' he asked.

'I don't think it's my place to tell her. But with a few carefully worded questions, I may be able to find out how much she knew . . .'

Billy knew it was a long shot. His Ma had never said anything so far, and if she *had* known something, she had clearly made the decision to bury it. It wasn't his job to rake up bad memories, or ruin lovely ones.

But he felt compelled to do something, anything.

'I'll come with you. Let's make an outing of it. We can take some ingredients around and make a lovely meal to share with her. You don't visit often enough . . .' he let the words trail.

Aidan knew that Billy hadn't explained the full nature of their friendship to his Ma. But at the same time, he couldn't bear the idea of him having to face this conversation on his own. He'd been through such torment over the years. At least he should be able to give him some comfort and support through this.

'I'm not sure, Aidan, whether it's a good idea . . .' Billy's mind was racing, wondering what his Ma would think if he turned up with a male companion and they made supper for her together.

'I think you've spent too many years trying to fight your demons and find your answers on your own. This is why I am here. To share your hardships and help you take the burden. Let me come with you. We don't need to explicitly say anything, Billy, we can keep it nice and light. I'm your friend, I'm coming over to help you cook. That's it.'

Billy looked at Aidan gratefully. He'd put it so simply, so logically, how could he find fault with the argument? There's no reason why it wouldn't feel natural, normal even.

'You're right, I'm sorry. I've tried for too long to carry all this alone. But there's nothing wrong with two friends visiting a mother. Nothing wrong at all. Let's plan the trip. What shall we cook?'

They plotted together and whiled away a happy hour discussing recipes and possibilities. It was the perfect distraction for Billy, who had felt deeply uneasy since discovering the locket. So far, he hadn't been back to the hospice.

They decided there was no time like the present, so made the decision to call Billy's Ma tomorrow and see if they could go over Saturday night.

She, of course, was delighted to hear that her son was coming to visit. Like most parents, she adored seeing her children, and felt these days as grown-ups she didn't see nearly enough of them. John and Simon had both given her grandchildren, so it was a special pleasure when their families came to stay, but the whole clan had scattered widely and she was the only one left in Tyneside.

She was still in the old house in May Close. Billy visited rarely. He'd been too wrapped up in the memories of what had happened.

So it was a wonderful surprise to hear that he was coming up, and bringing a pal. So she was going to meet him at last, she smiled to herself. She'd guessed Billy's secret long ago – the whole family knew, she thought – it was one of those unspoken truths. But until he wanted to talk about it, that was up to him. No one was going to make him feel uncomfortable.

She thought it was rather sweet actually. For getting on 15 years he's been mentioning Aidan this, Aidan that. It didn't take the brains of Solomon to work it out.

The main thing from her point of view is that her youngest son had clearly found happiness. What price that?

Lord knows she understood the value of love. Had lived and breathed through its sweet infancy, early friendship and deep, mature trust. Nothing in the world was more precious than love.

She tidied the house and straightened a few bits and bobs out. Smoothed the tablecloth and gathered together the crockery. She was rather frail these days but it didn't stop her wanting to fuss around, making the place nice.

Billy had said they would cook her a meal, that it would be a surprise. She could hardly wait.

She had been lonely for years. First felt its icy breath longer ago than she cared to admit. There had been a sense of neglect, of taciturn isolation. Conversations left unsaid, arguments brewing beneath the surface but never rising to punctuate the smooth calm.

Life had carried on virtually unchanged to anyone observing from the outside. Routines were maintained . . . food on table, children washed and dressed, everyone to school, chores done and dusted.

But she knew something was different. There had been a solid steadiness to her husband's gait, now there was a skip and a lightness.

Before, he'd been quiet but earnestly interested.

Now he was brighter, lifted somehow. An eagerness in his eyes and a healthy glow to his demeanour.

She, on the other hand, was retreating into a grey shell. Feeling lost and alone. Bereft.

It went on for a while, this disconnectedness. But then all the things that happened . . . happened. And things changed again.

She decided all she could do was to focus on her family, give them all of her being and devote her life to theirs.

Life lived selflessly was a life lived well, she thought. It may not have been the happiest of lives, but in our own way we are blessed.

Saturday arrived. The doorbell rang and two shapes were silhouetted at the door.

It took her a minute to make her way down the hallway, her feet rather unsteady and her body more fragile than ever these days.

She opened up and beamed at the pair.

'Well don't stand on the step all day!' she laughed, welcoming them.

'And you must be Aidan. I've been hearing all about you for years,' she cried, 'though he didn't tell me what a handsome young man you were.'

She gave her son a warm squeeze and planted a papery kiss on the cheek of his companion.

Aidan instantly saw that she knew, and smiled to himself. Poor Billy, worried all these years over nothing. It was obvious his Ma was pleased as punch for him.

They went through to the kitchen, and Mrs Harper put the kettle on. 'I'm thrilled to see you both, just thrilled,' she burbled away, contentedly.

She wanted to know all about how their jobs were going and how life in the City had been these last few weeks.

The hours passed happily and the men went about preparing supper. They had decided to do one of Aidan's specialities – roasted Welsh lamb with rosemary, prosciutto, lemon and garlic. Billy took on the job of being sous chef and chopped, sliced, peeled and diced away as Aidan prepared the joint.

They had made a stop off at the Waitrose on the way. Hopefully they had thought of everything. They'd also brought breakfast things for the next day. They wanted the visit to feel like a proper treat.

As the hours passed and cooking aromas floated in the air, garlicky citrus mingling with a lamby rosemariness, Billy said he would take the cases upstairs.

He always felt strange coming home. So many treasured memories, and yet so many difficult memories. Even in this very house – the games he and Gracie had played, the secrets they had shared, the sleepovers they had had. He fondly thought of that ridiculous time they had taken a sneaky peek at each other's private places. They had been so innocent then! Oh, how life had changed.

He took the luggage up and paused in the hallway, half-hearing her tinkling laughter. Half imagining her dashing silhouette, skipping around a corner.

He peeped into his old room – how tiny it was! – then realised with a start that he wasn't sure what the sleeping arrangements should be. He went into John and Simon's, which by now had been converted into a guest room with two single beds either side of a little table. On the table sat a squat blue lampshade and a glass vase with roses from the rose bush outside arranged into a little posy. And propped up against the vase was a card.

'To Billy and Aidan,' it read.

He opened it up quietly and pulled out an old-fashioned card with a picture of a love heart stitched with embroidery.

Inside it read:

'I am so glad you have found each other. Be blessed. Love Ma x'

He felt a slight lump in his throat and he sighed softly, wondering how long she had known. He felt ashamed about not having had the confidence to say something before.

But he felt touched and moved by her lovely words. He felt the slight hotness of tears collecting in the corners of his eyes.

He returned downstairs to find Aidan and his Ma roaring with laughter over something.

He walked over to her and tenderly kissed her on the forehead. 'Thank you, Ma,' he said, softly.

'I'm just very happy for you, pet,' she said, warmly.

Billy handed the card to Aidan wordlessly.

They exchanged a twinkly smile.

'So, the lamb needs to rest for another 10 minutes or so then we will be able to serve up,' Aidan said, knowing Billy would appreciate a burst of normal chatter at this stage.

It wasn't long before Billy was pouring the gravy and Aidan carving up the roast. Delicious scents wafted through from the kitchen, making everyone hungry.

They all sat down at the dining table and in an instant, Billy was transported back to another era. It was the same table – Formica surface, wooden legs, that his family had had when he was a little boy. The walls had changed colour these days – they used to be white and now they were yellow. But the dresser was the same and even some of the old plates decorating the dresser were the same as before. It was both reassuringly familiar and yet uncomfortably reminiscent of a difficult time.

Made more difficult with his recent discovery. He wondered whether his Ma had been completely in the dark or whether she had known, but accepted. She had always had a sunny nature, his Ma, and rarely lost her temper. He remembered as they got older and the Joe business got worse, she seemed to suffer too. It affected them all, he supposed, in different ways.

But she had always been kind and sweetness radiated out of her. How could his Da have done it?

Distracted, he didn't realise that Aidan had asked him a question.

'Sorry, what did you say, I was miles away,' he said, slightly guiltily.

'I was just wondering if you could pass the cauliflower cheese please, looks like you've done a top turn again.'

Aidan was doing a fine job nattering normally and keeping the sense of chit-chat going. He was always rather wonderful at making conversation with anyone and everyone, it was one of his gifts.

Billy was more grateful than ever that they had come here together.

On the way up, they had discussed the sorts of subtle questions they could pose to his Ma, to try to establish whether she knew anything but without giving anything away. The last thing either of them would have wanted to do was to reveal a horrible secret she hadn't been aware of and ruin her memories forever.

But similarly, they felt if she *had* known then it might have been a burden for her, protecting him all these years. Perhaps by now she may wish to talk about it?

They had fretted together and decided there was no point planning it, something would emerge, or it wouldn't. Life would evolve as it should.

Scribblings

Outside, white mistiness shrouded the canopies of the trees. Snowflakes fell, softly, hovering a moment or two in the air before finding a new home on the ground. Underfoot, a soft, thuddy crunchiness built up, layer upon layer. An absence of colour but an almost blinding bleakness as the purity of the new landscape bathed in a gleaming, winter sun.

Gracie was in her bedroom, staring out unseeingly, lost in thought. She had decided that she should start to make sense of her life by chronicling it. Perhaps if she wrote it down it would feel like a story – like someone else's story.

So there would need to be a beginning, a middle and an end.

Well, perhaps not an end, but certainly a beginning and a middle.

The silence outside created the perfect backdrop to a story-telling moment. She wished there was a roaring log fire to warm the place up. She could see her own breath and her fingers were frozen.

She reached for the blanket and wrapped its cosiness around her, tightly.

Then stretched out for the notebook she had found, and a

black pen. Warm up, hands, warm up . . . she willed her fingers to work.

She pondered how to start.

And then she did.

Once upon a time, she began, *there was a young girl called Gracie. She was born on September 4th, 1940. She lived with her Ma in May Close and had a best friend called Billy.*

Gracie didn't have a Da.

But she didn't mind very much. After all, her Ma loved her and she had no end of happy times.

Only one day, the happy times came to an end.

A bad man called Joe entered their lives. Her mother's brother. Only unlike families you read about in stories or see in other people's homes, this new-shaped family wasn't right. Wasn't right at all.

But let's not talk about that right now. Let's talk about the young girl's life before that day. I have decided to start writing a diary, and here we are. I found this blue note-book the other day so hello, diary, I am going to fill you with all my thoughts and my memories and my hopes and my dreams and I am going to try to remember everything. My name's Gracie and this is all about me. Welcome to my life, I'll try to show you around . . .

School days had their comforting routine but now the evenings were taking on a sense of predictability, too. Every day Gracie would rush back to put more detail into her burgeoning diary.

In between homework, helping her Ma with the cooking and tidying up, writing up her memories and luxuriating in whatever poetry she was reading that week, she was creating enough distractions for herself to try to blot out the dreaded feeling that sooner or later Joe would come back, to carry on with whatever it was he had started.

She had tried reasoning with her mother, but the deep look of shame that had etched her face that first time Gracie and Billy had overheard the awful attack in the kitchen seemed to be assuming a permanence that Gracie wasn't comfortable with at all.

The fear in those eyes had deadened into nothingness and her once placid face was newly crumpled into a criss-cross of lines. It was as if she was sleepwalking through life, barely participating.

Gracie hated the idea of bringing up the subject because she didn't want to inflict yet more pain. And she had great hopes that Mr Harper would be able to do something, but these were fading as there still didn't seem to be a plan.

She and Billy sometimes hatched plots to go to see the police, but every time they convinced themselves it was the right thing to do, they always felt the idea unravel when they remembered they were only children and no one would take them seriously.

There was nothing else for it – they would have to rely on the grown-ups, have to rely on Gracie's Ma. She would have to stand up to Joe, she would have to . . .

Leafing through the diary now, virtually every page was filled with scribblings and sketches and poems and lists. It was a thorough, meticulous piece of home-made history and it captured all the nooks and crannies of her life.

There were moments these days when its memories would take shape and paint themselves into reality. But they offered scant comfort, replete as they were with devastating reminders of all the lost opportunities that were wasted.

It was sunny outside, but that sort of silver sun you get in the depths of winter. The garden was crusted in twinkly whiteness, and you couldn't see a blade of grass or a thread of bark.

Shards of shimmery light danced onto the wall beside the bed, where she was sitting, leafing through the old book that had become her chronicle.

The faint smell of yesterday's dinner was wafting in through the corridors. It always seemed to smell like boiled cabbage, whatever they ate.

She tended to take her tea in her room. Didn't like going into the communal space – they always had the television on in there and they always put it on so loud. And for some reason, people were always arguing. It was the opposite of restful. There was one elderly gentleman called Bob who always insisted on sitting in the same chair, and got very cross if anyone else dared to sit there. There was a woman called Elizabeth who wore long, holey cardigans and spewed vile filth at whoever cared to listen. A pair of twins – Mildred and Margaret – always sat in the corner, squabbling with one another, sometimes even lashing out at each other and once attempting to pull each other's hair. They didn't seem to like one another very much.

It wasn't the happiest of places.

Not the carers' fault, of course, they did their best. It was clean enough and they often came around with a little glass of something cheering to lift the spirits of an afternoon.

But it wasn't the sort of place you would choose to live out your days. Too much time for wallowing in grief and in retribution.

Too many memories crowding in and hurting her head. Other days too few memories to make sense of any of it.

She knew it couldn't be long now. Thank goodness for Billy visiting as often as he could. Where would she be without dear Billy? She couldn't remember the last time he visited. Had no idea how many days would pass between one to another. But she was always pleased to have that connection with her past, even though she knew from the shadows of memories that she had, joining the dots with the diary, that the past most certainly wasn't the happiest of places, either.

She stared out of the window, unseeingly, lost in thought.

Plans

Joe was sentenced to 10 years. Would be allowed out in eight if he behaved himself. He had got away with manslaughter, managing to persuade the jury that the politician had been drunk and disorderly so Joe was acting out of self-defence. Just like he'd persuaded his Ma previously about what happened with Finnegan.

Beguiled by his clean good looks, and swayed by the testimony of some of the old stalwarts who'd been bored to tears by the young man at the pub, they accepted the story.

In the gallery, his mother wept. No one else came – no one else knew him and no one else cared. His sister didn't come, but no surprise there.

As the judge passed sentence, he sighed a small sigh of victory that he had got off lightly. In the same breath, an overpowering sense of disgust for the politician welled up an anger in him that began to consume him.

As he was led away, he didn't turn back to his mother, who was waiting, hesitating, to wave goodbye to her son. If he'd bothered to glance her way, he would have seen how broken she was. How wretched. And even if he'd seen, he wouldn't have cared a damn.

Instead, he made the effort to look at the jury, one to the other, to the other. Holding their gaze. And sneering.

For years afterwards more than half of them were plagued by doubts that they had reached the right verdict. Was it manslaughter – or was it murder? As his handsomeness morphed into a grim, hard-set stone, they saw him for what he was. And they felt sick.

It was the twenty-third of March, 1940.

Joe would go on to bide his time carefully in prison, keeping himself to himself and not causing trouble. He would relive his memories and had more than enough material to satiate his darkly growing appetites.

He didn't talk to the other inmates and he didn't engage in the plotting and the swindling the others did. They eyed him with suspicion, wondering who on earth he was and why he wasn't one of the gang, any gang. Unlike some of the others in there, he wasn't a wayward miscreant or a dodgy chancer. He was simply bad.

It suited him to dwell in his own world, watching and waiting. Sometimes training himself for weeks to hover in that sweet ecstasy of pleasure-pain, on the cusp of something that would sting in its intensity.

He found the time passed quickly. But he also found himself growing agitated, wanting to savour not just the memory but the reality of the contract with new accomplices.

He would devise exquisite new plans, imagining a series of scenarios to whet his thirst.

Days morphed into weeks, weeks into months, months into years.

With monotonous sameness, six years passed, and to his surprise, he was released even earlier than he had thought. He had barely appreciated that the War had come and gone in the time he was inside.

He was walked to a stark room with a large, wooden door. There, a wrinkly, bespectacled husk of a man handed him a small handful of belongings. The dungarees he had been wearing the night of the attack, the checked shirt, some coins and a key. A pair of brown shoes with laces. Spatters of dark brown crusty stains splattered over everything apart from the metal. They hadn't bothered to clean his stuff. But what did he care, he was free.

He changed into the clothing and walked into the foggy morning air. Money jangling in his pocket, a jauntiness in his gait that he wouldn't normally have. He breathed in deeply, inhaling the familiar ozone buzz of the seaside air. Hands stuffed deep down, he felt a piece of paper in the right pocket. He pulled it out. An address.

He searched his memory to try to work out who it belonged to – then he remembered – his sister.

He realised he could go to see her for some food and for some shelter. And more . . . But that could wait. First – there was stout to be drunk.

When he was imprisoned, the withdrawal pains of being denied alcohol were crippling. He would wake up with night sweats, throat parched and stomach wretched with agony.

He drifted in and out of consciousness, craving the taste and the sensation of black, creamy liquor.

It took about three months for his body to adjust to a new

regime – but he adapted with the same rigour and discipline he applied to his plans. He knew that by waiting, waiting, waiting – for the alcohol and for the new contracts he would make – the taste he would be rewarded with would be sweeter than anything he had ever tasted before.

So he set on his way to nowhere in particular. He was a man with no ties, no material belongings and no friends. It didn't matter where he would go. The change he had in his pocket would be enough for tonight and he would worry about getting some more the next day.

As he wandered down the country lane, the prison fading away into the distance behind him, he felt the excitement of freedom and possibility mount in him. A swirl of memories breathed in him as recently as if they had happened yesterday, as one accomplice after another drifted into view. He savoured the deliciousness of it all, and savoured the knowledge that his hardening desire for submission would be meeting its release very, very soon.

A tumbledown, stone-built pub with a welcoming light in the front porch way stood out up the lane. There weren't many houses around here, mostly empty spaces with plenty of dry stone walls dotted in outlines around fields and lining the roads, spikes of grass poking through. Squat yellow flowers poked their heads up along the sides of the lanes, with larger, swaying pink ones nodding thoughtfully in the breeze. There was a bleakness in the air, and a slight chill.

Silence was punctuated with the odd rustle of wind in the leaves – but there were no voices and no other audible signs of life.

He sauntered up to the pub – the Green Man – and pulled open the heavy, iron-clad door. A warmth rushed out to greet him and he bent his head down so he could step into the entrance way. It was one of those ancient places, built years ago, for men of another era. Today, it was crumbling somewhat on the outside but it had a cosiness about it that served well the men of today.

Inside, there were two old boys drinking together and another off to the side of the bar on his own. Joe made his way to the front and noisily sat himself down. He'd forgotten the spatters of brown, crusted blood that served as a vivid tableau of that dreadful night six years ago. By now anyone looking at him wouldn't be able to guess what those stiff stains were – with his youthful face and strong hands they would probably guess he was a labourer of some sort. He lacked the weathered tan of someone who worked outdoors, but there was plenty of other work so he attracted no undue attention.

He had had no trouble fitting back into his clothes – the only difference now was that he had built up his body so the lean-ness of his early twenties was now usurped by a rugged, muscular solidity. The proportions were more or less the same. But if you touched his arms, you would feel their strength. If you saw his torso, you'd think he had trained as an athlete. If you felt his grip, you wouldn't escape.

The black hair had been kept meticulously in check over the years inside – short back and sides with a floppy, boyish front that disarmed everyone from the prison guards to cooks serving up the slop. He always got extra portions of meat by winking at the ladies who stood at the hatch. Somewhat unusually, they had been brought in for a short time from the Women's Voluntary Service to give some much-needed assistance. And well, they thought he was just lovely. So handsome! So strong looking! They would admire the angular jaw, the breathtaking green eyes and the hint of muscle you couldn't help but catch sight of, stiffening under his clothing as he carried his tray or walked over to the table to eat. Even his table manners were impeccable in comparison to the other animals he was in there with. The ladies would gossip quietly behind their hands, trying hard not to look too often in his direction, but he was distractingly good-looking, and his hands had a grace and a strength about them you couldn't help but wish might one day caress your hip or hold you tight.

And then there was that voice! Oh goodness, that was something else. Like Sinatra himself had dropped in to prison. Or rather they didn't really know much what Sinatra would sound like if he talked, but they imagined that this was it. If this man talked, that smooth, deep unctuousness could lull you to sleep.

Several of the women rather fancied that when he got out, perhaps that's exactly what he would do – captivate them and take them to his bed. There was certainly the odd moment of flirting here and there, as they competed for his attention. Each and every one of them would nurse a desire to be in his gaze, with the possibility of serving him up a different sort of scrumptiousness when he got outside.

Joe of course was entirely unmoved by all this – all he cared about was that this tiresome flirting was his ticket to the possibility of more meat. The lamb chop sort.

He didn't experience sexual desires in the way other men did.

Others in the prison would be so desperate for release they would sometimes do it to each other. More often than not a younger, weaker prisoner was singled out for attack.

But there was also no shortage of rampant flirting (and more) with the serving ladies and the women in the laundry. The other prisoners were consumed with sexual frustration and took whatever they could. Some even found ways around the system to ensure their visiting spouses made the most of their time inside, as it were. Others discovered the clever tricks you could do to have a quick one with one of the ladies visiting someone else.

Joe barely considered the women as sexual beings and had no desire to use a man to release some primal urge, either. He had a far more disciplined, sophisticated approach, he thought.

The women would spend hours wondering why he was in there, speculating that he had been framed. How could anything as gorgeous as that be guilty of something terrible? He looked as if he could be one of those Hollywood film stars. There were rumours that he had killed a man. Not a single one of them believed he could have done it.

Meanwhile, oblivious to their ample and open charms, he would keep himself to himself. Inspiring jealousy and even more suspicion from the other inmates. They thought he couldn't be right in the head. It was the only way they could justify his lack of interest in girls and his refusal to smuggle dope, buy fags or join in the moonshine ring where you'd take turns to get your socks bundled up, keep back your potatoes from dinner and make paint-stripper alcohol to share around.

Everybody did it, even though it tasted like shit. But it got you high and it helped numb you away from this shitty life.

Joe wouldn't take part in any of this stuff. Dying though he was to have even one more drop of alcohol on his tongue, he had no sense of communion with the guys and no inclination to participate in anything they did. So he didn't.

All this got picked up of course by the warder who thought he was some sort of saint and gave him endless good write-ups to the inspectors and the chiefs. Joe was held up as some sort of model prisoner. Never smoked, didn't smuggle anything in, didn't get caught up in the moonshine ring and didn't attempt to take advantage of the ladies.

He was just about the best-behaved prisoner they had ever had.

Of course, if they could have taken a peek into that corrupted mind of his, they would have seen how on the money the other inmates had been. *They* thought he couldn't be right in the head. How devastatingly wrong he was though, was something nobody guessed.

He would while away hours on end, nursing his memories and making plans. Disciplined and sophisticated. He would think it a badge of honour to keep an erection alive for several hours at a time, just allowing himself a squeeze or a tug or a gentle stroke underneath from time to time. He dedicated his life inside to the perfecting and the prolonging of his aroused state. He would see it as training for outside – to use his own sense of desire and restraint, arousal and discipline – to develop an extraordinary ability to stay hard for hours.

When he did allow himself release, he would always think

back on one of his accomplices. The Finnegan memory was one he came back to time and time again, as was the politician, despite its unwelcome denouement. But Mr and Mrs Businessman was his favourite – he would dwell on the picture he had in his mind of what she would have done when he left.

It would drive him to a point of near release just thinking of how desire would have swelled through her body, how desperation for his touch would have compelled her to explore where he had explored, to touch where he had touched.

He would think of her looking at herself – the hard, round point of her dusky nipple, aching upwards and crying out to feel his touch. She would see that right breast exposed in all its creaminess, trails of her wispy cardigan brushed aside to reveal its full roundness. She would gaze at it, seeing what he saw, and feel her groaning sting rising inside her.

She would have to take hold of that roundness and stroke around it in circles – first tenderly, then harshly, working inwards to that tantalising first touch of nipple. She would judder in pleasure-pain as that pulsating gorgeousness would be bursting into hardness – that budding point unrecognisable in its tenseness from anytime she had ever seen it or felt it before. It was gorging with desire, needed hard, hard twisting – darting flashes of sheer ecstasy down inside her.

And with her other hand, slowly, that unfamiliar navigation to the places he had taught her. Surprised at her ready wetness, the folds of her warmness engulfed her third finger, copying his actions and feeling that darting connection with her twisting nipple.

She would be craving his hands, his touch. With every trace of her fingers, she would be feeling him.

But this was just 'near release' for Joe. He had no doubt in his mind of what would have ensued after he left. No doubt at all. The picture he had was so clear and vivid, it was as if he had watched it take place. If he had witnessed the truth, he would have seen Polly collapse into relief of an entirely different sort, holding her dear son and wretched on the floor of the nursery with fear and horror.

She vomited shortly afterwards, aghast that something so vile and unexpected could have happened in her own house.

But for Joe, the story in his head was playing out differently. He saw Polly, helpless with desire for him, bringing herself to ecstasy in waves of release. He saw her imagining him, desperate for his touch. He saw her continue to fantasise about him, as he did about her story, in a way that would destroy her marriage and wipe that smug smile off that smug face of Mr Businessman.

His was a long game. It wasn't just the idea of her flowering into a new understanding of arousal and pleasure with him and for him – it was the idea that this new understanding would inevitably weave its decaying path to the end of a happy union. He had despised the jaunty merriness of that man – something about him made him want to destroy him.

And so that was where the 'near release' became release for Joe in the story of Mr and Mrs Businessman. Thinking about the scene that would unfold as Mr Businessman got home, discovering his wife's passion for a passing stranger, seeing her lack of satisfaction with him and with her life . . . this was the scene that Joe would play out when he wanted to finally end his own engorged entrapment. To find his own release.

He had no idea whether or not his fantasy had played out into truth – but it almost didn't matter. In Joe's world – he had achieved what he had set out to accomplish and there was no doubt in his mind that that was that.

He had even managed to justify in his own mind that his current incarceration had been part of the plan – because without it he wouldn't have been able to train his mind and his body so effectively and so precisely if he'd been forced to go to war.

Everything had happened for a reason. And everything going forwards would happen for a reason.

Which was what brought him here tonight. He'd been walking for about five hours – wanted to break the link from his most recent past as forcefully as possible – so had relentlessly kept the pace up through lanes and streets and fields until he came across this lonely place with its tumbledown pub and its quiet stillness.

Joe asked for a pint of the black stuff.

He watched the lady at the bar pour it, slowly. He watched the liquid cream its way into the glass with a thick promise of bitter bliss.

He saw her pause, waiting for it to collect itself into a pool of softly undulating lather, then watched as she tipped in the last few drops, collecting as it did in a meniscus of dairy creaminess at the top.

The condensation collected down the side of the glass and the black liquid shimmered like oil.

He felt his saliva glands moisten in anticipation, the build-up of six years' worth of expectation. He pulled the glass towards him and lifted it up, dipped his lips around the rim and inhaled the familiar aroma. As his nostrils filled with the treacly, homely sweetness, he sucked in his first draft. Savoured it, slowly, in his mouth, without swallowing. Absorbing the sense memory of a thousand drafts before.

He smiled, then drank it down.

And that night, slowly, slowly, sip by sip, he began to slake one of the two thirsts he had been cultivating these last six years.

The other he would begin to slake tomorrow.

Possibilities

She sat there, pored over her book, entranced by this latest revelation. Rilke, again – how did he come to be so wise, when he died so young?

How did one young man learn so much truth and knowledge about the world? How did he know he was right? And for that matter – *was* he right??

She paused, staring into the distance, ruminating in what she had just read.

It was from a collection called *Letters to a Young Poet*. Although *her* book hadn't printed out whole letters from the 10-letter series, it had poignant extracts. This one came from the eighth letter, the same source for her newfound talisman.

Don't observe yourself too closely. Don't be too quick to draw conclusions from what happens to you; simply let it happen. Otherwise it will be too easy for you to look with blame (that is: morally) at your past, which naturally has a share in everything that now meets you.

Simply let it happen . . . well yes, that's exactly what she'd done, wasn't it. Time and time again . . .

Gracie couldn't help her habit of wondering why so much bad stuff had happened to her. She would fiercely question what she had done wrong, trying to work it out. She was sure pencil pockmarks stabbed into her arm must have happened for a reason. She was sure being trapped in a cold, dark, mossy prison must have been her fault. Sure not having a Da must be punishment for *something*. Sure her Ma's violent slap, that day of the pencil pockmarks, must be retribution for some unknown crime. Sure Joe's raven stare and soulless vileness must be recompense at her for some dreadful past unwitting crime.

Sure her Ma's refusal to tell the police about what was going on at home must be some ill-fated redress and reprisal for some mysterious misdeed of her daughter's. Why else would she not try to protect Gracie? Why not try to protect herself? It was a slow, shameful acceptance that whatever would unfurl had a purposeful inevitability. Not worth stopping. Not worth bothering to try.

It was this reluctance to act – to do – well – anything – against her own brother, even when he was hurting both her and her only child – that Gracie found most hurtful. She couldn't begin to fathom what lay behind her Ma's inaction. Her refusal to talk to the police, seek help from neighbours, ban him from ever coming again. It had to be some strange penance, it had to be.

Gracie was baffled and wounded and scared. That constricting feeling pressing hard on her chest, stopping her breathing, was something she began to experience more and more. Whenever she remembered . . . what happened . . . that familiar pressure would seize her chest and force the oxygen out of her. A few times now she had actually fainted with the dizzying blackness of it.

She was paralysed with perplexity. Didn't understand the bath business at all. Couldn't understand that her own mother's instincts weren't to roar into battle to safeguard her. Assumed there must be some dark secret she was unaware of but must somehow be responsible for.

She reread Rilke's prose.

Don't observe yourself too closely. Don't be too quick to draw conclusions from what happens to you; simply let it happen. Otherwise it will be too easy for you to look with blame (that is: morally) at your past, which naturally has a share in everything that now meets you.

She wondered whether the scrutiny she had subjected herself to was helping or hindering the situation. It certainly wasn't helping her feel better. And when she discussed it with Billy, they would go round and round in circles, him insisting nothing was her fault.

Only yesterday they had gone for one of their walks to the glade and had sat down to thrash it out again. The topic, as ever, was Gracie's Ma's refusal to deal with the 'Joe Issue' as they both called it. Gracie couldn't bring herself to call him uncle – that would have been as much a lie as calling this house a home. Uncles brought you gifts and played with you and told you you looked pretty in your dress. Homes were safe places where you could rest and read and bathe and play in peace. She felt she had neither.

As for her mother, she was nothing like the placid, kind woman her Ma had once been. Fear and shame had eroded that calmness and loveliness from her these days. Perhaps if he went away, forever, it wouldn't be too late for her?

He – on the other hand – was a sneering, stern, stygian presence that exuded threat and darkness.

Where sister had been soft and beatific like a sunbeam dancing on water, brother was hard and obsidian like an armour-clad raven.

Looking back at the diary entry on these observations years later, trapped in a lavender prison, the old woman would reflect that they had been the twin halves of a whole. She the light, he the dark. She was sure there was a name for that . . . Either way, they were bonded together, forever.

But today, they were there in the glade, Gracie and Billy, each trying out different descriptions to attempt to capture the essence of the problem.

They were both quite grown up now. Gracie a willowy, tawny 14; Billy – voice broken and getting quite handsome – a solid, proud 16.

Still the best of friends, the pair would potter off together to natter and try to solve the world's problems whenever they could. Since the incident a couple of years ago there had been several more visits from Joe. What had started in the bathroom was just the beginning. Gracie had tried to blank it all out of her memory. Each time was worse than the last.

So in the glade that autumn day, russet leaves intermingling with flashes of orange and dabblings of yellow, crunchiness underfoot, they resumed their mission.

Billy had brought lollipops for them to suck on as a pre-tea snack. He let Gracie pick which flavour she wanted. She smiled and pointed to the lemon one, leaving Billy his favourite, the blackcurrant. He should have known she would do that. But then, as she began licking her sweetie, the piquant fragrance of lemons hung in the air and reminded him, of course. Gracie and lemons. It was the scent he always associated with her. If Gracie was a colour, she would have been yellow – fresh and sunshiny and lemony, daffodilly and happy.

Only not so happy these days. The visits from – *him* – had been taking their toll on her. Even though she threw herself into her homework and her diary and her reading, there was still that sleep-awake time in the morning when you woke up before you got on with the busyness of the day – and there was still that dark, quiet time, alone in her room, when the memories would crowd in and chase out nicer thoughts. Fear and revulsion were her customary companions. She never knew when the next visit would be, or how far he would take it next time. All she knew is that she was beginning to feel a struggle and a torment others her age did not face.

Billy tried to convince her it wasn't some kind of unexplained punishment and that she hadn't done anything wrong. How could she? She was utterly lovely.

But Gracie felt there must be an explanation, and she cast her mind back through her life, observing herself closely, trying to draw conclusions from every twist and turn. She wondered how her Ma came to be in May Close in the first place; wondered who her Da may have been, and why she didn't know who he was; even wondered where Joe had gone travelling and whether he was like *this* before he went.

She had remembered that first night when he had arrived. She had only been about five but the memory imprinted itself on her mind. She recalled the intensity of his odour and the gruffness of his manner. The raspy, scratchy stubble itching her skin. The way her Ma seemed to be happy at the sight of him. Although she doubted her memory of this happiness now . . . The way her usual smiley face soon turned into something else.

And as for *him* – she had never seen him smile, or laugh. Not once. It was as if that sneer he had somehow set into his face permanently, oscillating from scorn through smirks to anger and back again. She wasn't sure if he knew what happiness was, or whether he ever felt it.

She breathed out these latest thoughts to Billy.

'I wonder if it all means something? Whether it all adds up to an answer?'

Billy shook his head, preferring as always to try to lift her mood.

'No, Gracie, it's a series of horrible coincidences. There was a brother and a sister and the brother was evil and the sister was too scared to escape. The sister had a young girl and the brother continued being evil and frightening them both. But luckily, the young girl had a friend, and the friend had a plan, and the good thing was it wasn't long before the plan could be put in place. Then the young girl and her friend would be able to run away and the evil brother would never find them ever again. And they would live happily ever after!'

He looked at her from below his lashes, wondering how his attempt at lightening the situation was going.

A slow smile began to cross her face, then a little laugh burpled up inside her.

'Oh, Billy, you are such a funny thing. I wish you did have a plan though, wouldn't that be just wonderful?'

'But that's the best part, Gracie, I really do have a plan. I've been working it out over the last couple of months. Do you think you can wait till the spring before we escape?'

'If it means really escaping, I can wait for as long as it takes! But what *are* you talking about?'

'I've been thinking about this for ages, Gracie. Your Ma just isn't going to do anything about it. If she refuses to deal with being hurt herself, that's her business, but she shouldn't be letting him hurt you. So I've got everything sorted.

'By the spring I will have earned enough money for us to take a train to London. I'm going to make my fortune there, Gracie, inventing things. At the moment the money from the docks work isn't much but it's going into a great big pot which will give us transport and lodgings for a few months until I find my feet and work out what to do next. We'll find you a nice school and I'll get a job building on the engineer apprenticeship I've been doing here. But we can't go just yet – I've worked it out, we need to have enough money to live on for several months so that we can feel safe and secure. What do you think of that, then?'

He looked at her with anticipation, expecting her to be pleased and excited.

Instead, large, lolloping tears started to roll down her childish cheeks.

The salty splashes smudged the bodice of her pale pink dress – little damp patches where she had wiped the wetness of her cheeks into her hands and onto the cotton.

'Oh no, what's wrong, what have I said?' Billy exclaimed, worried.

'Oh Billy, that sounds such a clever idea, you always have been so clever. But does it mean I will have to leave Ma, and you'll have to leave May Close? How can we leave our families? Wouldn't you be sad?'

He hadn't quite thought of it like that. But he was strong in his resolve.

'Some things are more important, Gracie. I am scared about what might happen. It's getting worse each time he comes. How many times has it been now, since that first time I disturbed him locked up with you in the bathroom? Maybe four or five over the last few years? He's not going to stop, Gracie, and who knows what will happen?'

She sighed, knowing he was right. But the idea of abandoning her Ma was truly awful. She was becoming a shell of her former self – lines etching onto her face and pain carved into her every expression. Gone was the soft, beatific placidity of times gone by. Gone were the days of bubbles in the garden and picnics. Gone were the happy times where life felt full of possibilities . . .

Only what Billy was offering her was a doorway out of this stifling existence into a life full of – yes, that's right! Possibilities.

She attempted a smile, gratefully.

'Anyway, that's the second part of my plan. Once I've got a good job I'll be able to come back and visit everyone here, and then in the future when I've saved up enough money to look after her as well, I'll come and fetch your Ma. I promise you, Gracie, I swear – that I will always, always, no matter what – fetch her and make sure she's okay. I'll make sure you are both okay.'

Gracie looked up at him, in wonder at his generosity and cleverness. He always had looked after her. Always been the knight in shining armour. Always rescued her in all their games. Now he was rescuing her for real.

'If you're sure, Billy, and as long as you think you'll be able to come back and visit everyone as often as you like, then what I think is – hurrah! We will be running away from this wretched place and we can have a home where we can feel safe and cosy. A home that will be warm and inviting. No more dragons . . .'

Gracie thought back to that moment now, with a leap of excitement in her heart. They had pledged to keep the plan secret. In the spring when the weather improved and when Billy had enough money, they would go to London, leaving notes to be discovered after they'd gone. And they would correspond all the time, letting their families know how they were. Billy had found out about a post box system where you could pay to collect your mail no matter where you lived. So they were going to be able to protect themselves from anyone knowing their address and tracking them down. Well, when they said 'anyone' they both knew who they meant. But they tried not to articulate it any more than was necessary.

So here she sat, with a new wave of possibilities washing over her, and this note from Rilke which seemed to be written just for her. Giving her permission to stop blaming herself for everything.

Don't observe yourself too closely. Don't be too quick to draw conclusions from what happens to you; simply let it happen. Otherwise it will be too easy for you to look with blame (that is: morally) at your past, which naturally has a share in everything that now meets you.

She remembered even yesterday, she had been scrutinising every memory for a clue to why her life had unfolded the way it had. Now she was being told she could *simply let it happen.*

It gave her an unexplored feeling – a sense of liberty and a renewed sense of optimism. She reflected on those other lines, from one of the other letters, that she had clung to so protectively, since she had first stumbled across them:

> *So you must not be frightened..*
> *If a sadness rises up before you ...*
> *... You must think that something is happening with you.*
> *That life has not forgotten you.*
> *That it holds you in its hand.*
> *It will not let you fall.*

For the first time since ... *it* happened ... she felt strangely comforted. She even found herself allowing herself a proper smile.

A calmness settled deep at her innermost being. She breathed. And she slept.

Revelations

Dinner at May Close had been a merry affair with much laughter and clinking of glasses. The conversation flowed nicely and everyone pronounced the lamb a triumph.

Aidan was just pottering away in the kitchen, clearing the main dishes away, and putting the finishing touches to pudding.

Back home, he had prepared a rustic apple tarte tatin. Now, he was tipping it out of the baking tin and onto a pretty serving dish he had found. He rather liked the old-fashioned green and gold swirls around the edge.

There was a matching jug, so he poured the cream into that and collected up some spoons and napkins.

He bustled back into the dining room, smiling at his partner and Mrs Harper. The room had a somewhat dingy air about it, but there were fresh flowers adding a dash of colour on the sideboard and another splodge of colour from a collection of bone china knick-knacks, presumably collected over the years. A deep purple china beetroot sitting alongside another porcelain trinket in the shape of an apple, with a tiny china mouse poking out from the base of a partially eaten china core. There was a postcard tucked at the back with a picture of a flamenco dancer. Someone had sewn a scarlet ruffle skirt onto the cardboard. There were seven or eight thimbles of different shapes and sizes, and another china ornament – a slice of Swiss roll with glossy chocolate china round its edges and another grey china mouse poking out through the middle, having cheekily taken a bite.

So despite the gloom in the room, the atmosphere was lively and the eccentric decorations gave the place a bit of character.

Billy and his Ma made appropriate oohing and ahhing noises as Aidan presented the tarte to the table.

'Doesn't that look gorgeous, Billy?' cooed his mother. 'Looks like you've found yourself a talented young man there, pet.'

She smiled warmly at her son, so grateful for the chance to see him and spend time together. Life had been lonely these last few years. It was good to see her Billy happy.

Aidan popped back into the kitchen to get a serving slice, leaving mother and son alone again briefly.

'Oh my goodness, I've just realised!' she gasped, clutching her mouth, eyes widening.

Billy wondered what was wrong.

'It's the dish and jug set, pet,' she said, noticing the china Aidan had rooted out from an old forgotten place in a cupboard to put the tarte onto.

Her voice dropped, and she spoke softly.

'Your Da gave that to me as a parting gift before he went to the War. He said it was for me to stay hopeful and remind me that he would be back, wanting more of my famous dinners in no time. That he would stay safe and come back to us just as soon as he could.'

Her eyes were filling with tears.

Aidan, unaware of the upset in the room, came marching back with gusto, declaring it had taken a while to find a suitable knife. He stopped short when he saw Billy's face and came around from behind Mrs Harper to glimpse her damp cheeks.

He rushed back into the kitchen and fetched a couple of tissues.

'Do you need me to, um . . .?' he began.

'No, pet, don't you go going anywhere. I think Billy would want you here . . .'

Billy wondered where this was leading.

Then it all came tumbling out.

'Billy, I've not spoken about this to anyone, pet, but I'm getting very old now and I want to make sure you know this in case . . . anything happens.

'It's about Gracie. There's something I think you should know.'

The silence hung in the air. Billy gave her an encouraging nod.

'Back in the late thirties, a young woman moved into the Close, taking the smallest, end house next to ours. Just a living space downstairs with a kitchen down one end and two small bedrooms upstairs, and a bathroom.'

'Gracie's house?' asked Billy, needlessly.

'That's right. Gracie's Ma was very shy but also very sweet. We became friends instantly and she helped me enormously when you came along. I was pregnant with you when we met and she cooked for John and Simon and your Da sometimes when I was feeling tired and unwell.

'She would pop over and make sure everyone was okay, and

often made extras of bread or stew or hotpot and would bring
it over. The night you were born, she even came here and stayed
the night with us, caring for the boys and looking after your
Da. She was a natural homemaker and I always thought it was
rather sad that she didn't have a man in her life.

'She was pretty and gentle and petite. I remember her lovely
dark-green eyes – do you remember them, Billy?' she asked.

He nodded. How could he forget?

'Then the first few months after you came along, I was
feeling was far more tired and far more unwell than I had been
with the others. Perhaps it was being a bit older when I had
you, I don't know, but it took its toll on me physically. I would
take myself up to my bed as early as I could and I stopped
making all the delicious meals I used to make. I was so
exhausted, Billy, and I found I couldn't stop crying. Years later
I read about postnatal depression in one of those magazines,
but I hadn't heard about it then and I know it was beginning to
wear down your Da and the boys. They wanted the old me
back – the one who smiled and laughed and cooked and kept
everything nice.

'As the months swept by, I was consumed by looking after
my new wee bairn and everything else seemed to drift by.

'I hadn't even taken in that your Da had started doing lots of
odd jobs for other people in the Close. And especially Gracie's
Ma. I barely saw it, Billy, but slowly it seemed to me that she
was coming over to us less frequently, but he was going over to
her.

'Now, I can't be sure of anything, but I began to have my

suspicions. Nothing was ever said to me, by him or by her. But there were times when I felt I just knew.

'Then, that devastating day came when we knew he was to be posted abroad for the War. He was being sent to serve in France, to start with – although as you know, he ended up soon afterwards in North Africa. None of us even knew where that was or what it had to do with the War.

'He sat with us all around the table – you were about one then, Billy, pet. And he told John and Simon and me that he would be back. He gave me a large, heavy parcel, wrapped in newspaper. Inside was the prettiest dish and jug set I had ever seen.

'Delicate green swirls and curls of gold leaf intertwining. The china gleamed on the table and we all looked at it, trying to take in the enormity of what was happening. I can remember the look in his eyes, almost as if he was sad, or regretful.

'"This is for you, darling Mary. When I'm back I want to see your lovely old smile back, I want you to feel better and be better. Boys, will you help your Ma? I want you to encourage her to start making her famous dinners again, alright boys, so that when I'm back we can sit around this table again, as a family, and we'll use this dish and this jug for beef mince and gravy, for stew and dumplings, for hotpot and roasts. Alright boys?"

'John and Simon agreed enthusiastically. I don't think it had dawned on them yet that their Da would be going away, and possibly never coming back.

'"Do you know when you'll be back?" I asked him, scared of the answer.

'"I don't know, I'm afraid. I don't know." A shadow of something passed across his face.

'I remember looking at the dish and the jug – sitting there so pretty and so proud – willing myself to give him strength and confidence that we would be okay.

'"I have to go and say my goodbyes to the neighbours now," he announced, and gave me a peck on the forehead before popping out into the Close and heading round to the smallest house at the end.

'He came back a couple of hours later, after the boys were in bed. You had gone down beautifully that night, so I was sitting on my own, listening to the wireless. Earlier I had packed together his things for him. I put in a photograph of the family, and I wrote him a letter telling him how sorry I had been for not being my usual bright and breezy self since the baby had come. I tucked it into one of his shirts for him to find when he was away. I hoped he would write to us and that God would keep him safe.

'When he came back, he was very tired, so we went to bed, preparing for the awful morning to come.

'He left us just after Christmas in 1939.

'So I don't know for sure, Billy, but all I do know is that in the autumn of the following year, Gracie's Ma had little Gracie. Nobody knew who the father was and she hadn't started having boyfriends. I can't be sure of course, I can't be sure, and I like to think I may be wrong. . .'

Billy sat in stunned silence. Aidan took his hand, gently, as the news began to sink in. Aidan more than anyone would know what an impact this revelation would have on him.

Billy worked it out carefully in his head. December to September, Gracie's birthday.

'So you think Da may have been Gracie's Da, meaning Gracie . . .' He let the words linger in the air. Wordlessly, he suddenly knew. He and Gracie were brother and sister. Bonded forever in a way they never even knew.

By now tears were rolling down his mother's cheeks.

'Maybe, pet, maybe.'

Billy went to hug her, hard, realising that she had known all along about the love her Da had felt for Gracie's Ma. What a terrible burden to carry all this time. And for Billy, a new discovery – he had no idea when Gracie and her Ma had come to May Close, no inkling that the love affair between his Da and her Ma must have started shortly after his birth.

There was a hot fugginess in the air as hugs and tears were exchanged.

Aidan understood at a deeper level the emotional impact not just the disclosure about Gracie would have on Billy, but the implications of his feelings about Gracie's Ma's behaviour. Somewhere in his innermost heart, despite the wretchedness he felt about her refusal to act – there were times when he felt he had despised her for her obstinacy – he had always managed to forgive her and somehow understood.

Perhaps there was some sort of unconscious collusion between them. Perhaps a tie, or a bond, where he had understood that she would have wanted him close by, the father of her child. His father.

Billy wondered whether Gracie's Ma had ever told his Da. Whether it was an unspoken, unacknowledged truth between them, or whether the toils of war meant the mathematical certainty of it hadn't perhaps entered his Da's consciousness.

Billy also wondered how his own Ma had coped. Had stayed friends with the woman who had betrayed her.

After all, it was Mary Harper who had young Gracie to stay and to play to help her friend out in times of need. The night of the miscarriage came to mind. He realised with a jolt – of course – that the baby who never came was likely to be his Da's as well.

And he wondered, momentarily, whether the constant nightmares he would have as a young child – scared the father he didn't know would not come back from the War – were somehow a product of any of this. Whether the anxiety the grownups were going through had somehow permeated his childish mind, fuelling his worries and his nightmares.

Even though he was now a mature, sensible person with a life well led and generally happy existence, tonight's revelations were uncomfortable and painful. Bittersweet, too. How he wished he had known before . . .

He didn't like to think about the life his own Ma must have led. He remembered her irritation at times when jobs around their own house didn't get done because Gracie's Ma needed driving somewhere or had chores that required the hand of a man to help. But as a child, he put it down to the fact everyone's mums get grouchy and moan a lot at their husbands. As far as he and his brothers were concerned, it was all nice and normal. They hadn't detected their mother's loneliness, hadn't seen her misery.

Then a few years after the War, Peter Harper ended up

succumbing to lung cancer, brought on, they said, by the grit and sand of the North African front. It had irritated his lungs horribly. The doctors had recommended he take up smoking to try to ease the pain, but the disease continued to spread and within a year his big, strong Da had died quietly and softly, fragile and skeletal in a hospital bed.

Everyone in the Close had rallied around, trying to help. And Mary was left alone with her boys. Billy realised now that she had been left alone for years before.

He couldn't remember how Gracie's Ma had taken the news of his Da's death. Whether she had visited him at the hospital. Whether she was at the funeral. He couldn't remember. At the time, his own life was in such turmoil, the suffering of others barely made an impression on him.

The dinginess of the room took on an even more sombre tone. The candles they had laid out on the dining room table were beginning to flicker their last.

The tarte tatin lay untouched.

So many questions darted around his mind.

But he reflected that he and Aidan had been right – if his Ma had wanted to discuss anything, somehow or other she would find a way. And now he had at least some of the answers. He wondered if there was anything he could do . . .

And then, as ever, Aidan was there, doing and saying the right thing.

He was comforting Mrs Harper, telling her what a wonderful job she had done raising her boys, how brave and kind she had been.

It put Billy in mind of Gracie's favourite poem – that line

about 'beautiful and brave'. And he thought about that other line she had taken comfort in a thousand times: *life has not forgotten you . . .*

Billy joined in with Aidan's sentiments, telling his Ma what an inspiration she had been to him. A war widow at such a young age, barely in her forties when she was left on her own. Billy had been 17, he remembered – so John and Simon would have been 18 and 20. All three had been working by then – him down in London – so they all made efforts to look after her and make sure she wasn't lonely. On reflection, he wondered whether they had collectively done a good enough job.

But before his mood darkened further, there was Aidan, slicing up the tarte and offering up portions to everyone. His Ma chuckled, saying, 'Go on, spoil me then, why not?'

They all tucked into the squidgy, syrupy, tartness of the apple, marvelling at its crunchy deliciousness.

But despite the bonhomie and chatter, Billy and his Ma couldn't help but dwell on a bittersweetness of another kind.

Belongings

Joe awoke on his first morning of freedom with a headache and numbness he hadn't felt for years. He felt dizzy and unsteady, an airy light-headedness causing him to sway and stumble. His head felt spongy and achey and throbbing.

This wasn't part of the plan.

He had slept rough, having been thrown out of the tumble-down pub just after midnight. But with nowhere to go, he found shelter in a barn nearby and hunkered down there on straw. He didn't have much need for physical comforts – after all, he'd spent the last six years on a springless mattress in an airless room with a slop bucket for a bathroom.

But even he was knocked back by the rank ripeness of the stench in that barn when he woke up. It wasn't helping his nausea.

So he made his way out tentatively, craving the taste of water.

The light outside seared his eyes, yellow and bloodshot from too much drink.

So much pain.

He found a stream not far away and drank with gusto. Then collapsed onto his side and snored away for another few hours, the beer coursing through his veins and pulsating into dilution.

When he woke for the second time, the light was duskier. He didn't have a watch so had no idea of the time. But his head was feeling less fuggy and he knew he had to advance his plans. The boring, logistical stuff you have to do – not the plans he had been crafting in prison.

For *those* plans to succeed, he knew he needed to get some decent clothes, tidy himself up and find lodgings and a job. Shouldn't be too hard. If he did it in that order. Good tidy up first.

He had spent all his money, so for the first couple of days he would need to rely on the kindness of strangers. It occurred to him that he could spin a line about being a war hero. That would get him drinks and sympathy and maybe a whole lot more.

He was good at spinning a line. Had had plenty of experience.

He thought back to the time with his sister.

His little sister had always been a sweet and shy little thing. He knew that where he had been blessed with confident good looks, she had a softer, inner beauty that only shone through when she laughed and smiled.

If he was being honest, she was a bit plain.

She wasn't the kind of girl to warrant wolf whistles in the street. But she did have pretty eyes, he'd give her that.

As she matured, she developed a slender, petite physique. She wasn't athletic in any way – but she had a sunny nature and she was caring and kind. They couldn't have been more different.

She had had the odd boyfriend, but nothing serious. She was independent spirited, though, and read endless books. From a very young age, she had set her heart on a life on the buses. Although she was shy by nature, there was something about meeting people in that fleeting, passing way that appealed to her. You could exchange pleasantries without having to go into deeper conversation or share too much.

It was a lightness of being that she carried with her, and working as a conductress allowed her to flower.

Once she had been working for about a year, she was able to afford to go and get her own place. She must have been about 18, he guessed.

Since she had been about 10, he had taunted and teased her. As he was growing his taste for submission in his accomplices, he practised his watching and waiting on her. He would lie in wait for her, to frighten her. He would seek out her bed, her satchel or her shoes and leave the disembodied head of a mouse, a bloodied hide of a hare, a roughly-cut pompom tail of a rabbit for her to discover.

He enjoyed seeing her squirm with disgust and cry out in revulsion. More than once, she had vomited at the sight of the presents he would leave for her.

She had decided very young that as soon as she could afford it, she would move away to escape this torture.

For her mother's sake, she put on a mask. But she knew she couldn't live a life like that forever. She needed to seek out peace and tranquillity, even if it meant being on her own.

It was that inner feeling of contentment she was missing. She knew others her age did not face such struggle, such torment.

And she couldn't understand why her mother didn't punish him or make him stop. What was *wrong* with her?

So as soon as she could, she started work on the buses and saved and saved and saved. She didn't tell her Ma or Joe what she was doing. She had everything arranged in secret, so that she could make her escape.

When the time came, she felt sad. The bank manager had helped her find a tiny place in a secluded Close, far on the out-skirts of North Shields. She gave him everything she had, and he arranged everything. All she had to do was go.

She collected her things together on a sunny Tuesday. Her Ma was on one of her regular trips out to the shops. Joe was out for the day. Probably on that construction site he'd been working on recently.

She wrote her Ma a short note, to explain. She couldn't decide whether or not to leave an address.

And that was that. On a bright, cloudless Tuesday in May, the teenager set off with her small bag of belongings and into her new life.

The year was 1938. Joe was coming under pressure to take on a steadier job. Nothing could have been further from his mind.

He wanted and needed to be in control of life – not just his own, but those he chose to make his accomplices.

He had been watching and waiting with his sister for years, practising his ability to tease out the torment for an agonising age. Savoured her fear and her distress.

She couldn't have known that he was building up to a de-licious denouement for her – the next stage in her story. He had been planning it for months, with every new bloodied gift a stepping stone to the grand finale.

Arriving back from work that Tuesday afternoon, his mood turned sour when his Ma told him his sister had gone.

Raw, monstrous rage swelled up inside him.

'What do you mean, gone!' he yelled at her, furious that his plans had been thrown into disarray, and murderously angry that the little slut thought she could defy him.

Think you can run away, do you, little bitch? Eh? He pictured her face. *Well, think again.* I'll find you wherever you are, Sweetie – you will never be able to be free. We are bonded, you and I, we are blood.

His Ma was distressed, weeping helplessly. First her husband had turned out . . . the way he had turned out. Then Joe had started developing a cruel, ugly aspect of his personality she recognised only too well. Like father, like son. Both charming. Both beautiful. Both deadly.

And now this. Her beloved daughter had abandoned her.

'Don't you think about anyone other than yourself, Joe?' she asked, despair in her voice.

Joe didn't care about that. He was boiling with fury.

'Where has she gone? Tell me!'

He pinned her against the wall and grasped her throat, applying more and more pressure to her soft, white skin.

Her eyes darted from side to side and he saw that familiar fear cross her face. That fear he'd seen a hundred times now. She let out a little sound and gasped, trying to shake her head.

'Tell me!'

Eyes widening, she slackened slightly against the wall. He let her go, disgusted with her. And disgusted with himself, that he hadn't moved faster on fulfilling his plan.

He had to think through how he could hunt that whore down. It wasn't going to be easy. The months slipped by, and his anger grew inexorably. If there was one thing Joe couldn't tolerate, it was defiance of his will. How *dare* she?

He simply couldn't believe she'd disappear into nowhere, leaving no trace. His Ma must know where she was, she must . . .

It occurred to him there had to be a note of where she was going, somewhere. Or a letter.

One day, months later, there was a particularly annoying news item on the wireless about missing relatives. He decided enough was enough.

He was going to find that bitch.

He started searching drawers, pulling them onto the floor and tipping their contents into a shambolic pile.

The elegant art deco walnut looked incongruous in this modest little house, and he knew his Ma treasured the furniture she'd inherited from her own parents. But he didn't hesitate for a second.

One of its legs twisted then creaked into splintery shards. Almost comically, it tipped over, slowly, then crashed onto its side, a dozen plates and water glasses tumbling out and shattering onto the floor.

Then, more insistently, he knocked over the walnut console in revulsion, shoving papers off the kitchen Formica. A china tea set, balanced perfectly on a cream melamine tray, crashed onto the linoleum. A cup bounced against the skirting board and smashed into pieces.

He flung an ashtray with the ash and remnants of a solitary

cigarette against a wall, a cloud of bitter, grey particles floating gently to the ground, incongruously delicate. A slow-motion mist wafting gently down as the carnage unfolded around.

Joe was getting into his stride now, punching anything and everything. His jaw jutted out with a determination like he'd never felt before. He marched up the stairs and pulled the fussy valances off the bed and tore down the curtains. A sea of beige frothy netting heaped onto the floor.

Becoming desperate, he seized his Ma's dressing table with both hands and emptied its contents. Some cheap looking trinkets scattered across the rug.

His eye alighted on a chest of drawers. That's got to be it . . .

With rage pumping through his veins, he pulled out the sweaters and the underwear and the scarves.

Nothing.

He let out a primal scream, then suddenly, silence. He composed himself as quickly as he had let himself descend into bedlam. A slow smirk crossed his face.

He looked around the room and admired his handiwork. All the furniture was tipped over or onto its side. All the clothes and papers were layered on top of each other in messy heaps.

He was impressed at what he'd achieved in just a few minutes.

But then he caught himself and remembered he was still no further on finding where his sister was. *You bitch, Sweetie. Just you wait. I will make you pay for this. Just you wait.*

He stomped down the stairs, his fury beginning to rise again. How dare she defy him. How dare she try to escape.

In the doorway at the bottom of the stairs, his Ma was

standing, wordlessly. Her beret perched at an angle on her set waves.

She was looking around the room. Destruction everywhere.

Joe had smashed apart some of the railings on the stairwell, and the dining room table was shoved against the wall, two chairs lying awkwardly on top of each other on the floor.

Broken china everywhere.

She caught his eye. 'Oh, Joe . . .' she said quietly, sheer lack of understanding paralysing her.

Then, more angrily, 'Joe! Joe! What the hell were you thinking?'

He had a coldness about him, a stillness. It was hard to believe so much fury had been unleashed by just one person. His calmness was unnerving.

He shrugged and raised an eyebrow. Then slid his back on the wall, looking at her, as he took each stair one by one.

There was silence between them, the only sound coming from the slight rub of his shoulder blades on the paintwork.

Then, suddenly, a clatter pierced the air as a picture frame knocked off the wall and cartwheeled down the stairs.

'Noooo!' His Ma let out a shriek, and moved to grab the small wooden rectangle. He saw flashes of green and gold and remembered the picture was a favourite of his Ma's – a farm-yard scene with some white geese.

And then, he saw it. A small piece of paper wedged into the back of the frame. He stretched down for it, snatching it out of his Ma's reach. She let out a moan, an agonising noise that penetrated the quiet. Joe ignored her and, taking his time, eased the paper out. Unfolded it. Then smirked for a second time.

He had it. The address.

A raven's hunger gleamed in his eye.

He snatched the note into his pocket, unseeing and unhearing. Marched past his Ma without a second glance. Oblivious to the chaos he was leaving behind, and unaware of the pained expression on her face, tears coursing down her cheeks.

He was a man on a mission, that focus and discipline already honed. All that mattered was that he could hunt his quarry.

He had been able to outwit the bitches, and now he would taste vengeance.

Snowflakes

Thinking back on it now, he smiled.

His head was still sore from the excesses of the night before, but he had his plans and all he had to do was tidy himself, spin some more lines and let nature take its course . . .

It didn't take him long to win the trust of the locals. He'd prepared well, raiding a number of washing lines on the way down and picking up a selection of trousers and shirts, a sweater and a coat. Everyone he met found the young man charming, handsome and beguiling. Drawing on the stories he'd heard in the tumbledown pub, he would tell his tales of being undercover in Germany, on a special mission for the army. Camping out day and night, alone, spying on the enemy and feeding back intelligence to HQ. His story was so deliciously far-fetched, he enjoyed embellishing it every time, safe in the knowledge anyone who had been in Germany on a spying mission wouldn't be talking about it. The beauty of this story was that no one could contradict him, and he didn't have to know any details.

It worked.

A job offer followed, and within a month of leaving prison, Joe had somewhere to live, an income and a nicely turned out appearance.

296

Nobody would have guessed he had managed to escape the War completely, living it out as he did in one of the most violent institutions Her Majesty could offer.

The job was back on the construction sites – he was happy with that. Physical labour was something he enjoyed, and apart from anything else it kept him fit and strong. And he would need his strength to continue his true life's work.

He was aware of the stirrings deep in his being, stirrings which wanted him to start slaking the thirst he had been nursing these last six years.

He decided to start where he had left off. Almost.

Not with the politician, the one before the politician. His sister.

He let his new group of buddies know that he was going to be away for a couple of days on family business, but that he'd be back by early next week.

He found that bit of paper with the address on, slung on his long, dark coat, and set off on his way.

He amused himself as he travelled, thinking about that night he had managed to track her down.

It was just after Christmas, 1939.

He knocked on the door. Waited. Knocked again. A moment or two later, skipping steps inside revealed he had found his quarry.

She opened the door brightly, not for a moment expecting what she saw.

By now, she had been living in May Close for a little while.

The snow outside made the place look picture postcard pretty. Not a scrap of colour anywhere, all winter whiteness.

A warm glow spilled out from her home into the evening air.

And her, looking fresh and rosy, wrapped in a yellow cardigan over a yellow and white woollen dress.

She stopped, dead, staring at him, unbelieving. She may have let out a squeal.

'I brought you presents,' Joe said, grinning softly, his voice tracing silky tones in the cold, December air. His breath hung in icy traces between them. 'I remember how much you like presents . . .'

He pulled out the head of a sparrow from one pocket and the paw of a rabbit from the other.

She retched, nausea overcoming every fibre of her being.

'Leave me alone!' she hissed, looking around the Close for signs of life. It was teatime so everyone was inside, no doubt eating. She wished Peter was still around. She winced, painfully, at the memory of their recent parting. He would have come to help . . .

'What are you going to do about it? Eh, little sister?' he sneered. Again, the icy breath seemed to hang there like a physical presence.

He hurled the sparrow and the paw into her hallway forcefully.

Outraged, she turned to him.

'You have no right to be here. Go away!'

He ignored her, pushing past her and making his way into her house.

'Joe, I'm warning you, go away – there are people here – they will help me . . .'

By now her pleading was beginning to sound a little empty. All the other little houses were closed tightly for the night, no outward signs of life, no one rushing to her rescue.

And the one person she needed right now was the other side of the earth, fighting a different battle . . .

Just a few weeks ago, she couldn't have been happier. Now everything was going wrong . . .

He closed the door behind him.

'You thought you'd run away, did you? Ma always used to call you Sweetie, didn't she? Well, what do you think of this, Sweetie? I've tracked you down and I will never let you be free. You will never escape, never.'

All the way there, his yearning for submission had been growing in him like an ache. He knew that it was the easiest thing in the world to frighten his sister, and she would be even more anxious when she realised what he had in store for her.

He imagined the quiver of her skin and the fear in her eye.

She held no sexual attraction for him whatsoever. She was about as appealing to him as any of his male accomplices. It was the experience more than the gender, age or physicality of a person for Joe. But for this to really hurt her – for her to really comprehend that he never intended setting her free – he needed to show her. And he needed her submission more than any other he had craved over the last few years. It was the denouement of her story. Her destiny.

So this would be the night he would consummate for the first time. He had been planning it for months, in his mind. Knowing that when he did hunt her down, she would bitterly regret running away in the first place.

So as the months passed, his longing for conquest grew. His desire and arousal were almost unbearable at times. The idea of her coming to that point of needing his release would be unimaginably sweet. He would harden and throb at the thought of it.

You will be mine, little Sweetie, and you'll learn you can't choose your life.

He turned the lock in the door and pushed her onto the floor, scattering some papers away.

She pushed him off, but where he was strong and muscular, she was petite and lithe.

He ripped her clothing off – first the cardigan and then the dress. He took particular delight in pulling apart where the buttons tugged over her breast and her hip, exposing her nakedness. Her childlike vulnerability.

She lay there, helpless, him shoved on top of her. This contract lacked the elegance and the measured pace of some of his previous experiences, but his anger towards her defiance drove him to an insanity he had rarely felt.

A few weeks later, it would be the same defiance he would see in the politician that would spark his murderous response.

Today, it wasn't murder he was about to commit. It was rape.

Outside, the snow fell softly, like fragile clumps of fairy dust, glistening in the night air. There was a slow languor to the Close. Cosy flickers of warmth could be seen at the window edges and under doorways.

Silence hung in branches, on pathways and between houses.

Pure white frothed over the landscape, like a bubble bath.

Seas of snow flowed over the Close, snugly enveloping every nook and cranny.

An hour later, the man left number 29 and the snowflakes quietly covered his footsteps.

Inside, the woman was bleeding and hurting and crying.

She had taken delivery of the message.

Fears

And now, all these years later, he was on his way back. Sweetie had had a lucky escape. He had intended intimidating her and violating her regularly. But the bloody politician had put paid to that.

Now it was April, 1946. War was over, and his new life was just beginning. He had landed on his feet better than anything he could have imagined.

So now it was time to start appeasing his appetites.

He trudged down the old pathways of the Close, scarcely recognising the place. Last time it had been bathed in soft whiteness. This time, an explosion of yellow daffodils decorated the lawns and crocuses bloomed in white and purple abundance. There was the budding beginning of white roses outside one of the houses . . .

This time he hadn't brought any presents, apart from himself.

The long, dark coat was keeping out the chill of the spring air and he remembered with satisfaction that the stubble on his face would give him a more menacing air than usual. He was also aware that he had built up the strength in his muscles during his time inside and that he looked even more imposing than before.

Vanity was one of his many vices, and he luxuriated in his own physicality.

He knocked on the door. A familiar skipping to the door. And a look of horror on her face. This time, she let out the squeal of an animal caught in a ripping, metal trap, pure terror in her eyes.

'Now play nice, Sweetie, play nice . . .' he coaxed her, gently.

She couldn't help but glance up the stairs to the little girl who had wombled out onto the landing and was clutching the banister with a chubby hand.

He saw where she was looking, and followed her gaze.

His breath caught as he saw a froth of angel hair damply curling onto the shoulders of the prettiest little thing he had ever seen.

'Well, Sweetie, aren't you going to introduce us?' he whispered to his sister.

'This is my daughter, Gracie,' she murmured, a thousand fears constricting her throat.

'Gracie, come and meet your uncle!' she called up.

The five-year-old toddled down the stairs, wrapped up in her rough peach towel.

She was about as sweet and precious and lovely as an angel.

Joe leered at his sister, silently communicating some wordless threat about her daughter.

'Give your Uncle Joe a kiss, pet,' he said, bending down to this lemon-scented child.

He swooped her up, a tiny towelled-up bundle, and his raspy, scratchy stubble itched her skin.

It was the beginning of a whole new chapter in the story . . .

Later that night after Gracie had been despatched to bed, Joe asked where her father was, said he didn't know Sweetie had got married. So who was the lucky chap, then?

Gracie's Ma didn't know what to say.

This was the first time in years she had laid eyes on the man who had forced his way into her home, and into her body. She could barely stand to look at him. His body and his breath stank of cigarettes and beer. His presence revolted her. And now she had a greater concern than just protecting herself. She thought about lovely, lovely Gracie and wondered what new tortures Joe had up his sleeve.

She had known he had been imprisoned, but she thought for 10 years, not six. Oh God, she prayed, deep in her being, make him go, please . . .

She thought of that last time they had been in this living room together. Thought of the endless happy memories she had experienced with her beautiful daughter since.

Thought of the violence he had brought into her life. Thought how he had violated her . . . *there* . . . in her most private of places . . . just a few days after Peter had come to say goodbye. Had come to see her, to *be* with her.

The truth was she didn't know who the father was. It could have been either of them. She hoped, dearly, that it was Peter. But she didn't know.

So now, with Joe asking, she didn't know what to say. She didn't know whether it would be better or worse for Gracie if he thought he was the father. She just didn't know. So she said so.

'I'm not sure,' she hesitated. Then added, quickly, 'I'm not married.'

'When was she born?' he asked her, peering intently and wondering at her nervousness. He was also thinking about the last time he was here, just after Christmas, all those years ago.

'September 4th, 1940,' she replied.

Joe worked it out carefully in his head. December to September, Gracie's birthday.

He sat in stunned silence. So that angel of sweetness was his own flesh and blood.

Curiouser and curiouser.

'Well, you know I've got my eye on her now, too, Sweetie. I'll never leave either of you alone. You will never escape. I will always find you . . . Always.'

Gracie's Ma hung her head in powerlessness. She had no idea what to do. She couldn't move again – he would only find her. And anyway, Peter had only just returned from the War – her other reason for living was right here, in this Close. And then there was Gracie's friendship with Billy. Perhaps Peter would be able to help her come up with a plan.

Perhaps they should go to the police?

While she was musing on this, Joe pushed her to the floor and walloped her across the face.

'I'm going to stay for a few days. This time. You get to cook for your big brother and give him a place to stay. And I'll be back, very soon. And if you tell a soul, believe you me, you would rather you didn't. Let's just say you know what I am capable of, and put it this way, Ma is getting fucking irritating in her old age.'

Joe was enjoying her discomfort, and could see the old fears mingling with new fears, dancing in her eyes. He felt the familiar hardening in his trousers as that old feeling of conquest flooded through him.

Gracie's Ma tenderly stroked her left cheek, still stinging from his touch.

'And as for that peachy daughter of yours . . . Well, Sweetie, we wouldn't want anything bad to happen now, would we. Remember those presents I left you when we were growing up?'

She nodded silently, recoiling at the memory and seized with terror for what this could mean for her Ma, and for Gracie.

The first of hundreds of purple bruises began to bloom.

And a dead weight hung in her heart.

Ramblings

Gracie couldn't have been more excited about the plan she and Billy had devised. Just a couple more months, then they would be free, forever.

A lightness skipped in her heart and her eyes began to shine once more with optimism. She was wallowing in that feeling of liberation, rereading that passage she had come across the other day.

Don't observe yourself too closely. Don't be too quick to draw conclusions from what happens to you; simply let it happen. Otherwise it will be too easy for you to look with blame (that is: morally) at your past, which naturally has a share in everything that now meets you.

She wondered what the bit meant about your past having a share in everything that now meets you, and decided that because you had to 'simply let it happen', whatever lay in the past wasn't your fault, so you shouldn't carry the blame for it. Whatever dreadful crime she may have committed unwittingly in the past was something she should stop fretting about. Any moral blame buried deep in her story was something that could be quietly forgotten. Was evil born or made? She had no idea, but she had a heartfelt conviction that she was good, really.

And the important thing was to concentrate on the future, to make plans!

For some reason, she turned to the little box on her dressing table and took out the crucifix. She decided that even though the chain was unbearably fragile, it would be a good idea to start wearing it, to get her through these last few months.

Perhaps God would be able to find her and look after her more easily if she wore his special sign.

She clasped it around her neck, and glanced at the mirror. It looked pretty. It hung quite low so she would probably wear it underneath her dresses, she thought, but she felt safer somehow.

The days were getting darker and colder. And with each new dawn, Gracie would count off the time to their departure. They had planned it would be the beginning of March. It was December now.

Even this house had begun to feel more like a home again. Her mother was singing in the mornings, and had started to smile more, started to give her daughter hugs and kisses again.

Endless weeks had drifted by where she had merely stared into space, shame hovering like a veil around her.

But it had been months and months since Joe had visited, and with each passing day her Ma was becoming more like her old self.

She had even started taking rides out with Mr Harper again. He'd stopped coming for a while, which Gracie's Ma got cross about. Gracie just assumed he had lots of things he had to do in his *own* home – after all he had three children. But her Ma had been getting cross about anything and everything. Gracie wondered whether it was guilt, eating into her.

When Gracie was feeling less than generous, she would blame her Ma for their situation. It was perfectly straight-forward to go to the police and report what was happening. She couldn't fathom why she didn't just do that.

She had heard about children being taken away to Dr Barnardo's if there were bad people in their life, so she half thought perhaps her Ma didn't want her to be taken away. But she still thought they should do what was morally right. And clearly the morally right thing to do would be to tell on him.

Gracie leafed through the book again and spotted the red dress poem. She smiled and remembered how clever she had felt, making mind shapes and joining the dots to understand what it all meant.

Today, she felt inspired again to write her own poem. It would be something to capture her excitement about escaping, but without giving anything away in case someone accidentally read it.

She wanted to find a metaphor that would work, or a clever turn of phrase.

She picked up her diary and saw with relish how packed it was already. She had decided the other day that she would bring it completely up to date – the chronicle of Gracie Scott, in time for their departure. So it was brimming with memories and snatches of conversations and sketches for poems and lists upon lists upon lists.

She wondered if she would find any inspiration for her escape poem in her diary.

She reread large chunks of it. Her ramblings were a bit all over the place, but they were always sincere.

'Billy is obviously my best friend, but my overall best friend is Mam. Sometimes she is grumpy and cross. In fact over the last few years she seems always to be grumpy and cross. But I know that underneath the grumpiness there's a soft and lovely person who loves me and wants to be loved back.

'I worry about her so much. Everyone else either has or has had a husband. Other women in the Close and some of the mothers at school have lost their husbands in the War, but it seems as if Mam has never had anyone to love her other than me. I'm not sure it's enough for a grown-up.

'I sometimes think perhaps I should try to help, but I wouldn't know where to start. What do I know about getting a boyfriend! And anyway, she always seems so sad and upset all the time, I don't think anyone would find her very much fun. She also isn't as pretty as she used to be. It's strange, because she's not very old at all, but her face has got lines on it like someone much older. I think it's all her worries, scratching away at her skin.

'I'm sure she must still love me very much, even though she doesn't want to do anything to stop *him* coming back. I wish I was a grown-up and able to understand what she's thinking.

'But then at other times I wish I was just a little girl again. Things were simpler and nicer then. Happiness was blowing bubbles, reading together with Ma, seeing spring flowers on a sunny day.'

*

The old woman closed the diary shut, finding it hard to stop the tears coming.

The childish scrawl felt so familiar. Read a hundred times, maybe more.

Capturing the essence of the girl she had been with a wisdom and an incisiveness that you wouldn't expect.

And she wrote exactly as if she was chattering away to you. If she strained hard, she could still hear her teenage voice.

She pulled the small box towards her and looked at the crucifix, a beautiful pendant without a chain. How did it go missing again? She wondered. And nestled inside, the brown, wrinkly rose petals curling up together.

She remembered the Little White Pet rose, her rose. Even today, there was the faint musky scent lingering in the air.

White roses had always held a special place in her heart. There was a purity and a freshness about them. And she remembered the words the young girl had written in her diary. 'One day,' she had said, 'I will have a garden filled with white roses, their big, nodding heads floating in the breeze and wafting fragrance into the air.' One day . . .

The locket was tucked away underneath the petals. She opened it up, watching the golden curl tumble out. Then she looked at the inscription, tracing her fingers over it, searching her memory for some meaning.

The curl of angel hair felt as soft as spun silk, and looked like it, too. It wasn't hard to stretch back and reach for this particular memory. She glanced at the photos on the shelf. There, but not there.

She opened the diary at another point, wondering what memory may be unlocked here.

There was a poem.

There is an absence of presence.
A beauty in the stillness of the night.

Being, unbeing.
A journey begun.
A heart awakened.
The sense of the sun.

There is an absence of presence.
A calmness in the quiet of the bright.

Shards

The quest for a metaphor was like trying to solve a puzzle, only you weren't quite sure what the puzzle was. So it was extra hard.

Having decided to try to secretly capture something around her excitement about their escape plan, Gracie fell to the task of trying to extricate a story or a happening that would do the job.

Her thoughts turned to dawn, to waking up, to that wonderful feeling you get when you know you are going to start a fresh new day, full of possibilities.

Then she thought wouldn't it be good to hint at the beginning of a journey – the travels she would take to her new destiny.

She imagined what it would be like. They'd sneak out in the dead of night, slowly, quietly into the still, dark air.

They would scarcely exchange a word, throats thick with heady anticipation.

They would cover miles and miles, getting further and further away.

Dawn would eventually break, warming her skin with its enveloping presence.

Then, inspired by the thought of the sun's presence – a thing you just *knew* was there even without opening your eyes – she realised she could do a bit of word play with the idea of something being there, but not being there. She thought that's what it would be like, when she wasn't there anymore. She would be, but not be. There would be a big Gracie-shaped hole where Gracie had been, as if her absence would have substance. But it didn't mean she wasn't actually not there – she would be miles away in London, going to her new school and making new friends, living a new life.

Her thoughts were whirring into a dozen mind shapes as the dots flew together faster than she could keep up.

It wasn't long before she was sketching her ideas down and playing with rhythm and concept.

She knew she couldn't begin to compete with the Rilkes and the Wordsworths of the world, but she derived enormous pleasure whiling away hours in poetic endeavour. When she eventually got something down she was happy with, she read it out loud to herself, to test it on the air.

Satisfied, she reread it, slightly louder, with slightly more conviction.

She liked the way the words rolled around her mouth and the way she had spun a sense of calmness and stillness into the atmosphere. She liked the way she had captured something of the galloping of her heart and yet had managed to weave a sense of quiet into the poem.

She felt exhausted. Outside, the stars were twinkling hellos and good evenings to each other. Her bed looked especially soft and appealing. She thought she could just lie down for a tiny moment, to rest her weary head . . .

On the drive back down to London, Billy was quieter than normal. Aidan was doing the driving, bless him. So Billy had plenty of time to gaze out of the window, staring out absent-mindedly, scarcely noticing the gorgeousness of the countryside.

It was a yellow-golden autumn day. One of those sumptuous, chilly breeze days where you feel extra cosy either being inside tucked into the warm, or outside, bracing the cold, but wrapped up nicely with comforting layers.

Sunshine was bathing the horizon in a buttery goldenness and birds were circling in the sky.

None of this attracted his attention in the slightest, eyes fixed as they were in unfocused thought, somewhere in the middle distance.

Aidan glanced at him, wondering how he was taking everything. He had seemed to react surprisingly well last night. But Aidan was glad they had brought a second bottle of good claret to take the edge off the news.

It can't have been easy.

It wasn't. Billy was still silently reeling from an invisible blow that seemed to leave an imprint of physical pain. He was thinking about that Tuesday night in January. He couldn't help it. He usually succeeded in blotting out thoughts of it, but after last night his memories were flooding every nook and cranny of his mind like mercury.

He pictured everything as if it was yesterday. Could remember the smell of the winter air, could even remember that he'd set off from home at seven thirty precisely because they'd just got to the end of a programme on the wireless and the announcer had given the time.

He had raced over to Gracie's house, eager to tell her the good news. That he had very nearly saved enough money for you-know-what.

Rapping on the door once, twice. Then a third time. No answer.

He nudged it open, slowly, and saw bedlam had returned.

He sucked his breath in, wondering if Joe was still in the house. Furniture was splayed onto the floor, shards of broken things lay scattered in pointed accusation.

'Gracie?' he called out, hardly daring for the answer. 'Gracie?'

He slowly started to explore, inch by inch, wondering what he would find. In the kitchen area, Gracie's Ma was lying, lifeless on the floor.

Billy rushed to her and tried to shake her. 'Wake up! Wake up!' then ran into the street, calling for help at the top of his voice. Even if Joe was inside, people should find out what he was capable of. Enough of everyone hiding the truth. He saw doors opening in the Close and spotted his Da speed down the road towards him. Thank God.

He ran back inside, and tried to see if she was breathing. Her skin was still warm, which was a good sign, but she wasn't moving and seemed horribly heavy. Something wasn't right.

His Da came in and Billy looked up at him. 'I think she might be ... dead ...' he said, quietly, 'and I don't know where Gracie is.'

His Da let out a sound that was somewhere between a gasp and a scream. He sat next to her, on the floor, and pulled her softly onto his lap, looking for signs of life.

He had fear and horror in his eyes.

Billy meanwhile was likewise filled with anxiety. He tiptoed up the stairs and peered into every Gracie-shaped space to see if she was there, possibly hiding in fright.

Nothing.

Joe had visited several times over the last year or so. But not for several months. Billy searched his memory – he thought maybe September. He thought about the first time Gracie had properly talked to him about it. In the spring.

He remembered her telling him that his stench reeked into every room, lingering there for days. Ash and bitter treaclish revoltingness. She despised everything about him. How he had stood there, in her house, permeating what was once her home with a soulless cold hate.

Gracie had told him how she had been getting ready for school. It was a sunny, blustery kind of day. She had been staring out of the window at the hazy view – thought she may have seen crocuses and daffodils outside. Rain one moment, splashes of sunshine the next.

And then my heart with pleasure fills,
And dances with the daffodils.

Then, the sound of that familiar gait traipsing onto the gravel outside.

She had frozen, she said, 'Oh God, please no, not again . . .'

Her heart raced in desperation. Inside, she knew she just had to get through it. Again. Deep breaths.

Gracie had told Billy how even the daffodils that her Ma had picked the day before smelt strangely chemical after he arrived. As if he drained everything of its beauty and loveliness.

Like the last time, he had wanted her to go outside with him. And like the last time, he had enjoyed watching her discomfort and horror as she knew she couldn't run away but had no idea where they were going or what they were doing.

He thrived on her unease, taking more visceral pleasure in the sight of her big, fearful eyes than anything he had so far experienced. Especially with those long eyelashes, dewing with water in the drizzle. The sight of her slender form – so pretty – so small – made him feel like he could conquer the earth.

He could snap her like a twig. And one day, one day, that was exactly what he was intending to do.

But Joe being Joe, it was the careful, patient watching and waiting that was building up in him over time that so exhilarated him. Gracie had no way of knowing that he had a long-term plan for her. He, on the other hand, knew he would keep taunting her like this for the next year or two then do what destiny told him was his rightful path.

He knew he could wait. Watch and wait. His other accomplices would slake his thirst until then. But this heavenly girl –

his Gracie – would be his finest prize. He just needed her to watch and wait, too, and then he would take what was his.

Gracie couldn't breathe, the pain in her heart was so intense. Forced to accompany him to a quiet, unknown place. Forced to sit on the ground with him. Forced to remove her clothing, piece by piece, watching his eyes hungrily tearing into her, as if he was a starving man and she the first food he had set eyes on.

Her embarrassment melded into her fear, and her fear melded into her embarrassment. He would stroke her jaw, softly, feeling the child-like curve of her cheek, the peach softness of her skin.

And his raven eyes would bore into her body, drinking in its possibilities and savouring the taste of her nightmare.

Every time, he would take it slightly further – how long he made her stay with him and how much of her physicality he touched, and where.

That spring day was the day Gracie decided her Ma was to blame for all of this. She could have protected her. Could have stopped him. Could have saved her from this twisted wreckage of a life.

It was the day her resolve hardened on needing to do something about all of this.

Later, when she was back at her house, she had asked Billy to come over to talk. It was the first time she properly opened up to him about what had happened. From that first time when he had forced her to sit in the bath to today.

He wasn't used to seeing Gracie cry, but big, sloppy tears rolled softly down her face. It was the first time she asked him for help, begging him to do something. She was sitting cross-legged on her bed, he close by on the chair next to the dressing table. He sort of wanted to go over and hug her but wasn't sure if she would want him to. So he patted her hand, gently. She smiled, gratefully.

That spring day was the day he started working on a plan in earnest.

Echoes

Of course, the picture she presented to the world was a mask. What choice did she have?

Melting snowflakes trickled slowly into dropleted patterns down the glass. Rivulets making their cautious descent – fat luscious large ones and tiny, sparkly, little ones – still crystalline with snow. A kind of lethargy which echoed the mistiness of the day.

Outside, the view was hazy through the fog of snowfall. Splashes of green and grey. The odd moment of brown and beige.

Winter then.

Her heart was beginning to beat with that familiar anxiety. Inside, she knew she just had to get through it. Again. Deep breaths.

There was a straggly set of pansies squatting in a white china vase downstairs. The Formica gleamed. A scent of polish lingering in the air. Harpic and Jeyes fluid. Bitter. Piercing. It was a house that looked like one of those dream homes you saw in pictures. But this wasn't a place anyone could call a home. Wasn't *home* meant to mean something warm and inviting? Safe and cosy. Hearth and heart. Home, sweet home.

This house was a dream that never was. A game of make-believe. Of nightmares.

The pansies looked defiantly on with their cheery yellowness. She bowed down and smelled them. Strangely chemical rather than floral.

I wandered lonely as a cloud . . .

A whisper of a thought crossed her mind but disappeared in a vapour.

'You ready, then?' he asked.

She looked up, nodded.

The sense of not quite being able to breathe constricted her. She wasn't sure if she could speak.

He wore a long, black coat and a long, stern face. Had slightly raised eyebrows, as if questioning.

She collected her things and walked through the door he held open for her. Snowflakes lingered on her cheeks and clung to her eyelashes. Her soft hair began to feel damp.

Crystals

He couldn't help but think of that spring day when he started working on a plan in earnest. But today was another day. A bleak, winter's day where the wind stung you and whipped around your ears. Months on from that April showery day when Gracie felt her world close in.

And now Gracie seemed to be missing.

He wondered whether she had run away, managed to escape from Joe, or whether Joe had her somewhere for one of his weird sessions where he forced her to do . . . things, unspeakable things.

Billy shuddered. But it wasn't due to the cold.

Downstairs, his Da was pushing a glass of brandy against the lips of Gracie's Ma. He seemed to be hugging her tight to wake her up and make her say something. She was still lolling in his arms, still and quiet.

'Can you get some help, Billy, please, son,' he said, his usual knowing-exactly-what-to-do spirit battered into something cautious and frightened.

Billy ran out of the house to see what help he could find.

The rest of everything blurred into a haziness. Somehow, Gracie's Ma was alive, but she had suffered a catastrophic blow to the head and would never be properly the same again. For-ever after her memory would come and go – pockets of light filtering through the dusty cobwebs. Sometimes clear as day, her mind's filing system would bundle everything into a tumble of clarity. Her life, her daughter, her brother . . . what happened . . . would sharpen into focus and sting her with its vividness. On those days, the pain was excruciating, like a migraine piercing her consciousness.

Other times – most times – there was a pleasant fog, a sort of unknowingness that she didn't find altogether unpleasing.

Still others, there would be shadows of memories that would poke through. In some ways, these were the worst times. Because during these times, a sadness would overwhelm her, more profound than anything she could imagine.

Somewhere in the back of her mind, she would get the sense that life had not forgotten her, that it would not let her fall.

But the sadness would rise up in her, subsuming her soul. A darkness would sink into her, and a veil of shame would descend.

So while the remnants of skeletal leaves rustled underfoot, crunched into snow, Billy noticed nothing. As people bustled by, on their way somewhere and anywhere, Billy noticed nothing. His mind, lost in another time, was clearing the haze of a life lived long ago.

He had run out for help for his Da and Gracie's Ma. Then he turned to what was truly important. How to find Gracie?

It was getting dark and there was no sign. All anyone knew was that there had been a worse struggle than normal. Anyone could see that by the detritus strewn over the ground floor of their house. Gracie's Ma had been taken to hospital. Billy's Da had shadows of grey across his face, as worry lines crinkled into etchings deep into his features.

Billy didn't know what to do. The police had been called and he made sure he got to speak to them. He decided once and for all someone needed to stand up for what was right. Someone had to stand up for Gracie.

So he gave them the whole story, as far as he knew it. He spoke with revulsion of the gradual intensity of Joe's attentions, how he forced Gracie to take her clothing off and do strange things. How Gracie described him, raven-like, soulless, some-how hungry for her. Ballbearing eyes boring into her and piercing her humanity.

He told them how Gracie's Ma refused to stand up to him. How he attacked her, violently, whenever he visited. Like he was compelled to strike her, push her down and crumple her, as if it was some sort of ritual. A game.

Billy had observed his attacks on Gracie's Ma had grown more frenzied, and told the police. He told them every last detail he could grasp.

He felt exhausted.

His Ma had sat with him as he explained what had been going on over the last nine years. Mrs Harper looked uncom-fortable, and sad.

The ruddy-cheeked policeman told him he needed his rest because Gracie would need him to talk to and be with when she was back tomorrow.

That thought comforted Billy. He'd thought back to earlier,

when he'd rushed over to let her know he'd nearly saved enough so that they could make their escape later in the week. He had decided that very day that it's no good hanging around, waiting for just the right amount of money to feel safe and secure. As long as Gracie was here, she was in danger. He would have to save her because it didn't look like anyone else was going to.

At that stage, he had no idea that the blow on the back of Gracie's Ma's head would have such devastating consequences. For now, he just knew that he needed to accelerate his plans and protect Gracie for good.

Billy sat in the car, the world rumbling by in rushes of oranges and russets, musing on that thought, blinking back the tears. If only. If only.

He'd gone to bed that night with strengthened resolve and an optimism in his heart. The policeman assured him that Gracie would be alright, that she would be back in the morning. There was nothing to fear.

He had the rumblings of an old nightmare stir him in the night – a sense memory of the days as a little child when he would wake up in sweats, fearing the father he had barely met would never come home from the War.

That night there was a moment when the nightmare gripped him, but he shook it off, safe in the thought that in the morning, everything would be alright.

Only it wasn't.

The morning came and went. No Gracie. The afternoon came and went. No Gracie. The twilight fell over the powdery landscape, cascades of snow softly whitening the land. No Gracie. Night drew in and the moon shone down, magically.

Silent shadows rippled across the Close. Everyone watched and waited. No Gracie.

The next few days passed in a slumber of haziness. No one slept. No one ate. Billy's Da visited Gracie's Ma, along with the other neighbours in the Close. But *he* had a particularly tender way of looking at her that softened his eyes, a look that was private.

Billy went to see her, once. He saw the helpless form, nestled into the crispness of the hospital sheets. She looked pale and thin. She wasn't wearing make-up – so her lips were faint lines and her eyes were sunken deep, as if they were missing an out-line to prop them up. Billy realised he had probably never seen her without her make-up on before.

Part of him felt such disgust for her, he could hardly look at her. It was her fault that Gracie was gone. She should have stopped him. She could have, she should have.

But another part of him was consumed with pity for her. After all, she had been subjected to years and years of beatings and who knew what else. Billy didn't know what to think. He was so, so very tired.

And still no Gracie.

After the fifth day, the ruddy-cheeked policeman came back again, this time wearing a sorrowful expression that seemed to rearrange his face.

He spent some time murmuring to Billy's Ma and Da in the hallway. Glancing up at Billy with an acknowledging nod. Billy nodded back.

Then he left.

Outside, crystals of snow clung like lacework to the tops of the trees and sparkled in the moonlit sky. The stars above seemed to twinkle with them. A communion of light.

Wondering what on earth was going on, Billy drew closer to his parents. They looked at each other, and told him to come into the living room and sit down.

And then they told him.

Branches

The pristine ground was soft, fresh snow having settled in the night. A silver sun hung low in the sky. Powdered whiteness bleached the horizon. Seas of snow shimmered into the distance.

Silhouetted against the brightness, a powerful beak was tearing into something. The arc of a wing rose up, each armour-clad feather catching the light like metal.

Steel eyes squinted, hungrily. Branches overhead cast shadows, eviscerating the landscape. A low, guttural kraaa pierced the air and echoed into nothingness.

Something glinted on the ground, discarded in the snow.
A gold crucifix, stripped of its chain. Half buried.
And a raven was attacking the earth, ripping violently, deeply.
A trace of something lingered on the breeze.

Redness began to stain the snow.

Roses

White petals folding in
A calmness resting
Quietly
Stillness in sorrow
Buried gently, softly,
The sweet, sweet calm of a new day

The chill of a wing's breath swooped past.

Epilogue

She stirred from her sleep, and realised she must have dozed off while sitting on her chair. Looking down through bleary eyes, she saw two ancient rose petals nestling in the creases of her hands. Sepia in colour, brittle in texture. She lifted them up and breathed in the musky scent of rose.

Her rose. Her Little White Pet. Her daughter.

She realised the little box was open. Inside, the crucifix glinted. She pulled it out and traced her finger around its engraved edge. A fleeting memory of something flickered in her.

She had grown even more frail these last few days. That husk of a body, its skeletal frame was tiny. She felt weary.

A pot of purple chrysanthemums smiled prettily into the room. But even the sight of the sun dappling onto them, casting lacy shadows onto the far wall, failed to lift her spirits. She felt profoundly uneasy.

Then the diary hove into focus, on the bed next to her. It had been placed page side down, open at a spot near the end.

Drawing it up, she peered down at the childish scrawl and read.

Her eyes alighted on a particular passage:

. . . But then at other times I wish I was just a little girl again. Things were simpler and nicer then. Happiness was blowing bubbles, reading together with Ma, seeing spring flowers on a sunny day.

The flicker of memory began to take shape in her mind, like a migraine crowding in her head. The pain was excruciating.

She saw a little girl with golden curls and an angel smile.

Piercing pain.

Saw a tall, handsome man with beautiful green eyes and a cruel mouth.

Throbbing, throbbing.

Saw an apron-fronted woman with tears in her eyes and blood on her hands.

Agonising! Stop it!

She realised the apron-fronted woman was her, and the rest began to fall into place. Her Gracie, what happened that day. The beginning, the middle and the end.

The little girl would forever be a little girl. Life stolen from her. Snatched. Clawed away.

She suddenly remembered the epitaph Gracie had written in her diary, and turned to it with a clarity of purpose. The sad, sad words held more meaning than the young girl could possibly have imagined.

Her small body had been found five days after she had gone missing. Buried in a shallow grave of soft snow. There had been a tree in a clearing, and a blood-stained mound. It was clear some feral creature had attacked her.

Death itself had been strangulation, they thought. No one knew why. But everyone knew who.

And a clear memory pierced into her consciousness. Joe. Her brother. What he had done, the man he had become.

It didn't take the police long to track him down. And with a second killing under his belt, one of those a child, the judge had no qualms about sentencing him to death by hanging.

Her thoughts crystallised in anger. Death was too good for that man. How could he have done what he'd done to her Little White Pet? Her rose.

Then another memory clawed into her, tearing at her heart.

Somewhere deep inside, she knew that this was all her fault.

The diary had revealed Gracie's joyful plans for escape. How dear, sweet Billy had come to the rescue, gallantly. Gracie's Ma reflected briefly on the promise he had made to Gracie, recorded in her diary that time, to look after her Ma no matter what – and felt grateful that he had kept his promise. Just this week he had visited her in this godforsaken place again. He was a good boy. He kept his promise. She suspected the purple chrysanthemums may have been a gift from him. But she couldn't remember.

The diary showed how he had come up with a clever scheme to whisk Gracie away into her new life. Just another few weeks and perhaps she would have been safe. But it was a mother's job to protect her daughter, to take her to that safe place she deserved – and this she had failed to do. She had stood by and let him permeate his cruelty into their lives. She remembered she had tried to escape him, once. But he had searched her out and held her his mental prisoner for years. But it wasn't good enough. She should have fought back.

She paused, wondering whether that's what Gracie had done, that January night when he took her for the last time. Fought back. She recalled that the one thing that would trigger blind rage in Joe was defiance. He couldn't countenance anyone standing up to him. Perhaps Gracie had been so focused on her escape plans that she felt she could try to stop him, or try to run away.

Nobody would ever know. Her darling Little White Pet. The absence of presence.

A veil of shame descended over her, submerging her being. Sadness seeped into every pore of her body. She reached for the locket, opened it, and stroked the lock of blondeness, still luminescent with life.

Her eyes gradually dulled and she found herself looking at the metal thing she was holding in her other hand. The thing the curl had been contained in. What was it called now?

So much going on, she couldn't keep up.

She read the inscription: 'Forever yours, PH'.

She wondered who PH was, and what it meant.

Heavy-lidded with tiredness, she found herself sinking deep into her chair. Bones brittle and heart slow. Barely breathing.

Her left hand let the locket drop to the floor.

Her right hand clasped, tight, the silken keepsake.

She closed her eyes.

The End

Acknowledgements

It's hard to know where to start. The inspiration for the book began many years ago when I was leading the BBC News coverage of a high-profile case. The police officers I worked with were extraordinary human beings – Chris Stevenson, Andy Hebb, Gary Goose. The people running BBC News at the time who trusted me with the work and gave me the opportunity – Richard Sambrook, Mark Damazer, Roger Mosey, Peter Horrocks, Frances Weil. And the utterly brilliant Kristin Hadland and Fiona Bruce.

My learning journey in the field of psychology continued as I trained and qualified as an Executive Coach on the BBC's in-house training programme, which is accredited by the Association for Coaching and the International Coach Federation under the amazing Liz Macann.

Seas of Snow was written over several years in my holidays. The wealth of talent, support and expertise at Unbound has been a delight to discover and work with. From my initial meeting with Dan Kieran to Mathew Clayton who was there on filming day (shout out also to Mark Bowsher from Rabbit Island Productions) to the wonderful (and ridiculously ingenious) Jimmy Leach; and Georgia Odd, DeAndra Lupu,

Isobel Frankish, Paul Fulton and the peerless John Mitchinson. Very, very special thanks also to Mark Ecob for the stunning cover artwork and Scott Pack for being the most brilliantly incisive, sensitive and supportive editor I could have hoped for.

Beyond that there have been a number of unsung heroes I would like to thank – for being there in so many wonderful ways and helping me when it counted. Alf Bowles, Caroline Cowie, Ruth Francis, Rebecca Sutherland, Rebecca Hoyle, Anjula Singh, Cathy Drysdale, Rikki Kraftchenko, John Ray, Michael Wilson, Amanda Thirsk, Martin Harriman, Helen Bunker, Maggie Philbin, Debbie Forster, David Cleevely, Olivia Lockyer, Andrea and Kevin Stanford, Helen Jacks, Leigh Pottinger, Kamal Ahmed, Bronwen Roscoe, Sherry Coutu, Annika Small, Georgia Hewson, Gi Fernando, Josie Macrae, Bethany Koby, Rowena Goldman, Eddie Morgan, Priya Lakhani, Matthew Jukes, Fernando Peire and Ajaz Ahmed.

And finally, my family who have stunned me with their support and belief. Thank you so much Caroline Bansal, Paul Gage, Andy Gage and Carole Gage.

Supporters

Unbound is a new kind of publishing house. Our books are funded directly by readers. This was a very popular idea during the late eighteenth and nineteenth centuries. Now we have revived it for the internet age. It allows authors to write the books they really want to write and readers to support the writing they would most like to see published.

The names listed below are of readers who have pledged their support and made this book happen. If you'd like to join them, visit: www.unbound.com.

Kamal Ahmed
Vikki Andrews
Spencer Ayres
Jason Ballinger
Caroline Bansal
Vik Bansal
Hatti Bartlett
Nicola Beckford
Ralph Beliveau
Ian Blandford
Graham Blenkin

Alf Bowles
Julie Bowles
Mark Bowsher
D. Brown
Helen Bunker
Paul Burman
Ollie Burton
David Calcutt
Stephanie Chappell
Jane Clancey
David Cleevely

Andrew Conroy

Sherry Coutu

Caroline Cowie

Olivia Coyle

Bob Cryan

Zoe Cunningham

Nick Darley

Jessica De Pree

Kent DePinto

Clare Dodd

Cathy Drysdale

Margaret Duncan

Nyasha Duri

Phil Eckardt

Jennie Ensor

Eddie Farahar

Amy Finch

Eleanor Forder

Debbie Forster

Ruth Francis

Paula J. Francisco

Oliver Franklin

Angela Frier

Andy Gage

Carole Gage

Matt Gage

Pat Gage

Paul Gage

Jill and Brian Garner

Alexandra Gee

Sarah Gibson

Laura Gillespie

Janet Goggins

Rob Goodsall

James Green

Paul Groom

Tiffany Hall

Nick Harrison

Peter Hawkins

Janel Hayley

David Hebblethwaite

Lizzie Hedges

Thomas Hetherington

Simon Higdon

Tim Hipperson

Daniel Hirschmann

The Hooper Family

Sophie Hoult

Jordan Howells

Edwina Humby

Johari Ismail

Helen J

Susannah Jackson

Aleyne Johnson

Emma Johnson

Cambridge Jones

Tom Kenyon

Dan Kieran

Saul Klein

Jim Knight

Krissy Koslicki

Erika Kraftchenko

Naomi Ladenburg

Pri Lakhani

Andrew Lassetter

Jonathan Lassetter

Graeme Lawrie

Paul Lindley

Ian Livingstone

Olivia Lockyer

Will Longhill

Lizz Loxam

Peter Macann

Barton Macfarlane

David MacLeod

Josie MacRae

Yvonne Maddox

Camilla McCusker

Mary McEneely

Judy McInerney

George McIntosh

Brett Metelerkamp

Georgia Metelerkamp

Jodi Meusel

Alexandra Tessa Mills

Juliette Mitchell

John Mitchinson

Maree Mottin

Emma Mulqueeny

Archie Myrtle

Carlo Navato

Marie-Jose Nieuwkoop

Karen O'Connor

Jane O'Hara

Scott Pack

Beth Parks

Kathryn Parsons

Zarin Patel

Richard Pattison

Maggie Philbin

Tim Plyming

Justin Pollard

Leigh Pottinger

Nick Purnell

John Ray

Yonatan Raz-Fridman

Helen Rees

Ralph Rivera

Steven Roberts

Adrian Ruth

Rosemary Scott

Tim Scott

Malcolm Scovil

Sanjay Shah

Daniel Shakhani

Russ Shaw

Stuart Sheppard

Amy Shrimpton

Anjula Singh

Annika Small

Michael Smith

Phil Smith

Justine Solomons

Andrea Stanford

Jason Stevens

Andy Sumpter

Rebecca Sutherland

Sebastian Thiel

Claire Thomas

Hedley Carolynn Trigge

Sophia Ufton

Emma Virgilio

Molly Doyle Waiting

Rupert Ward

Tony Ward

Andy Wilson

Michael and Deborah Wilson

Melanie Windridge

Anne Winfield

Kat Wong

Robin Worrall